I0771316

Shadow Work

Also by Montana Carr

Beyond the Scent of Sugar: A Memoir by Billie River

Marti Starova Erotic Thrillers

Drowning in Broad Daylight (Book 1)

Coming Soon!

Rain-Soaked (Book 3) – November 5, 2025

Almost (Book 4) - January 16, 2026

The Familiar Dark (Book 5) - March 11, 2026

Shadow Work

A Marti Starova Erotic Thriller Book 2

Montana Carr

Northshore Noir Press

This is a work of fiction. All names, characters and incidents are the product of the author's imagination. Any resemblance to real persons, living or dead, is entirely coincidental.

SHADOW WORK. A Marti Starova Erotic Thriller Book 2. Copyright © 2025 by Montana Carr. All rights reserved.

Northshore Noir Press and the Northshore Noir logo are copyright and used with permission.

Northshore Noir upholds the principles of free expression and recognizes the significance of copyright protection. All rights reserved. No part of this publication may be reproduced, distributed, or transmitted in any form or by any means without the prior written permission of the Publisher, except for brief quotations incorporated into critical articles or reviews. Your adherence to and respect for the author's rights are sincerely appreciated.

Northshore Noir Press
Toronto, Canada
www.northshorenoir.com

ISBN: 978-1-998648-21-4

eBook ISBN: 978-1-998648-22-1

For more information visit: northshorenoir.com

Contents

Chapter 1

"Who the fuck is screaming?" Marti shouted out the bedroom window, eyes bleary, voice hoarse, cigarette dangling from her lips though she hadn't lit the damn thing yet.

"Fuck you, bitch!" someone hollered back. Laughter followed: drunken and stupid, like gravel scraping down bone in a blender.

Marti leaned out far enough to consider how many floors it would take to kill a man with gravity and spite. Three stories wasn't enough. She sighed and slammed the pane shut hard enough to rattle the cracked glass.

Sleep? In Falls City? That was a fucking fantasy.

She turned back into the apartment, toes catching on a half-crushed beer can that wasn't hers. Neon from the strip club across the street blinked through her blinds, painting the walls in migraine pink and hellish green. It made her peeling wallpaper look as if it were flaking skin. The air stank of wet concrete and fried grease, the city's own cologne, and it had seeped into everything she owned. Even her favorite hoodie smelled like mildew and regret.

Once upon a time she had a badge and a name that meant something. Now she had rust stains in her sink and a stack of cheating spouse files collecting dust on her coffee table as if waiting for someone who gave a shit.

She ran a hand through her cropped black hair and hissed when her fingers caught on a knot. "Assholes," she muttered to the ceiling. A siren wailed nearby: either an ambulance or another cop beating someone to death over a traffic stop. Marti didn't care which.

Another burst of laughter floated up from the street. She kicked at a laundry pile on her way to the kitchen nook, stepping over a half-eaten takeout box that might've been noodles or possibly boiled rat. Hard to tell anymore.

"Falls City," she muttered, "where dreams go to overdose."

The faucet groaned when she cranked it, coughing up chalky water as if it resented being useful this late. She let it run over her hand but didn't bother drinking any. Her mouth tasted like cotton.

She turned away from the sink and grabbed the cigarette pack off her bedside table: a crumpled mess of receipts, empty pill bottles, lint, and one half-loaded Glock that liked to whisper things when she was high enough to listen.

"Fuck it."

She lit up and let that first drag kiss her insides like an old lover who smelled of danger and disappointment. Her lungs burned. It felt honest.

The gun sat beside an open case file: missing girl, seventeen, probably dead but no one had found her body. Marti stared at it before wrapping her fingers around the grip.

Too easy.

She could hear what they'd say: "Washed-up PI loses it," or "Former detective guns down teenagers in drug-fueled rage." Clickbait headlines wrote themselves these days.

And none of them would mention how tired she was.

She dropped onto the couch like week-old meat hitting linoleum. She took another drag, eyes fixed on nothing while sirens wailed somewhere distant; not distant enough.

"Get it together," she muttered between clenched teeth, tapping ash into an overflowing tray where old filters stuck together like little corpses holding hands.

But even as she said it, that familiar whisper curled around her spine again; soft and sticky as tar: You're better when you're worse. You know that.

Marti sat there surrounded by old coffee cups and un-slept nights. Laughter floated in through broken blinds as if some cruel serenade from a city that never stopped taking things.

She wondered if maybe Shadow wasn't killing her fast enough.

Marti crawled into bed and yanked the blanket over her head as if it could smother the entire goddamn city: Falls City and its noise, its bullshit, its never-ending parade of broken glass and testosterone-drenched dickwads playing king of the block at two in the morning. Tomorrow, she'd deal with it. Tonight was supposed to be hers.

Then came the crash: bottle against concrete, or maybe a skull. Hard to tell from up here.

Voices rose in a chorus of fuck-yous and manic laughter. A shout. The pop of something metal. Then glass again, louder this time. Windows or bottles? She didn't care.

She stared at her ceiling for six seconds. That was generous.

"Fuck this." She kicked off the blanket, rolled out of bed, and grabbed the gun from the table. Cold steel, old comfort. Better than a fuck buddy, less needy than a girlfriend. The weight settled into her hand like it belonged there.

Barefoot and pissed, she padded toward the window.

"You wanna screw with my sleep?" she muttered, thumb brushing safety off. "Let's fucking dance."

She shouldered past moth-eaten curtains and cranked the window open with a screech loud enough to qualify as its own warning shot. Leaned out far enough to get an angle on the chaos below.

Four assholes circled a hatchback as if it could fight back. One had a bat. Two had attitude. All of them had that untouchable swagger that came with youth, testosterone, and no working brain cells between them.

"Hey!" she shouted. "Shut the fuck up or I'll put holes in your stupid little bodies!"

One of them looked up and flipped her off. "Fuck you, cunt!"

"Cool," Marti said, then pulled the trigger three times.

The flash lit up their faces like camera bulbs at an execution: wide eyes, frozen mid-laugh. A beer can dropped and rolled across pavement.

"Holy shit!" one screamed as they bolted down the alley like rats spotting fire.

Marti leaned on the sill and watched them scatter with all the dignity of wet cats hit by a hose.

She smiled. "Sleep tight, dipshits."

The window slammed shut behind her as she turned back toward bed: gun on nightstand, shoulder cracking as she flopped face-down onto damp sheets that still smelled like frustration and cheap detergent.

Her heart thumped like someone else's bad decision echoing in her ribcage. Satisfaction didn't even begin to cover it.

Was it legal? Probably not. Definitely not.

Did she give a shit? Less than zero.

She exhaled into her pillow and whispered: "Sweet dreams, assholes."

* * *

Two hours later:

A pounding knock tore through whatever half-dream she'd managed to assemble in the dark.

Marti groaned against cotton sheets that now felt like sandpaper soaked in regret.

"Open up! Police!"

Of course it was.

She swung her legs out from under the covers and shuffled across splintered floorboards as if someone dragging their soul behind them on a leash. Hoodie over tank top. Gun tucked under mattress this time; not smart to flaunt evidence when badge-wielding morons came knocking.

She cracked open the door to find exactly what she'd expected: Officers Driver and Davidson in matching scowls and state-issued leather jackets three years out of style.

"Morning, boys," Marti said around a yawn, leaning against the doorframe just enough to show she hadn't brushed her teeth or given a damn in quite some time. "You here about my fireworks show?"

Driver didn't smile. Davidson looked constipated with authority.

"We got multiple calls about shots fired near this building," Davidson said through clenched teeth. "Witnesses say someone fitting your description was seen firing from their window."

"Oh no," Marti deadpanned. "Someone with tits and insomnia? Must've been me."

"You wanna try again?"

"I mean…" She swept an arm behind her in mock presentation of her shitty apartment: unmade bed, flickering kitchen lightbulb threatening suicide every five seconds, ashtray overflowing beside an empty bottle of rot gut. "Do I look like someone who'd waste bullets on dumbasses breaking windows?"

Driver stepped forward until his badge tried to intimidate its way into her space.

"You've got priors," he said, too calm, and Marti considered spitting directly onto his boots just to see if he'd flinch.

"And you've got bad breath," she replied.

Davidson rubbed his temples as if Marti's existence gave him migraines by default. "Listen closely: if you're caught discharging a weapon again."

"Allegedly."

"Without cause."

"Oh I had cause," she grinned. "You ever try sleeping through four junkies beating up a car?"

Driver pulled out his notepad but didn't write anything down. He just held it as if tension meant business.

Marti folded her arms under hoodie sleeves gone threadbare at the cuffs and sighed loud enough for half the hallway to hear it echo back down the stairwell.

"Well," she said, "if you're done scolding me for allegedly defending myself from noise pollution, I've got dreams of peace and quiet calling my name."

Neither cop moved, which was annoying but not unexpected.

They stared each other down another five seconds before Davidson grunted something about checking security cams across the street and Driver snapped his notebook closed hard.

"Don't test us again," he said over his shoulder as they walked away down hall tiles sticky with years of other people's problems.

"I would never dream of it," Marti called after them before slamming her door shut just loud enough to count as punctuation on the whole conversation.

She leaned back against it for one long breath before pushing off toward bed once more.

Tonight she'd almost gotten sleep between gunfire and threats of arrest: a personal best lately. Falls City didn't scare easily, but neither did she.

The black case hit the counter with a thud that echoed. Marti's hand lingered on the latch, her knuckles pale and tight. She stared at it for a second, as if maybe it would apologize for not being full enough. She flipped it open. Slim metal inhalers gleamed inside, nestled like bullets in an assassin's kit.

She grabbed one and pressed it to her lips. She never knew if she was going to hit the jackpot or lose it all.

Inhale. Hold. Wait.

Shadow hit her bloodstream like a back-alley kiss: too fast, too familiar, too perfect. The warmth unspooled through her chest and spine, smoothing over the jagged edges Knox and Driver had left behind. Useless cops. No sense of nuance, no instinct, no fight. They were what happened when bureaucrats dressed up like soldiers.

"Fuck them," she whispered, voice hoarse from the cigarette she lit without thinking. First drag scraped up her throat like sandpaper dipped in tar. Second one tasted like bitterness she didn't want to name.

The combo: Shadow's chemical lullaby and nicotine's throat-punch nostalgia, wrapped around her skull until everything outside her kitchen faded to static. Anger? Still there, sure. But distant now. Like a dog barking in another room.

Chapter 2

She flicked ash into an empty mug, turned on the rattling coffee maker with her elbow. Liquid bitterness dribbled into a stained cup, the same shade as despair but somehow more comforting. She took a sip and popped two slices of bread into the toaster with force. The appliance groaned in protest. So did she.

By the time breakfast materialized: a piece of toast as if it begged for mercy, Marti was through her cigarette and committed to finishing both out of spite.

Cigarette: dead. Sink: full of gray water that hadn't moved in three days. She dropped the butt in and watched it sizzle as if from a noir short film nobody watched.

None of it mattered.

The memory of those badge-wearing idiots kept circling back like acid reflux, no matter how high she got or how much caffeine she threw at it. Once upon a time, she'd worn the badge too; a younger Marti who still gave a shit about rules and justice and all that bedtime-story crap.

Now?

Now she burned bridges before they were built.

She muttered "jerks" like it was a curse and prayer rolled into one word, then set down her mug hard enough to crack porcelain. The anger hadn't left. It had changed shape, gone cold around the edges like old soup or fresh corpses.

And beneath that cold? Purpose.

Martina fucking Starova didn't sulk when things went sideways. She adapted, recalibrated, rearmed. This day wouldn't be different.

The Shadow was fading; the stuff never lasted long enough, but its whisper stayed behind: You need more. You always do.

Yeah, she did.

Not just to level out but to get ahead, to stay faster than whatever was trying to catch her: guilt, memory, someone with a badge and a vendetta.

"Kransten Park," she said, testing the name in her mouth as if expecting it to bite back.

It didn't.

Kransten Park meant product: quiet deals traded under burned-out streetlamps by men with smiles too wide to be honest.

For Marti, she'd rented this shithole for its proximity to that particular brand of salvation.

Her knees cracked as she stood, aching joints reminding her this body came with mileage and scars paid for in cash and consequence, and headed over to where yesterday's wardrobe lay abandoned on the floor like battlefield remnants nobody claimed after the war ended.

Pajama pants hit the laundry pile. Her jeans were next: ripped at the knee from something she couldn't remember, involving running or fighting or falling down while too high to care. T-shirt followed, black once but now faded enough to look blue under harsh light, and clung to her ribs as if no fabric should unless it had consent first.

She didn't care about flattering angles or fashion statements; this wasn't about hot looks or handsy club stares. This was about efficiency and availability: could she reach her gun without snagging on denim? Yes? Good enough.

Gray hoodie, fraying at the cuffs, and leather jacket layered overtop until she looked street-level dangerous instead of vulnerable or broken or whatever else Lori might've said during one of those therapy-inspired heart-to-heart ambushes over lunch breaks Marti pretended not to enjoy.

Gun slid into place against the small of her back like a familiar itch. Cigarettes vanished into hoodie pockets beside fingers that trembled when idle too long.

"Let's do this," she said, tired, and pulled on boots scarred from years of chasing things that never wanted rescuing.

The key turned behind her with a metallic finality as Marti stepped into the hallway's gloom. Unlike earlier that morning, now there was direction behind her walk and fire simmering behind every step.

She needed Shadow, and anything standing between her and Kransten Park better believe she'd walk straight through them if they tried slowing her down.

The air outside slapped her like a wet glove. Rain came down in sheets, soaking through Marti's jacket in seconds and gluing her shirt to skin that wasn't in the mood for this kind of intimacy. One of these days she'd buy a raincoat; maybe the same day she started flossing or believing people didn't deserve what they got.

Falls City looked like hell's waiting room: neon signs smeared across the puddled sidewalks, flickering pinks and greens bleeding into storm drains too clogged to swallow anything but dreams. The gutters had more color than most funerals. Fitting.

She lit a cigarette with shaking fingers, glanced back at her apartment building, and squinted at the sidewalk. No blood. No splash pattern. No body sprawled in a dramatic pose under broken streetlight glow. Just water and disappointment pooling in all the wrong places.

"Well gut me with a rusty switchblade," she muttered, letting smoke curl between her teeth. "Not even a goddamn splatter."

She shoved her hands deeper into damp pockets and moved fast, boots slapping rain-slick pavement with purpose if not grace. Around her, Falls City groaned; sirens wailed distant, traffic hummed like an exhausted lover trying to finish anyway. Voices shouted somewhere behind her as if it could've been a drug deal or somebody losing their lunch over bad sushi and worse decisions.

Didn't matter. It was all white noise now.

Her brain played reruns: the itch behind her eyes pulsing to the beat of Shadow withdrawal. Twenty hours since her last hit and counting. Her nerves? Shot to hell. Her muscles? Tense enough to snap steel cables. Her next dose wasn't just a craving; it was survival.

Another cigarette burned down to filter before she noticed. She flicked it away without ceremony. Hit someone in the leg? Oops.

She turned the corner and spotted the bodega at the end of the block, Carlos's place, a flickering OPEN sign buzzing as if it wanted out just as badly as she did. She had a craving for citrus, something sharp and sweet, to stave off the craving for Shadow for just a bit longer.

The man himself waved from inside: gray-bearded, wearing that battered Raiders hoodie he claimed was lucky, despite all visible evidence to the contrary.

"Hey, Marti!" Carlos called through the cracked door as if nothing was burning inside her head. "Long time no see!"

She pushed the door open hard enough to rattle the bell above it.

"Can't talk," she snapped, voice sharp. Soft edges were for people who didn't have corpses on delay.

Carlos raised both hands as if she'd pulled a gun instead of words. "Easy there! I know that face: you're on a mission."

Marti didn't respond. What was there to say? Yeah, I'm jonesing for Shadow so bad I'd suck dick in an alley if someone hinted they knew a guy?

Instead of probing further (thank God), Carlos ducked below the counter and came up holding an orange. He knew the cravings.

He tossed it underhand toward her as if they were playing catch instead of flirting with narcotics dependency.

Marti caught it mid-air without looking; reflexes still sharp even if everything else was fraying. The fruit felt warm in her cold fingers. Soft skin under calloused palms made her stomach lurch with something close to feeling.

"You serious?" she asked.

Carlos shrugged with that shit-eating grin he always wore when he knew he'd won some small battle for humanity today. "Vitamin C builds character."

Marti stared at him one extra second: a long enough pause that something between them threatened to soften. She rolled the orange against her palm as if it might explode if squeezed too hard.

"Thanks," she muttered, voice between gratitude and disbelief.

Carlos leaned back against his fridge full of off-brand cola and expired yogurt drinks as if he had all day to wait her out.

"You look like you needed something real," he said. "Even if it's just fruit." Then added: "No strings attached."

That was probably bullshit, but nice-smelling bullshit at least.

Marti gave him one final look before turning toward the exit: soaked hair dripping onto cracked tile floors, orange cradled against her chest like contraband or confession.

Outside, Falls City hadn't changed, but for half a second, something inside of her almost had.

Marti stepped out. The rain punched her in the face. Cold, hard, insistent, as if the sky had something personal against her. She ducked under the crooked awning of a rundown bakery that smelled like mold and disappointment, pulled an orange from her coat pocket, and started peeling it with focus usually reserved for disarming bombs.

The skin came off in wet flaps. Juice dripped down her fingers, sticky and sweet, mixing with city grime in a way that was probably biohazardous. She didn't care. It was the first good thing to touch her mouth in days. She bit into it skin-on like some feral thing, rolling her teeth over the flesh until all that was left was pith and pulp. Not gourmet, but it beat chewing nicotine gum until her jaw clicked.

She tossed the remains into a trash heap that may or may not have been organized by species. Wiped her hand on her jeans. Citrus and diesel clung to her fingers.

Then came the crash: her high slipping away, the orange glow of sweetness replaced by the gnawing black pit at the center of her chest.

Her jacket pocket gaped open. No inhaler. No lifeline.

"Fuck me sideways," she muttered, patting herself down like a junkie version of a TSA agent.

This was bad. Her stash was gone, burned through two nights ago during a bender that ended with someone else's blood on her boots and no memory of how it got there. Without Shadow, she'd spiral fast. The edge came back quick without it: jagged thoughts, shaking hands, old ghosts with knives at her throat.

And now she had to walk through this piss storm to meet Boot-Face in Kransten Park before every addict within ten blocks cleaned him out.

Slick sidewalks glared up at her as she moved fast down Delroy, shoes squelching with every step. Her brain did barrel rolls around one thought: get to Shadow before the city chewed you up again.

"Goddamn freezing," she spat through clenched teeth as wind smacked her in the face as if it had a grudge.

By the time she hit Kransten Park's west entrance, her clothes were soaked and her nerves tighter than Lori's ponytail on a court day.

The park greeted her like an open grave: twisted trees clawing toward gray skies, paths littered with broken glass and lost hope. Whatever passed for landscaping hadn't been touched since before Marti quit whatever passed for normal life.

She spotted him under a busted streetlamp: tall guy, shoulders hunched as if he'd spent his whole life bracing for punches. That boot-shaped face hadn't gotten prettier since last week, and his hands still looked like they came with felony charges.

"You holding?" Marti asked, voice rough from too many cigarettes and not enough Shadow.

"Three hits," he grunted without meeting her eyes. "Same price."

He fished around in his torn coat while Marti pulled out cash; bills damp but still legal tender unless he tried to get fancy about things.

She tossed them at him. He caught them one-handed like he'd done it his whole life. He probably had.

"Here." He handed over three canisters so small they looked laughable compared to their gravity.

Marti slid them into her coat pocket as if they belonged there more than anything else ever had. She didn't bother saying thanks, just gave him a nod and turned back toward the exit without looking twice.

She could feel Shadow humming against her ribs: warmth in an inhaler, salvation with a side of self-destruction.

At least now she could make it through another night without stabbing anybody who didn't deserve it.

Probably.

Chapter 3

Marti stalked away from the dealer, the taste of orange still sour on her tongue. Shadow tucked deep in her pocket pulsed like a second heartbeat. The park path stretched ahead: cracked pavement, yesterday's trash caught in the gutter weeds. She passed a rusted bench someone had tried to tag with a broken pen. Real art.

The mist clung low across the grass, thick enough to swallow sound. Still Marti heard it: footsteps that weren't hers yet were somehow following her. Memory, probably. Or guilt.

Then she saw her.

Lia Fisher stood by the fountain like a ghost who'd forgotten how to haunt: solid in body, but wrong in time. Her coat flared open enough to show the burgundy collar of that same shirt she'd worn last winter when Marti was still pretending she could get clean for love. For Lia.

They'd burned hot once. Nights pressed against cold windows, hands buried in each other's hair as if knots could hold things together. They didn't.

Marti slowed, boots scraping at the gravel as if giving her one last chance to turn around and disappear into another bad decision.

She didn't take it.

"Lia," she managed, voice husky from too many dry hits and not enough sleep.

Lia turned sharply, eyes rounding before settling into something softer. Recognition with restraint layered over it like frosting no one asked for.

"Marti?" Her voice was quieter than it used to be, or maybe it only seemed that way now that Marti wasn't screaming inside her own skull. "This is... unexpected."

Understatement of the fucking decade.

Marti nodded like that meant something and stepped closer to the fountain. The thing gurgled behind them, spitting water as if it wanted an award for ambiance. Concrete cherubs watched their reunion with blind little eyes.

"I thought about calling," Marti said. She hated herself for saying anything at all.

"You didn't."

"No."

Lia tucked a strand of hair behind her ear and didn't smile this time. "How've you been?"

That question should've come with a warning label, two paramedics standing by.

Marti shrugged one shoulder. "Still vertical." She jammed her hands into her coat pockets as if she could stuff down everything else hiding in there: shame, hunger, a crumpled photo booth strip where Lia had kissed her cheek and ruined Marti forever.

Fingers brushed cold metal and plastic; her inhaler. The one thing that still kept her steady when nothing else could hold weight.

She pulled it out without thinking.

Lia's face changed: not disgusted exactly, but disappointment sharpened into something surgical and precise.

"Don't," Lia said, as if keeping her voice soft enough would stop Marti from breaking again on the bricks.

Marti froze; her thumb paused on the trigger valve of oblivion.

Her jaw tightened. The fog wrapped around them both, thickening every breath into something gelatinous and wet.

"I can't have that around me," Lia added, voice cracking like old tile under pressure.

Right. Because Lia had managed to move on to nuance and growth and fucking kale smoothies or whatever people did when they weren't mainlining memories of missing hearts at 7am in a city that never forgave you for being soft once.

Marti nodded once, sharp as a snapped bone.

She slid the inhaler back into her pocket with fingers she couldn't unclench. It trembled against her thigh like a ticking bomb, or maybe just withdrawal setting up camp behind her eyes.

Lia hesitated as if she wanted to say more but didn't trust herself to mean it. She turned away. Her footsteps faded on damp cement, swallowed by mist and Marti's rising panic until both were gone.

Marti stood there alone before fury kicked in: familiar and hot and safer than whatever hope had tried wriggling loose when Lia smiled at her like something might still be salvageable.

"Fuck," Marti muttered under breath she couldn't catch.

She yanked the inhaler out again and hit it hard, sucking bitter fumes into lungs already half-collapsed from regret. The burn was immediate; acidic comfort sliding down her throat like broken glass in warm milk.

The world blurred sideways at first, the way things always did when Shadow got mean. Then it snapped into focus so bright it felt religious in its cruelty.

Her legs carried her without permission deeper into the park, past where normal people walked their dogs or bought weed shaped like cupcakes from teenage dealers who thought they invented sadness.

She found cover beneath a cluster of half-dead trees, the kind of place kids dared each other to enter after dark, not because anyone believed in ghosts but because they knew people were worse anyway.

With shaking hands she took another hit without counting seconds or consequences this time.

The taste was sewage sweet: coppery and chemical tangled up in notes of rot. It settled inside just long enough to remind her why people called it Shadow instead of what it really was. Goddamn surrender bottled up small enough to fit between your teeth but big enough to ruin everyone you ever loved if you let it linger too long on your tongue.

Which she'd done already. Plenty of times over.

Okay, let's go. Third time's a charm.

The hit slammed into her chest as if it were a car crash she'd almost wanted. A sharp sting followed by syrupy darkness rolling through her limbs. Shadow didn't whisper relief; it kicked in the door and took what it wanted.

"Thanks, assholes," Marti muttered, voice flat. "Really needed that." She was talking to Davidson and Driver, though they weren't dumb enough to be standing nearby. Waking her up to scold her for firing shots at a trash can or whatever it had been. She couldn't remember, didn't care. "Reckless" wasn't exactly a new accusation.

Another hit. Her hands trembled as the warmth bloomed under her skin, melting muscle from bone. Self-loathing flickered underneath, stubborn and familiar, like an old ex you kept circling back to even though they keyed your car.

She staggered toward the nearest bench as if the pavement had turned against gravity. She collapsed onto damp wood slick with last night's rain and someone else's regret. Her spine screamed but her nerves didn't care; they were too busy floating somewhere above Falls City where nothing mattered except not feeling shit.

Marti leaned back, eyelids heavy, heartbeat slow as syrup. "Fuck it," she whispered to no one worth naming.

The world could burn itself down without her help tonight.

Then came footsteps: wet soles slapping concrete with too much rhythm for coincidence. Marti stayed still, head lolling to one side as if her brain had left early for vacation. But her fingers twitched toward the pistol tucked under her jacket, as if it had always been there waiting for this moment.

"Hey lady," some breathy goblin of a man rasped nearby, stinking of wet socks and desperation. "Gimme your cash and whatever you're riding high on."

Marti opened one eye.

The guy looked as if he'd lost a fight with a clothes donation bin: patchy jacket, sneakers three sizes off from each other, face half-shaved like he got bored halfway through remembering how mirrors worked.

He reached out.

Wrong move.

Her hand shot up and latched around his wrist with enough violence to express disinterest in being robbed today. She twisted until she heard something pop and brought her other fist up in a tight arc straight to his throat.

He stumbled back sputtering like a broken pipe, eyes wide and watery. Coughing turned to dry heaving turned to whimpering.

Marti sat up, shaking out her hand like someone had offered her a truly offensive handshake. "Run," she said. "Or stay and we can try that again."

The guy blinked at her as if language had become optional and backed away fast enough to trip over his own shadow before disappearing into the fog of alleyways and bad decisions.

Marti stared after him a moment longer just in case he wanted bonus rounds, then leaned forward with an exhausted groan.

"How long was I out?" she asked the concrete.

No answer, obviously.

Her fingers trembled in tiny aftershocks as adrenaline filtered out through tired veins, leaving behind that hollow throb of almost dying but not quite exciting enough for headlines. She existed somewhere between street corner junkie and urban legend, with slightly better hair.

She pushed herself upright with all the grace of a soggy shopping cart and took two wobbly steps toward somewhere that resembled safety: her office, her sanctum of expired coffee pods and emotional repression.

Falls City didn't stop moving just because she tried to check out early.

Engines roared past like angry beasts; horns echoed off years of rust-stained buildings; people laughed about things that probably weren't funny; sirens screamed their way uptown looking for someone else's corpse for once. She walked through it all half-there, dragging the weight of herself behind every step like an uncooperative suitcase.

Water fountain on Ninth was still broken; cold stream running sideways into cracked concrete. Marti bent down anyway and dipped her palm into its metal mouth. The water was filthy enough to qualify as sentient, but it grounded her better than Shadow ever could.

Somewhere overhead, a radio crackled garbage about missing kids while birds screamed at traffic as if they were part of a union strike no one cared about anymore.

Marti straightened. She froze.

Had she seen Lia?

There'd been something earlier: a flash of denim jacket maybe. Or it could've been just another trick Shadow liked playing when sobriety wasn't invited to the party. She squinted toward rooftops too far away to matter while trucks bellowed past and laughter echoed from people who hadn't watched anyone bleed out this week.

"Sure," Marti said. "Why not?"

And then she kept walking toward whatever mess waited next; because what else was there?

Marti shoved her way down the alley as if it had insulted her mother. Falls City didn't get darker after sunset. It just stopped pretending to be anything else. Neon signs blinked like they were dying, trash swirled in damp circles around her boots, and the scent of hot grease and human failure clung to the air like a drunk uncle at a funeral.

The Shadow inhalers in her coat pocket tapped against her thigh with every step. Not heavy, not loud: just persistent, like guilt with a rhythm section.

"Focus, Starova," she muttered through clenched teeth. Her voice cut through the background hum of power lines buzzing overhead and distant shouting that might've been a fight or just someone enjoying themselves too hard.

Cigarette smoke ghosted along the back of her throat, stale and sharp as regret. Her mouth was dry enough to crack. She needed whiskey more than sleep.

Somewhere behind her, glass shattered. She didn't jump, just let her hand drift toward the knife in her boot. Falls City demanded constant readiness, like a jealous lover who might stab you just for blinking at someone else.

The air was thick with rot and resignation. Sewer fumes soaked into the city's pores and marinated there until the whole place smelled like old sins reheated for breakfast.

She passed familiar faces slouched in doorways or curled up under broken signage. Most looked through her or past her, but one set of bloodshot eyes tracked her movement with clarity.

"Marti," he croaked, his voice shredded by smoke or something worse.

"Eddie." She gave him a nod without stopping. He'd once tried to steal from Driver and Davidson: Falls City's answer to what happens when cops go feral. Marti had pulled him out of that mess with three phone calls and one specific threat involving a stapler.

"Keep it together," she said, stepping over a puddle filled with cigarette butts and something that might've once been coffee.

Eddie didn't reply. He probably couldn't tell if she meant his sobriety, his spine, or both.

Chapter 4

She made it to the office without getting stabbed or propositioned (miraculous by local standards) and paused outside the battered glass door that read "Martina Starova, Private Investigator" in gold paint that thought it was classier than it was.

Inside smelled like paper mold and stronger things: old coffee grounds, burned toast from three mornings ago, Lori's floral shampoo that never matched her mood. Marti shut the door behind her and tossed herself into the dented leather chair.

Lori glanced up from her laptop. "That bad?"

"Some jackass tried to mug me in Harlan Park," Marti said as she lit another cigarette from the crushed pack in her coat pocket. "Didn't check my face first."

"Rookie mistake," Lori said, pushing a cup of tea across the desk as if it was some holy offering instead of steeped leaves in hot water.

Marti ignored it.

"You okay?" Lori asked without looking away from whatever spreadsheet or stalker log she was reviewing today.

"I'm fine," Marti said. Then added: "Just another day in scenic hell." She flicked ash into a cracked ceramic bowl shaped like an owl wearing sunglasses; Lori's attempt at whimsy, probably salvaged from some yard sale run by witches or lesbians with garage space.

"What's on today's menu?" Marti asked, rubbing at the bridge of her nose until she saw stars. "Tell me we've got something exciting."

"Cheating spouse," Lori said. "Wilson."

Marti groaned.

"Another cheating spouse," Lori continued. "Johnson."

"Oh fuck off."

"And one potential car insurance fraud."

"Be still my fucking heart."

Lori smirked and dropped three folders onto Marti's desk loud enough to make a statement but soft enough not to spill tea on anything important. She knew how to hit that sweet spot; had known for two years now exactly how far to push before Marti snapped or started making out with people she shouldn't.

Marti stood. The chair squealed under protest.

"Give me five," she muttered, crossing into the inner office without waiting for permission, which would've been weird anyway since this whole place belonged to her.

She shut the door behind her and pulled the inhaler from inside her coat lining. No label anymore: just gray plastic worn smooth where she'd held it too tight too many times. It clicked when she primed it.

One deep drag later and everything blurred around the edges just enough to feel manageable again. The itch under her skin quieted. The noise in her head fell back into its usual dull roar instead of screaming static.

She exhaled toward the ceiling fan that hadn't worked since last July.

For one perfect moment, Marti Starova wasn't tired anymore.

Marti blinked hard, but the walls rippled as if someone had dunked the office in gasoline and tossed in a match. Her chair tilted back with a creak as she let the Shadow sweep through her bloodstream: hot, electric, invasive. The ceiling peeled open above her like a slow grin. She didn't smile back.

Then: tap tap tap.

She sat up, ears twitching. A soft sound, barely there, like fingernails on drywall. But Shadow didn't let things stay subtle for long. Every nerve sharpened to glass.

The tapping came again. Louder this time. More insistent.

Marti stood, blood thick with synthetic fire. Her head filled with static; one part euphoria, two parts impending doom. She stalked to the door and pressed her ear against it. Nothing at first.

Then: tap tap tap.

Too rhythmic to be weather. Too soft to be cops.

She slipped open her drawer and pulled out the Beretta. Checked the mag: full. Safety off.

No hesitation this time.

She flung open the door and raised the gun like it was an extension of herself, only to be met with a startled yelp and a face she knew far too well.

"Lori?" The name dropped from her lips like a curse.

Lori sat at her desk, arms up like she'd walked into a stickup. "Jesus fucking Christ, Marti!" she snapped. "You trying to put a hole in me?"

Marti didn't lower the gun right away. Her brain was still trying to match Lori's image with the threat Shadow had conjured outside that door. Finally, muscles slackening, she exhaled and dropped her arm.

"Fuck," she muttered. "Sorry."

"You think?"

"Thought you were someone else."

"Yeah? Who? The goddamn Tooth Fairy?"

Marti pushed past her and stumbled back to her desk, rubbing at her temple as if that might squeeze reality back in place. "Goddamn," she mumbled. "That was some fucked-up batch."

"No kidding," Lori said, brushing dust off her shoulders as if Marti's paranoia might be contagious.

Back in her chair, Marti tried to focus on the case files glowing on her screen: standard spousal gig. Wife suddenly doesn't need hubby's money, and he wants to know what she's up to.

Marti hoped she found the source, but had to make a purchase to know for sure. Click, click, done.

"Lori? Invoice Petrie for $500, miscellaneous," she shouted through the open doorway.

A grunt signaled Lori had heard, and Marti turned to the next case. Cheating spouse.

She clicked through grainy photos: a brunette slipping into Room 12B at the Gallant Oaks Motor Inn. She tried not to imagine what that beige wallpaper had seen over the years. The guy's face was always turned away from the cameras as if he knew which angles mattered.

Her concentration barely had time to come back when Lori reappeared in the doorway again, this time keeping an extra foot of distance between them.

"You've got a visitor," she said. "Rat."

Of course it's Rat.

Marti waved him in without looking up from her notes.

He slid into the room as if roadkill learning how to walk again: gray skin, sunken cheeks, an oversized jacket that looked like it hadn't been washed since Bush was president, the first one more than sixty years ago. His eyes jittered around the room before locking onto Marti with something halfway between hope and fear.

"Hey," he said, voice worn raw from pipe smoke and sleepless nights.

"Rat," Marti nodded, folding one file closed and pushing it aside. "You look worse than usual."

Marti had met Rat back when she was still chasing murderers for a paycheck, not just for personal satisfaction. The case was brutal; some asshole had offed a couple and taken off with their kid. Marti had been running through the piss-slick alleys of Falls City chasing that fucker when he lost her. Disappeared.

But she saw Rat: a junkie hunched near a busted-out lamppost, movements twitchy, eyes wild. She looked, he responded. He tilted his head toward a grimy little coffee shop and said something that might've been "there." Turned out he was right. The bastard had ditched the girl there like lost luggage.

She never filed that detail in her report. Some debts you don't repay with paper. Sometimes you repay a junkie by leaving them alone, and being forever grateful.

Rat's cough died halfway out of his mouth. "LaLoLa's gone," he said.

Marti froze mid-reach for her coffee cup.

"She's what?" LaLoLa was one of the most reliable and kind-hearted dealers in Falls City, so of course she was missing.

Marti's mind flashed to the last time she'd seen LaLoLa, silver forearm crutches tapping a rhythm against the wet pavement as she approached through the neon-streaked darkness.

A brutal attack three years ago had taken her left leg below the knee. It hadn't touched her smile, the only genuine one left in Falls City. LaLoLa dealt in chemicals and dreams, but unlike the other vultures, she never preyed on desperation. "Everyone's broken enough already," she'd once told Marti. "I just help them forget for a while."

"Gone-gone," Rat said, scratching at his neck until it reddened beneath grime-covered fingernails. "Haven't seen her since Thursday night."

Marti leaned forward but kept her voice even. "Did you check The Sinkhole? Or that squat near Ninth?"

"No one's seen her." He ran both hands through his greasy hair and looked up at her with something close to panic now. "It's not just that she disappeared. It's quiet out there, like people know something but won't say."

She swore under her breath and lit a cigarette with shaking fingers, second one since a breath ago, and took a long drag before speaking again.

"LaLoLa doesn't ghost people," Marti said. "Not unless someone made sure she couldn't crawl back."

Rat nodded fast, too fast, and stuffed his hands deep into his pockets like they were keeping him upright.

"I need your help," he said. "I liked her."

"Know her government name?" Marti stared at him through smoke-haze and denial for another second before sighing hard enough to rattle dust off her desk lamp.

"No. Just LaLoLa."

"She's probably just holed up somewhere," she said without conviction. "Shacked up with someone new or hiding from heat."

Rat didn't believe it and neither did she, but saying it made it easier not to feel how heavy this was becoming.

"Don't bullshit me, Marti."

She didn't answer right away, not because she didn't have anything to say but because all of it sounded hollow when spoken under flickering fluorescents and stained ceiling tiles.

Shadow still kissed around the edges of her vision like a hungry ghost, whispering other possibilities no rational person wanted echoing out loud yet: not until it was too late to deny them anymore.

"Tell you what, Rat," Marti said, cigarette balanced between two fingers, ash blooming like frost over the rim of her mug. "I'll help you find LaLoLa."

Rat blinked at her as if she'd offered him a house and a sandwich. "Seriously? You will?" His mouth curled into something that tried to be a smile but got lost halfway there.

"Yeah. Don't ask me why." She flicked ash onto the floor next to a coffee stain shaped like the Virgin Mary. "Free of charge."

"Thank you," he said, clutching his chest as if someone had handed him a beating heart on ice. "Marti, really, thank you."

"Stop thanking me. Save it for when I drag her skinny ass back here," she muttered, grinding the cigarette out on the desk. "If we find her alive and not strung out behind a dumpster, then yeah: we'll throw a fucking party."

She glanced at him. Still doing that wide-eyed baby possum thing. Made her itchy.

"Alright." She turned in her chair with the grace of a drunk ballerina in combat boots. The city outside coughed up smoke as a truck groaned past the window. "Where do we start?"

Rat scratched his chin with fingers that looked like they'd been dipped in nicotine and regret. "Well... there's the Handsome Dove," he said. "She used to go there sometimes. MethLumina is too techno for me, but she liked it."

Marti raised an eyebrow. "And?"

"She turned tricks, sold low level, did some licks. Survival stuff." He shrugged. "Went to pop-ups near the university. Someone there might've seen her."

"So she likes overpriced drinks and can vanish into thin air," Marti said.

"She's slippery," Rat admitted with a nervous laugh.

Marti stood, stretching the kink from her back and rolling her shoulders until something popped loudly enough to make Rat wince.

"I'll start with those pop-ups," she said, reaching for her coat. "Ask around, turn over some rocks."

She opened the door. It was time for him to leave.

"For you, Rat."

His voice cracked like thin ice under cheap boots. "It means something, Marti. Really does." He hesitated again: classic Rat. Then added, "LaLoLa... she used to sneak me sandwiches sometimes. Turkey on rye, no mustard. Always told me I looked too skinny to be functional." He smiled at his shoes. "Sounds weird when I say it out loud."

"Nah," Marti said, lighting another cigarette off the stub of the first one without breaking eye contact. "It's just rare these days to find someone who gives enough of a fuck to feed another human being."

For once, Rat didn't try to make things awkward by hugging her or crying or some other bullshit that would have made Marti light herself on fire from secondhand discomfort. He nodded once and held out his hand.

She shook it hard enough he'd remember it.

"Careful out there," he murmured as he let go and shuffled toward the door as if he already missed whatever piece of himself LaLoLa took when she vanished. He turned back before leaving, his eyes shadowed and tired.

"This city..." he started and sighed instead of finishing.

"I know," Marti said without asking what he meant.

But he kept going anyway: "It's always hungry, right? Just chewing through people until there's nothing left but bones and bad stories. You be careful."

"Oh honey." She blew smoke toward the ceiling fan that hadn't worked since 2016. "I haven't been digestible in years."

The door clicked shut behind him.

Marti stared at it. She kicked aside an empty energy drink can and headed for her files, or maybe nowhere at all, when Lori slipped into the room like static electricity in human form.

Her arms crossed as she leaned on the closed door with one hip cocked, her eyebrows already judging something Marti hadn't done yet.

"New case?" Lori asked.

"Not exactly." Marti dropped into her chair with the enthusiasm of someone accepting their fate via guillotine. "Rat wants me to find his dealer: LaLoLa."

Lori blinked, unimpressed but amused.

"LaLoLa?" she asked.

"Mmhmm." Marti took another drag and stared up at the water-stained ceiling tiles as if they might hold divine insight if she smoked hard enough.

"And you're doing this 'cause...?"

Marti shrugged one shoulder under layers of leather and sarcasm. "Because I'm a bleeding heart when I'm bored."

"Well then." Lori stepped into the room as if she was about to critique decor choices. "You're not going alone."

"I can handle myself," Marti said.

"You can barely handle breakfast," Lori shot back with a grin that could've melted industrial paint stripper off walls.

Marti narrowed her eyes but didn't argue; technically Lori wasn't wrong.

"I'm serious," Lori said more gently as she perched on the edge of Marti's desk, legs crossed at dangerous angles. "You dive into these things head-first with no backup and next thing I know I'm fishing you out of some alley smelling like burned plastic and poor decisions."

"That only happened once," Marti muttered.

"And we both still smell it."

Marti exhaled smoke toward Lori's face. Lori batted it away but didn't move from her spot.

"You done being noble?" Lori asked.

"I wasn't ever noble," Marti replied.

Lori tilted her head, smiling without showing teeth: a smile that meant trouble or tequila or both if Marti wasn't careful tonight.

"Well then." Lori uncrossed her legs with grace. "Let's go find your phantom sandwich queen before someone else does and ruins it all with incompetence."

Marti stood again with less effort this time and gave Lori half a smile: the kind only handed out after midnight or at funerals.

"Fucking aye," Marti muttered, tugging on her leather jacket. The weight of her pistol under her arm wasn't comfort; she didn't do comfort, but it sure as hell was familiar. Outside, rain smeared the city into something feral and mean. Perfect night to dig up whatever secrets were still rotting behind LaLoLa's smile.

Lori appeared in the doorway as she shrugged on her raincoat, fumbling with the zipper as if it had personally offended her.

"I've got a feeling we're in for a long night."

Marti didn't blink. "You say that like it's a problem."

Lori blushed. "I like spending time with you."

Marti lifted an eyebrow but didn't answer. She reached for the door and yanked it open, letting the cold slap them both in the face. Behind them, Lori locked up as if they were leaving something worth stealing.

The city's wet breath curled around them, thick with exhaust and neon and things better left unnamed. Falls

City welcomed its own like a stray dog: snarling and sharp-eyed but harmless if you knew how to play nice.

Chapter 5

The diner looked exactly how Marti remembered it: half-lit neon buzzing like it needed life support, windows fogged with grease ghosts, and the flickering sign promising FOOD 24 HRS like a threat or a dare.

She shoulder-checked the crap-streaked door open, setting off the bell that screamed instead of chiming. Lori trailed behind her like someone entering enemy territory without backup.

"Jesus," Lori muttered as they slid into one of the cracked vinyl booths. "Health inspector must cry himself to sleep over this place."

Marti looked around, but mostly at Lori's ass. The itch behind her ribs wasn't just nerves, it was hunger. And not for information.

"Colin Bonner," Lori said as she stared at the green 'pass' health card stuck in the window. She wondered briefly how much his signature cost.

The place smelled like regret fried in old oil, onions, pancakes, something egg-adjacent all layered under that eternal tang of stale coffee and despair. It clung to your skin fast as guilt.

Marti liked it here.

Not liked-liked it, but this diner had served more stake-outs and post-shootout pancakes than any therapist could count. It was part of her damage now. Some people had mothers who made casseroles; Marti had 3am hash browns and blood on her boots.

She leaned back against the duct-taped seat cushion and closed her eyes just long enough to remember why she never properly left this place: predictable misery beat new disasters every time.

A waitress appeared: youngish, with an over-caffeinated smile pasted beneath tired eyes. She poured them both coffee without asking. Yoga pants so tight they should've come with a warning label hugged every curve she wasn't allowed to flaunt in whatever hell passed for management here.

Marti slid her cup forward. "White toast," she said. "Unbuttered."

The waitress nodded and walked off; Marti watched her go long enough for Lori to notice.

"I think if more women wore yoga pants, there'd be world peace," Marti said, deadpan as ever.

Lori snorted into her coffee cup. "Maybe not peace, but I wouldn't mind living in that version of reality."

Marti grinned as if sharp teeth lurked behind soft lips and let her eyes drift after the waitress again like she was tracking movement on a firing range.

"There's just something about tight fabric stretched across a great ass," Marti said. "Doesn't solve geopolitical crises or anything but damn if it doesn't make things easier to survive." Marti smirked and tapped ash into the coffee saucer instead of an ashtray because there wasn't one. There probably hadn't been since smoking laws changed fifteen years ago.

Marti leaned across the table and flicked a non-existent toast crumb off Lori's collar. "Maybe we should try yoga pants," she said, deadpan. "See if world peace breaks out."

Lori blinked. "That where you're going with this?"

"Obviously," Marti said. "Spandex diplomacy. Real cutting edge."

The waitress dropped two sad excuses for toast onto the table, their edges curling as if trying to escape the plate.

She smiled like she hadn't just committed war crimes and walked off.

Marti licked the air in her general direction.

Lori choked on her coffee, coughed, laughed. "Jesus, Marti."

"What? That's how I flirt."

"You have issues."

Marti shrugged and dug into her jacket, pulling out a crumpled photo and laying it flat on the table with both palms as if she was about to perform a séance. LaLoLa stared up at them from the sticky surface: dark eyes, defiant smirk, a single hoop earring glittering like a middle finger at the world.

"Rat says she's been missing for a couple of days." Marti didn't look up. "Thinks someone grabbed her."

Lori stirred more sugar into her coffee and took another sip. Still bitter. Still weak. "Rat thinks everyone's out to get him."

"Doesn't mean he's wrong."

"Or she just left town." Lori tapped a hangnail against her cup. "Maybe got bored of Falls City and moved somewhere quiet without all the collapsing buildings and unlicensed gunfire."

"Or maybe she's dead," Marti said, meeting her gaze with those ice-chip eyes that made Lori feel like her spine had taken an unscheduled vacation.

"You know this city." Marti lit another cigarette and spoke through the smoke. "People vanish here all the time. You hiccup wrong next to the wrong person, they find your shoes floating in a gutter three days later."

Lori looked back at LaLoLa's photo, at the grin too bold for safety, and let out a slow breath. "We've got enough shit of our own without chasing ghosts."

"I owe Rat." Marti leaned forward again, voice low now, quiet in that way that meant deadly serious or about to punch something. "And I don't leave friends behind."

"Even if it gets us shot at?" Lori asked, failing to keep it casual.

Marti snuffed her cigarette in the overflowing ashtray. Ash spilled over onto the toast like seasoning.

"Especially then."

Lori hesitated long enough for two thoughts she wouldn't say aloud to tango behind her lips: one about how bad this idea was, another about how much worse it would be not to follow Marti into it.

She nodded once.

Marti pulled another cigarette but didn't light it yet. She twirled it between her fingers as if a priest swinging incense before a ritual.

"Rat said last sighting was south side," she said. "Dump of a motel next to some place selling deep-fried kale chips in recycled shoe boxes."

"Sounds legit," Lori muttered.

"We'll ask around," Marti continued, eyes scanning something invisible outside the diner window: maybe possibilities, maybe bodies nobody had found yet. "Check pop-ups, poke some dealers who owe me favors. Something'll shake loose."

"I'd prefer not to be one of those things that shake loose," Lori said, watching LaLoLa's face grin up at them from beside an old syrup stain.

Marti smirked sideways, as if danger was something she swiped right on for kicks.

"You remember last time?" Lori added. "Mayor ended up face-down in fall's pool and you hallucinated your own funeral."

Marti grinned. "Golden Shadow," she corrected. "Gotta include the 'Golden.' Branding matters."

She reached out and let her hand rest on Lori's forearm; warmth crept under skin, steady despite everything fraying around them.

"We've been through worse," Marti said; not soft, never soft, but real.

Lori swallowed hard around whatever answer tried to rise up first.

"You always do this," she murmured.

"Yeah?" Marti arched an eyebrow.

"Make me say yes when I want to say fuck no."

Marti winked. "Call it charm."

Coffee drained, still awful; toast untouched; photo rescued from syrup purgatory and folded back into Marti's pocket like a vow.

Lori reached across and snagged half of the cold toast before it could mold in protest.

"All right then," she said around a bite that tasted more like cardboard than commitment, but would have to do for now. "Let's go find your missing girl before she ends up as another mural on 8th Street."

Marti stood and cracked her neck as if they weren't about to walk into hell armed with nothing but instinct and bad attitudes.

"Twisted paths are our thing," she said over her shoulder as they left the diner behind them and stepped into whatever passed for morning.

The sun melted behind the skyline like a busted yolk, bleeding gold over Falls City's busted rooftops and rusted billboards. Marti lit her cigarette with a flick that said fuck this day and kept walking, Shadow inhaler in her other hand. The hit didn't help much. It turned her headache into a throbbing buzz and gave everything sharper edges.

Lori walked beside her, arms crossed tight like she was holding herself together with elbows and spite. She didn't say anything about the Shadow. Again. Just narrowed her eyes at every stranger they passed, scanning faces for a ghost.

"Christ," Marti muttered, stepping around a puddle that might have been rainwater or piss. "Smells like someone deep-fried a corpse."

"Falls City's finest cologne," Lori said.

* * *

The city was alive as if an infected wound: hot and festering and full of things that shouldn't be moving. Alleys twisted between buildings like veins. Trash spilled from bins like drunken poetry. Somewhere in the darkness, music throbbed from a busted speaker half-submerged in gutter water.

Marti's gaze snapped to a hunched figure pressed against the wall of an abandoned shopfront, just another lump among the graffiti and grime. He was staring at them as if he half-recognized something human.

She strode toward him without looking back at Lori. "Hey! You know LaLoLa?"

The guy blinked up at her through bloodshot eyes, pupils wide and wrong. He scratched at his arm, skin flaking off around raw scabs. Up close he smelled like rot and peppermints.

"LaLoLa?" he echoed, thick as syrup. "Yeah... saw her maybe... week ago?"

Marti crouched beside him, flicking ash onto the curb. "Where?"

Lori kneeled next to her, voice soft enough to sound harmless but with that blade-under-silk edge Marti loved too much for comfort. "Where'd you see her?"

The man pointed down an alley so narrow it could've been stitched shut with wire.

"By that old motel," he said. "Think it was the Whimsy... 43rd and Rockland." He coughed into his sleeve, wet and phlegmy, and added, "Girl was lookin' bad. Heard she owed people money... real wrong people."

"The Whimsy? Never even fucking heard of it. There's a goddamn army of motels in this hellhole," Marti muttered.

"Pretty sure it was the Whimsy."

Marti tossed him a few crumpled bills without waiting for thanks. He grabbed them as if they were burning holes through the concrete.

"Let's go," she said to Lori without looking back.

They cut through the backstreets Ironhook , coated in damp fog and graffiti layer cake until the Whimsy loomed ahead like something out of a fever dream trying too hard to look normal. The neon sign buzzed overhead; its pink W flickered so it pulsed: himsy... himsy... himsy...

A couple of bodies loitered in the parking lot: too twitchy to be asleep but not alert enough to give a shit about anything happening around them.

Marti stopped short at the curb.

The Mac Town neighborhood.

Fuck.

The memory made her stop cold.: blood on linoleum tile, sirens slicing open the night air, a broken body sprawled across a mattress that should've been burned years ago. The same peeling green paint clung to the walls like dried snot. Same black plastic garbage bags taped over windows as if anyone here still cared about privacy anymore.

This place wasn't just another dead-end tip. It was the place. Her first major case. Her first real ghost.

Her cigarettes tasted like ashtray dust now instead of nicotine and relief.

Lori watched her without speaking, lips parted like she wanted to say something but didn't know whether now was the moment for comfort or claws.

"This is where it happened," Marti said, as if Lori hadn't already picked that up from the way she went stiff as rebar.

"What happened?" Lori asked.

"Rape-homicide," Marti replied. Two words delivered like gunshots to the face. "My first."

She crossed into the cracked lot because if you stop walking in Falls City you start sinking instead. She wasn't ready to be buried yet.

Inside her ribcage, something twisted: a knot of dread pulled tight by time and memory and all the things she hadn't managed to outrun yet.

Some places don't forget you even when you beg them to.

And this one?

This one remembered everything.

"Keep your eyes up," Marti muttered, flicking her cigarette into a puddle as they stepped around a half-squashed rat. "This place smells like moldy ass and trauma."

"Duly noted," Lori said, voice tight. She hugged her notepad to herself as if it might deflect bullets or bad memories.

The alley narrowed before spitting them out in front of the Low Tide Motel, what passed for hospitality in this part of Falls City. Neon letters buzzed overhead like they were trying to give up the ghost. The rain had slowed to a sulk, but the air clung damp and sour.

Inside, the front office felt like stepping into a forgotten ashtray. Stale beer, old smoke, and something sweeter rotting beneath it all. A man hunched behind the desk, beard gnarly enough to house wildlife, flipping through yesterday's paper like it was interesting.

Marti rapped her knuckles against the counter and said, "Looking for LaLoLa."

Scraggly Beard blinked up at her, eyes bloodshot and unfocused, as if he was trying to remember if that was a name or a fever dream.

"LaLoLa?" he said, scratching his beard with fingers that hadn't seen soap since Clinton left office. "Yeah... rings a bell. Dealt stuff around here. Haven't seen her in days though."

"And?" Lori asked, pulling out her pen.

He sniffed. "Word is some of her clients bit the dust: bad batches. OD'd right in their shitty little rooms. Then someone said she offed herself after that."

Marti stiffened, instinct tightening in her gut. "Where?"

He shrugged. "Don't know. Not here; that's for damn sure. I run a clean business." He took a swig from a metal flask that said otherwise.

Great. Another dead end soaked in bourbon breath.

He jabbed a thumb toward across the street. "Try Athena's Palace: hair joint over there. Owner knows every-one and their grandma."

Marti slid him two crumpled bills without breaking eye contact, payment for information and silence both, and turned on her heel.

Rain greeted them again with renewed spite as they dashed across the street, puddles slapping cold water onto their ankles.

"Let's hope Athena's more informative than beard-boy," Lori muttered, teeth chattering.

Chapter 6

The crossed the street, dodging cars that were aiming for them just for fun. A flickering neon sign reading simply "ATHENA'S" buzzed above the entrance. Below it, taped to the glass door, was a weathered handwritten sign in faded marker: "Specializing in natural styles, braids & locs. Black-owned since 2041. No appointments needed for sisters."

The salon door opened with the cheerful jingle of bells that didn't belong in this neighborhood. Inside: warmth, soft jazz murmuring over the hum of dryers and gossiping women who barely glanced up from their mirrors.

And then there was her.

Fuck me.

Standing near the back wall in a dress so tight Marti could chart the rise and fall of every breath beneath it. Beautiful didn't cut it; this woman looked carved out of sex appeal and late-night mistakes you didn't regret until morning.

"Well hey there," she purred before either of them spoke, eyeing Marti first, then Lori, then back again as if she was picking dinner off a menu.

"I'm looking for Athena," Marti said, though careful thoughts were being slaughtered by whatever sparked between them.

"That's me," she said with a smile sharp enough to leave marks. Her gaze slid down Marti's frame like honey before locking onto her eyes with challenge. "You two cops?"

Marti laughed once: a dry bark meant to clear tension but failed under that gaze. "Nope. Private investigator."

"Aha," Athena breathed, stepping close for casual conversation but not quite close enough to make it illegal. Her perfume wrapped itself around Marti like liquid temptation: jasmine and danger. She leaned in until Marti could feel breath on skin.

"Nice to meet you," Athena said, voice brushing soft along nerves Marti forgot existed. Then came the smile again, knowing now, and one brief glance at Marti's lips as if she could already taste them if she tried hard enough.

"We're looking for someone," Lori chirped, oblivious to the rising sexual tension.

"I can help you," Athena said as she held Marti's stare. "But we'd better talk in my office."

Marti knew she should keep things professional, but fuck that. Or rather, fuck this. She found herself nodding while heat bloomed between her thighs. She was half-haunted already; might as well kiss something living.

"Yeah," she managed, clearing her throat like that would fix anything inside her skull or below it. She turned toward Lori without meeting her eyes.

"Interview whoever looks scared or nosy," Marti said. "I'll be... talking with Athena."

Lori raised an eyebrow but didn't say anything; she smirked as she drifted toward a cluster of stylists mid-gossip session, but all exchanging knowing nods as they glanced at Athena.

Athena walked ahead like she owned the place. It was her name on the door after all. Marti followed, pretending not to stare at the curve of her hips, the way her silk dress clung as if it had secrets to protect. The narrow corridor opened into a room at the back, lit and more boudoir than business office: two soft chairs angled close together under the hum of a lamp that flickered as if it had a headache.

"Have a seat," Athena said, voice velvet-wrapped steel. She shut the door with a soft click that sounded loud in the quiet room.

Marti dropped into one chair, trying not to look like she was sinking. Athena lowered herself into the opposite seat as if it was a throne, every movement deliberate. Her dress rode high on her thigh and dipped low at her chest: just enough to suggest, not enough to explain. Their knees nearly touched. Marti didn't move hers.

"So," Athena said, leaning forward. Her necklace caught what little light there was and swung toward Marti's face before settling right between her breasts. "What brings you here, honey?"

Marti tried to focus anywhere else and failed.

"I'm following up on a case," she said, voice scratchy from disuse or smoke or something worse. "I heard you might have seen someone I'm trying to find."

Athena gave her a grin like she'd heard this story before and didn't buy the ending. "You gonna tell me who this mystery woman is?"

"LaLoLa," Marti said. She held up the creased photograph and pretended not to notice how her eyes kept drifting toward Athena's hemline. She was failing at it.

"She come through here recently?"

Athena tilted her head, crossed one leg over the other slow enough to count as foreplay. Her shoe brushed against Marti's calf: just a whisper of contact, but deliberate. Too deliberate.

"Honey, I have no idea," Athena said flatly, like she was bored. One finger traced circles into the armrest like she was carving time out of the upholstery. "Blonde then? Platinum tips? Deep part?" She looked up through lashes like stage curtains dropping across an act. "Doesn't ring a bell."

Silence hovered for a second too long.

"That all you wanted?" Athena asked, letting her voice drag along the bottom of the question.

The air between them twisted: thick with heat and mistrust.

"There's... another matter," Marti said. Her throat felt dry but she didn't swallow.

No blink from Athena this time. Just a step forward.

"What kind of matter?" she asked, hand dropping onto Marti's thigh like she owned it or expected to soon enough. Her fingers curled just enough to stir blood without raising alarms. But Marti's pulse was hammering like someone had called last call on control an hour ago.

"You're beautiful when you're pretending not to be nervous," Athena murmured as her hand shifted upward: lazy as cigarette smoke curling toward a ceiling fan.

Marti didn't answer.

Couldn't.

Athena smiled into the silence like someone who liked breaking things just to check what they were made of. Her fingers skated down Marti's arm, warm as whiskey, soft as threat, until goosebumps prickled in their wake.

"Go ahead," she whispered. "Say what you need."

Marti leaned forward before her brain caught up with her body; tension snapped hot between them like static looking for a ground wire.

"I need you to fuck me," she said.

Each word cracked out like evidence read into record.

Athena's expression twisted into something toothy and amused. "All business until you aren't, hmm? I like that in a woman."

Marti exhaled sharp and low, legs pressing together on impulse alone.

"I think LaLoLa won't mind," she added, rough now around the edges. "You going to fuck me?"

"I thought you'd never ask."

Then everything tilted.

Athena stood fast and dragged Marti up by her jacket lapels like gravity had traded sides just for them. She slammed into velvet wallpaper, softened only by memory and adrenaline, and Athena's mouth claimed hers hard enough to short-circuit thought.

"Now," Athena muttered against her jawline between kisses that bit as much as they begged, "why are you looking for that girl?"

"Friend of a friend." The words slipped out between gasps and tongue flicks across pulse points. "She's gone missing… he's worried."

Athena's laugh hit low against her throat as one hand found its way around and grabbed a handful of denim-covered ass without apology.

"There was someone came through… might've been her," she said between kisses that refused to stop long enough for full sentences. "Snorting chemtrails… muttering surveillance paranoia crap… tried to hide under the sink… we tossed her out two weeks ago."

Marti shuddered hard, and not from arousal this time.

She moaned when Athena slid warm hands beneath fabric built more for threats than seduction, even if this felt like both at once.

A lead's still a lead, even if it left teeth marks behind.

Athena broke their kiss with something close to satisfaction before brushing lips against Marti's ear in something that sounded intimate if you didn't know better.

"I want to taste you," she breathed: quiet but sharp enough to cut through muscle memory and whatever resistance was still pretending to stand guard inside Marti's chest.

"But keep your voice down next time," Athena added as she yanked on Marti's belt loop. "Scare off customers otherwise."

Marti nodded; speech was overrated right now anyway. Her hands went under Athena's dress, palming over one breast then another until Athena groaned through clenched teeth like it cost something personal to keep quiet here too.

Then Marti let herself go lower: down over thighs tensed with intent until Athena grabbed her wrist. Not to stop her but guide her homeward instead, placing skin against soaked fabric without ceremony or shame.

Heat swelled under Marti's palm: the kind that promised destruction dressed as invitation. Athena rocked into it once like punctuation at end of sentence neither of them had bothered finishing yet.

Athena grabbed Marti by the waist and pulled her flush again, hips aligning like loaded dice thrown across cheap carpet, and kissed hard again while furniture scraped behind them under pressure neither cared enough to ease off from now.

Marti pressed back harder than necessary; took bruises as proof-of-contact while desk edges dug into flesh made tender by attention rather than absence.

Then Athena stepped back without warning and pulled off Marti's shirt in one smooth haul; bra followed with nothing but finger familiarity and erotic detachment before tossing it aside like laundry in someone else's story.

Marti found herself topless on an office desk that smelled of burned coffee and lye while Athena dropped between her legs like a prayer had been replaced by ritual with teeth instead of faith behind it all.

A kiss landed over bone; another lower; then teeth honed in on nipple while one hand pressed against spine until arching became imperative. Not choice but reaction worn raw by need masquerading as control one last time before giving up.

"Fuck..." It came out cracked wide open when nothing else would form anymore worth saying aloud.

Her fingers fumbled at denim fly stiff with sweat but Athena slapped them away with: "Let me."

She guided Marti forward like she was opening a file folder: quick, efficient, with just enough cruelty baked into care that it stopped being legal somewhere along the line but no one cared anymore anyway. Not in here. Not now when everything reeked of lust and unfinished business in equal parts measureless width apart from each other across skin still catching up to itself mid-motion.

"Lift."

The command landed low but solid; not request bglut necessity dressed casual in silk tones slick enough not to notice they were orders at all until obeying became automatic again.

Marti lifted herself onto elbows while jeans fell away with metal brushing linoleum beside gunmetal weight she'd forgotten about.

Her sidearm clunked onto deskwood hard enough for reality check-in.

"Fuck, I..."

"I don't care," Athena clipped while sliding metal skyward off desktop with two-finger ease before tossing it aside without reverence or concern alike: proof she'd handled more frightening things than this before breakfast every day since puberty probably. "We'll put that over there."

"Yes..."

But no more words were given space past that because Athena stepped back between spread thighs with precision built from bad intentions done well.

Sliding forward fast, lifting cotton aside like peeling away someone's last lie, and then teeth again first, then tongue, and nothing else mattered except heat threading along nerves too frayed from years spent pretending power didn't feel like this.

The underwear didn't survive long.

One push back too firm sent Marti into memory: motel floor blood-slicked linoleum flash-stamped behind eyes shut tight too late now.

"You okay?" came muffled against inner thigh.

"Yeah." Lie-shaped answer barked out fast before guilt could catch up.

She let go again anyway.

Let fingers replace friction; let tongue find everything lost in-between sense and surrender; let breath stutter out across ribcage where pain used to live rent-free until pleasure chased it screaming down side streets lined with neon regret wrapped tight around one good fuck disguised as interrogation tactic gone rogue.

"Oh fuck yeah, I uh... about Chemtrails..."

But speech blurred out again behind suction precise enough for confession; each flick sent thought scattering through skull walls thickened by bourbon regrets and love never survived.

"Concentrate," came voice low against clit now flushed pink beneath expert pressure drowning logic inside need turned feral fast.

"You don't multitask well enough for questions right now."

And then?

"Concentrate, honey. You don't multitask well enough to be asking questions right now," Athena said, voice flat as a file and twice as sharp, just before her mouth found Marti's clit.

Marti came hard: like steel snapping under pressure. Loud. Unstoppable. The kind of release that didn't ask permission or wait for grace.

Her hands clutched at Athena's shoulders sometime after the peak, seeking purchase, maybe penance. When sensation loosened its grip enough for thought to crawl back in, Athena was standing again, a crooked grin on her face like she'd tasted something forbidden and liked it too much to admit it.

She kissed Marti then: slow and sealing, like closing a case file no one would ever open again.

Marti didn't move right away. She looked wrecked in the most human way: skin slick with sweat and sex, breath coming back in broken stutters while her body tried to remember what normal felt like.

"Jesus." It came out hoarse, like she'd smoked it through regret.

Athena draped an arm around her waist with casual possession, as though this was some kind of shared prize instead of two women tangled across office furniture that reeked of stale toner and late nights gone bad.

She pressed lips to Marti's forehead, not tender so much as territorial, and leaned back on her heels between Marti's legs like she had every right to admire the ruin she'd left behind.

"You're beautiful," she said. Her voice didn't waver; it wasn't praise so much as simple inventory.

Marti snorted through what could've been disbelief or denial. She didn't argue though. Just let the edges of a smile curl into shape as something warm flickered low in her gut. Not flash-fire lust this time but something slower burning... dangerous because it lasted longer.

"We both know you're the beautiful one here." She paused then added: "My turn to fuck you?"

Athena laughed: a low sound built for smoke-filled rooms and locked doors. She tossed her hair out of her face like none of this would cost her anything in daylight.

"Yes," she said again like maybe saying it twice made it stick harder. "Yes."

Then quieter: "I need more of you."

Marti didn't move right away. She just reached for Athena like gravity had rules again, hands finding hip-bones that felt sharper than they had any right to be at this distance.

"I need to fuck you," she said flatly: just the facts, no embellishment. She kissed whatever skin she could reach next like punctuation on a sentence no one else needed to read aloud.

"Marti?"

Fucking Lori.

Mart's head hung down, defeated.

"Work calls? You know, girls like you come hard and leave harder," Athena said as she grabbed a tissue from the box on the desk. She dabbed at her lips.

"I think you'll need a touchup," Marti grinned.

"Take my number," Athena murmured near Marti's collarbone, voice gone velvety but still clear enough to cut glass. "Call me... come to me... fuck me. When we have more time."

And just like that it unmoored something inside Marti again: not lust this time but ache, that fragile shapeless thing kept buried under sarcasm and narcotics.

She inhaled through clenched teeth as she sat up straighter on the desk, legs still shaking from orgasm but mind already drifting somewhere less tender than before.

Her jeans were pooled near one ankle so it took effort bending far enough to reach into the pocket for what came next: small, metallic blue inhaler tucked behind some StimGum and a small Fentafill pill.

Across from her, Athena sucked her teeth. "Don't call me when you're high. I want my pussy clean." Her warm eyes narrowed just enough for judgment to curl between them.

"No worries. It's just currency for intel," Marti lied. She exhaled through parted lips and tucked the inhaler back where it belonged: close enough to reach for again if things got complicated later, which they always did.

"Thanks for making me feel good," Marti said, still catching her breath. Her fingers fumbled at the buttons of her shirt, sliding them through the holes as if it was a sin to move too fast.

Athena watched with the smug calm of someone who knew she'd rocked somebody's axis. "Pleasure was mutual," she said, brushing a damp strand from Marti's face.

It wasn't just a farewell line, not with the way her eyes lingered: intense, like Marti was a puzzle worth solving.

Athena adjusted her blouse with the kind of ease that should come with a warning label. She slipped a card into Marti's back pocket, fingers trailing just enough to make sure Marti noticed. "Personal number's on the back."

"Call me if you find LaLoLa. Sisters are vanishing every day."

"I will," Marti said before she could think better of it.

Marti didn't move. Some moments dared you to ruin them by moving.

Then came Lori's voice, slicing through whatever spell they'd spun between expert hands and spread legs.

"Hey, Marti. We should go," she called. "Got another lead across town."

Marti stepped back as if it hurt; maybe it did, just not in any way she'd say out loud. One last look passed between them with unfinished business written all over it. Marti ran a hand through her hair and slapped her work face back on.

When she emerged from the back room, Lori gave her one of those looks but didn't say shit about the flushed cheeks or the swagger in Marti's walk. Some stories wrote themselves.

They left the salon together, door clicking shut behind them like punctuation. Outside, the streets of Mac Town sucked up the rain and spit back steam and neon reflections. Falls City smelled like moldy pavement and bad decisions no one regretted enough to stop making.

Marti pulled up her hood against the downpour as they pushed into the dark.

"Did she give you anything useful?" Lori asked, trudging beside her with cop energy barely contained under civilian clothes.

Marti smirked without turning. "She gave me an orgasm."

Lori choked on that one; not quite a cough, not quite innocent anymore.

"I mean," Marti added; "her nipples are going to haunt my dreams in a good way."

"Marti." Lori tried for stern but landed closer to scandalized schoolteacher.

"What? You asked."

Lori scowled ahead. "Seriously though: anything useful about LaLoLa?"

"Maybe she came in a couple of weeks ago. Maybe she was on some new drug named Chemtrails. Maybe so fucking high she had no idea what was going on," Marti said, grin fading as reality reasserted itself like an overdue bill.

Chapter 7

Rain beat down like debt collectors with grudges. The sidewalks shimmered with garbage water and god-knows-what else as Marti and Lori huddled beneath a busted holo-hourglass sign that pulsed warm and gold. Marti swore it was mimicking the rhythm of the orgasm Athena had provided.

Across from them stood The Handsome Dove: a drug den dressed in peeling neon and false promises. People slinked around its entrance like ghosts looking for bodies to borrow.

"Last time we were here," Marti muttered around her cigarette, "that fucker shot me."

"You got paid for it," Lori said as she pulled her coat tighter.

"That doesn't make me any happier."

"The man who set you up is dead," Lori countered.

"Feeling happy now," Marti said and blew smoke in Lori's face.

"We've got this," Lori said beside her, scanning faces as if she had x-ray vision baked into those librarian glasses. "You're not getting shot again. Or kidnapped."

"Aw," Marti grinned crookedly, tapping ash into a puddle before flicking the butt into traffic. "You do care."

"I'm not dragging your bullet-riddled ass out of another shootout unless I get hazard pay," Lori replied.

"Says the woman who bolted without so much as a flesh wound last time."

Lori deadpanned back at her. "I told you I don't do bullets."

Marti scanned the crowd and found him: a young guy leaning against cracked brickwork, cradling his arm as if he'd pissed off someone who played rougher than he did. Face drawn tight around too much pain and not enough hope.

"He looks stab-resistant," Marti said, nodding his way.

Lori followed with a glance and gave her a tiny nod, the kind that meant 'try not to scare him off'.

They moved in together, two rain-soaked women in black boots and sharper intentions, toward the man bleeding misery onto some back-alley corner of Falls City.

He looked up at them; eyes tired enough to make Marti feel almost apologetic just for showing up alive. Almost.

Marti flashed a smile that had gotten her into better conversations than this and worse. "We're looking for someone. Thought you might feel helpful today."

The kid shifted, sneakers scraping on wet pavement. Sweat pooled in the hollow of his throat despite the chill. "Sure, for a price. Depends who you're after."

Marti stepped close. Close enough to smell the sour tang of nerves clinging to his hoodie. She held out the photo.

"LaLoLa."

His eyes darted toward the alley wall as if he thought it might rat him out. "Oh fuck, yeah, I saw her." He leaned in, whisper rasping like sandpaper. "Couple days ago. She was going down on some guy back there."

"Back where?"

He tilted his chin toward a garbage-stained doorway behind them.

Marti raised a brow. "And this is information you just happened to stumble across?"

He shrugged, but Marti caught the guilt twitching beneath his jawline.

"Waiting for your turn? Okay, describe the guy."

"Fat guy, bald, limp dick," he said without flinching. "Had trouble getting it up, so she laughed at him."

Marti blinked. "Did he get mad?"

"Not really. I think he was on Blue Star; giggled like it was a sitcom rerun, then let her finish him off anyway." He scratched at his arm.

Marti fished a few bills from her pocket and pressed them into his hand. "Thanks for not filming it."

"Didn't have enough battery life," he quipped.

She almost laughed.

They walked away under a canopy of rusted fire escapes and sagging laundry lines.

"You think maybe the guy did something to LaLoLa?" Lori asked beside her, voice low but tight.

Marti lit a cigarette with steady fingers. "Doubt it. He got what he came for and then some. But our friend over there watching from the shadows? That's more interesting." She scanned the street again. "Who's next?"

Lori nodded toward a woman parked on an upturned crate, skin like old parchment and hands twitching in slow earthquakes. "Maybe her?"

Marti had no time to answer before something shifted at the edge of her vision; movement threaded through the crowd like a needle stitching trouble into fabric.

She grabbed Lori's wrist hard enough to stop her mid-step.

"There." A sharp nod toward the man leaning against a graffiti-tagged wall like he owned it. Balding. Fat. Probably a limp dick: Detective Damian Kane. The ex-partner who was with Marti the night she let Charlie Gomez escape custody. The night Gomes killed Sabrina Kogoya. The night Marti's life fell apart.

He was talking to Hitchcock, one of those dealers who thought selling spice made him untouchable.

"What the hell," Lori muttered beside her, eyes narrowing as she recognized Kane's face beneath the streetlight glow.

"Yeah," Marti said, voice dry as ash. "That's Kane."

"What's he doing here?"

"Whatever it is, it smells bad and has graft in it." Marti didn't take her eyes off him.

Kane turned mid-conversation and scanned the crowd, then locked eyes with them.

Her stomach clenched hard.

"Fuck me," she hissed under her breath, then louder: "Now."

She pulled Lori with her, slipping between two buildings as fast as their legs would go without drawing attention. Trash crunched underfoot; neon light from a busted sign flickered overhead as if it was judging them both.

A cardboard box loomed out of nowhere, too fast to avoid. They went down together in a mess of limbs and half-muffled curses.

The alley stank of old piss and moldy paperboard and something metallic that could've been blood or just city rot.

"Fuck me," Marti said again through grit teeth.

But Lori wasn't hearing her anymore, not really. Somewhere between surprise, adrenaline, and Marti saying fuck me with that voice, all logic had exited stage left.

They were tangled close: legs overlapped, chest to chest if anyone blinked twice. Lori could see every fleck of silver shot through Marti's storm-colored eyes.

"Fuck me."

Did she just say...?

Lori froze mid-breath. Her mouth parted as if kissing Marti now might make gravity stop working altogether.

It didn't matter that they were lying in garbage juice with Kane circling outside like a shark with a badge. Lori wanted to kiss her anyway.

More than anything else in this city full of addicts and missing girls and ex-cop ghosts.

She kissed her.

Marti blinked at her once: the kind of blink that meant don't.

And yet didn't quite mean stop, either.

Marti cursed under her breath. "Thought Kane looked our way. We can't risk getting spotted."

She shoved herself off the damp concrete, brushing grime from her jeans like it had offended her.

Lori stayed crouched a beat longer, eyes fixed on Marti's hand; the one that had gripped hers too tight to just be tactical. She swallowed whatever idea was clawing its way up her throat. A kiss wasn't going to solve anything. Would've made things worse, actually. Way worse.

"Yeah," she said, standing up beside Marti, voice tight around the edges. "Let's avoid any more surprise cameos."

"Goddamn right." Marti scanned the alley again, already mapping exits and scenarios in her head. No matter how Kane's name came up, it still rang wrong in her ears, like chewing on tinfoil. Something was off, and she needed answers before someone ended up dead. Again.

They cut across three alleys of wet pavement and city stench before slipping back toward The Handsome Dove. Marti kept low behind a stack of garbage cans slick with rain. Lori flanked her without a word.

Kane stood outside the rear entrance, talking to Hitchcock as if they were trading stock tips instead of secrets.

Too far to hear anything useful, but they both saw it: the subtle handoff of something small, a package, an envelope. Could've been a birthday card or powdered death in wrapping paper.

"Did you see that?" Marti muttered.

Lori gave a curt nod. "What the hell are they doing?"

"Drugs," Marti said. "Has to be drugs."

"But Kane?" Lori squinted at him through dripping bangs.

"Exactly," Marti said. "Which means either I never knew him or he's gotten real good at hiding his rot."

"So do we follow them or…?"

Marti didn't answer right away. Her gaze tracked Kane's hand disappearing into his jacket pocket.

"He's carrying," she said.

"So are you," Lori shot back.

"Yeah," Marti said, "but I don't get government permission slips for murder."

Lori raised an eyebrow. "Never stopped you before."

Marti smirked and looked away.

"So what now?" Lori asked.

"We avoid that asshole," Marti said, already moving. "Don't give a shit about Kane." Her jaw tightened. "But I do want to know why that asshole is crawling around my neighborhood."

"You think he is going to become a regular on the scene?"

"Nah. I'll start spreading the word that he's unreliable. Junkies trust me. C'mon." Marti jerked her head. Time to go.

They peeled off from the alley, boots slapping against rain-slicked asphalt as they melted into the city's shadowy veins: half ghosts, half stormclouds with unfinished business.

In a recessed doorway, a woman with hollow cheeks counted invisible objects, her fingers twitching in the air as she muttered calculations only she could understand.

Nearby, a cluster of addicts huddled around a burn barrel. One man extended gnarled hands toward the flames, palms bearing the characteristic chemical burns of someone who'd cooked their own supply.

A pair of sex workers leaned against a corroded fire escape, their outfits a strange collision of practicality and fantasy: mesh tops revealing the outlines of protective vests underneath, stiletto boots reinforced with metal plates.

The streets of the Redspan District reeked of wet garbage and desperation; neon signs bled color onto puddles like open wounds. Nobody spoke for two blocks.

Then Marti stopped walking.

At first glance, Rat looked barely human, slumped under the busted overhang of an abandoned bodega as if he were landfill with a pulse.

"Shit," Marti breathed. She moved before the thought finished forming. "Rat!"

His head lolled when she crouched beside him, eyes glassy and far too blue for this world anymore.

"What the fuck happened to you?" she asked, slapping his cheek, not enough to hurt but enough to demand life find its way back in there somewhere.

Rat gurgled something between a sob and nothing at all.

"Fuck." Marti pressed two fingers against his neck, felt the slow thud of something trying not to die.

"He's overdosing," she snapped, fury pulsing through her usual calm like broken glass.

Lori fumbled with her phone, hands shaking so bad she almost dropped it twice before finally punching in 911.

"Don't you fucking dare," Marti hissed, gripping Rat's shoulders. His eyes fluttered like a dying streetlamp. "You better not make me write a eulogy for your sorry ass."

"I've got dispatch," Lori called, fingers tight around the phone. "911, yes, possible overdose, northeast corner of Fifth and Larimer. Send someone now."

"Help's en route," came the operator's voice, tinny and detached. "Please stay on the line."

Like hell she'd hang up. Lori nodded, knuckles white, even though No-Name McDispatcher couldn't see her.

Rain kept hammering down as if it had something to prove. Cold seeped straight through their coats; it didn't matter. Marti barely felt it. Her focus was locked on Rat: pale lips, twitching hands, heartbeat playing hide and seek beneath clammy skin.

"Where did you get this bad shit, asshole." She muttered it into his hair as she cradled him against her knees, voice low like a threat or a prayer. "You don't get to die just to piss me off."

Sirens shrieked through the night as if the city itself had stubbed its toe. Lights slashed across the alley walls. Uniforms were everywhere: boots splashing through puddles, gloves snapping on, voices blurring into static.

"He's breathing but fading. Get oxygen on him!"

A stretcher appeared like magic, and Rat was gone before Marti could finish the sentence lodged in her throat.

"You two coming?" one of them asked over the flap of doors and hiss of hydraulics.

Marti stared at the open ambulance as if it had teeth. She shook her head once and turned.

"He'll live," she said to Lori as they walked away, because if she didn't say it out loud, maybe he wouldn't.

"He'd fucking better."

The ambulance drove off with a scream too loud for an empty backseat.

Chapter 8

They didn't speak again until they hit Seventh. Rain kept sulking behind them, turning neon signs into bruises across wet pavement. Guilt trailed them like a third shadow.

Back at the office, everything smelled damp and burned: fried circuits from old machines that didn't appreciate sudden resurrection after patrol in monsoon conditions.

Marti kicked her door open and dropped into her chair as if gravity was her lover. "Rat knows his shit. Must have been a bad batch. He needs LaLoLa," she said over her shoulder as she pulled up the terminal. "Let's see if the wires are talking."

"I'll get started." Lori peeled out of her wet jacket and slid into her seat without comment. The screen flickered to life slower than usual, a stubborn mule of a processor, and she silently dared it to challenge her patience tonight.

Lori slammed the Enter key as if it had personally insulted her, then stared down the screen as if intimidation might speed things up. The loading bar inched across the glass as if it had all fucking day. When the files finally blinked into existence, she leaned in, eyes flicking over each header as if they might suddenly scream out "Here's your smoking gun, dumbass."

They dove headfirst into digital rot: forgotten forums littered with conspiracy theories, half-deleted news clippings buried under paywalls, glitchy archives held together by obsolete code and duct tape. Every link felt like a middle finger. Every search spat back static or dead ends disguised as deep dives. Nothing but shadows and rumor scraps. Still, they kept going. If LaLoLa had left a breadcrumb trail, Lori was ready to tear through the whole damn internet to find it.

"I'm expanding my criteria," Lori announced.

Marti smirked. "That's what I said to that dominatrix I met last month."

"Perv. It doesn't surprise me if LaLoLa isn't online under her name. I'm going to see what gossip I can find on Kane. Junkies will name him."

"Why Kane?"

Marti didn't wait for results before lighting up a cigarette with hands that weren't steady. She paced the office while smoke curled against cracked ceiling tiles.

"Why not? Maybe if he's taking bribes from that Hitchcock guy, he's helping him get into LaLoLa's territory," Lori said as she slammed her fingertips on little black squares.

"It's a stretch," Marti said. Then she shrugged. She had no other ideas.

"Come on come on come on…" Lori muttered as progress bars crawled uphill.

Finally: text populated. A mess of unverified sources, conspiracy threads wrapped in pseudonyms and paranoia, sketchy leads that smelled fake from three VPNs away.

"Fuck this," Marti grumbled as she headed into her office. She dug into her coat pocket and pulled out a red Shadow inhaler just for comfort.

Lori walked in just as Marti let the vapor settle deep in her chest.

She didn't say anything at first, just leaned against the doorway watching with arms crossed tight enough to hurt herself; not tight enough to stop caring.

Marti caught the look but didn't apologize. That ship had sunk years ago when she'd chosen this cocktail over therapy or retirement or anything healthy.

"You know," Marti said after a pause, voice soft but still edged in steel, "most people who don't use treat me like I'm ticking."

"You are ticking," Lori said, dropping into the chair across from her. "But I've seen worse explosions."

Marti smiled around another drag of Shadow-induced calm, the kind that numbed just enough without fixing shit at all.

"Besides," Lori added, glancing at the files loading as if moving with continental drift, "you're damn good at what you do."

Marti snorted. "Good? This gig's just babysitting with extra bullets."

Lori leaned in, elbows on the desk as if she was hearing gospel. "Bullets and babysitting?"

"Mostly just losers who can't keep it in their pants or assholes who borrowed money from people with more tattoos than mercy." Marti swirled the cigarette between her fingers. "It's not the life plan I sketched out during career week."

Lori tilted her head, watching her as if trying to spot fracture lines. "Ever think about doing something else?"

Marti blew smoke toward the ceiling and shrugged as if change sounded too exhausting to consider. "Not really. I do this well enough. No family connections, no trust fund, no backup plan. Just me and my bad decisions."

"You're selling yourself short," Lori said, voice sharp as a papercut. "You're smart in that scary way: like you'd know how to dispose of a body and make it look like someone's crazy for thinking the person ever lived."

Marti smirked. "Compliment accepted."

Lori smiled in return, and it lingered. Just long enough to be dangerous.

Lori ambled back to her desk and blinked at her screen again. Shook her head with a groan. "Still nothing."

Marti wasn't listening. "But Kane's a cop," Marti dragged the ashtray closer. "Ever since the last Chief of Police got his face rearranged by a car bomb, they scrubbed officer names from public records. Can't have civilians knowing who's a target."

"Charming world we live in," Lori muttered. Lori began browsing the the Falls City Police Department's social media feed. Missing. Missing. Drug cache found. Man found on sidewalk. Reports of a woman screaming.

Marti opened her desk drawer as if she was expecting treasure but settled for poison. She yanked out a half-empty bottle of whiskey and two mismatched glasses. She crossed over to Lori's desk, perched on the edge.

"Drink," she said, pouring like they'd earned it. "We're gonna need all the help we can get before this turns into another dead end."

Lori just stared.

Marti tilted hers back without hesitation, let it burn deep enough to remind her she still had nerve endings.

The cursor blinked on Lori's screen while Marti's mind ran circles around itself: Hitchcock paying Kane to clear LaLoLa's territory? Or was Kane paying Hitchcock? Of what they saw had nothing to do with LaLoLa and it was just coincidence. Dead ends everywhere and she hated coincidences.

"Keep going," Marti said, eyes on the screen but seeing nothing useful. "Kane works Homicide; not Narcotics, not Vice, and he doesn't use, far as I know." She tapped ash into an old coffee mug doubling as an ashtray. "None of this fits unless there's something we just aren't seeing."

She slid the whiskey over to Lori.

Lori slid her glass back across the desk untouched. "I don't do whiskey," she said, typing. "But thanks for trying to corrupt me."

"You're missing out," Marti murmured.

"That's what you said about Shadow," Lori shot back without missing a keystroke.

Marti chuckled but didn't argue.

Then Lori stiffened in her seat, scrolling faster until she jabbed at something on screen with a triumphant gasp.

"Got something," she said, eyes wide now. "An old article: it's Kane arresting Hitchcock. Years ago."

Marti leaned over, closer than necessary, and stared at the grainy scan. Kane looked green but proud in uniform, gripping Hitchcock by the arm as he shoved him into a cruiser.

"Well I'll be damned." Marti stared at the photo as if it would give her answers. "So they go way back."

"Still nothing about LaLoLa," Lori muttered, chewing the inside of her cheek.

"We'll get there," Marti said, refilling her own glass and lighting another cigarette.

Lori had been clicking keys like a woman possessed for two hours, eyes narrowed, mouth set in that determined little line that meant either she was onto something or about to lose her shit. She set up alerts for LaLoLa, Hitchcock and even Kane. Let the bots do the searches without her.

Marti had stopped pretending to be helpful somewhere around the third cigarette. She paced. Sat on the edge of the desk. Stood up again. She poured herself more coffee just to pour half of it out and burn her tongue on the rest.

Screenshots, mugshots, glamor shots: Lori scrolled through them all as if she was auditioning for some fucked-up casting call. Marti watched her with irritated admiration. Maybe there was such a thing as too competent.

"Found something," Lori said, voice jittery with caffeine and proximity to breakthrough.

Marti leaned over her shoulder. "Please tell me it's not porn. Or maybe that it is porn."

"That was thirty-seven browser tabs ago." Lori tapped a thumbnail image. "Reverse image search on Rat's photo finally coughed something up. Took forever, but this mugshot is close enough to pucker my nipples."

Marti looked. Lori lied, they weren't puckered.

The photo unfolded on the screen: sagging eyes, sharp chin, haunted expression.

"Who is it? A brother?" Marti asked.

"LaLoLa used to go by Terrance Henderson," Lori said. "Her transition was two years ago. Under this name, her deadname, she got picked up for possession twenty-three times."

Marti let the name hang there a moment, bitter and dry in her mouth. "Terrance fucking Henderson," she muttered, letting it sting before she spit it out again. "So LaLo-

La's been running these streets longer than we thought, making way more enemies than we knew about."

FCPD's social feed kept scrolling with live updates while they talked. Dumpster fire reported. Deceased body found in park. Report of gunfire. Demonstration stopping traffic at Lorten and Victor Streets.

"LaLoLa could've been targeted for being trans," Lori said, eyes still glued to the screen's glow. "Wouldn't be new around here."

Marti nodded once, jaw tight enough to crack bone. "Email Johnny Tangle at Baker Center. Ask if they've seen any uptick in queer bashings lately." She didn't look away from the window where rain smeared streetlights into bruises against the glass. "Don't mention names yet."

"On it." Lori's fingers flew, clacking out chain mail in digital form while Marti lit another cigarette with hands that wouldn't steady.

Outside, people slipped and ducked through puddles like rats abandoning ship; slower, heavier somehow. The weight of bad choices hung low in the clouds tonight.

Inside, Lori cursed and clicked open a FCPD post. "Shit."

"What now?" Marti asked without turning around.

"Deceased body in Kransten Park identified. Frederick Hitchcock, 24," Lori said.

"Is he our Hitchcock"

"Yep."

Marti turned fast enough to knock a mug off balance: not hers. She watched it shatter against tile like punctuation. "Overdose?"

"Doesn't say," Lori said, tapping a nail on the monitor.

"I mean..." Lori shrugged but didn't look convinced either.

"So if Kane saw us seeing him with Hitchcock..." Marti muttered around her cigarette. Smoke curled above their heads as if it had somewhere better to be.

"You wanna check it out?"

"Nah," Marti said, grinding ash into ceramic. "Cops can bag his corpse without me holding their hands."

"But...?"

"Go home, Lori. It's getting late." Marti jabbed a finger toward the screen without looking at it, her eyes fixed on the case notes spread across her desk. "But keep that police feed running. If Kane shows up at Kransten, or if anyone so much as breathes LaLoLa's name near that scene, I want to know about it."

Lori was already shrugging into her coat, the fabric rustling in the quiet office. "Finally." She paused at the door, watching Marti's hunched form. The harsh fluorescents caught the deep creases between her boss's eyebrows, the slight tremble in the hand that reached for another cigarette.

"You should get some sleep too," Lori said, her voice softer than usual.

Marti's laugh cracked like thin ice. "Sleep's overrated." She didn't look up from LaLoLa's file photo, thumb tracing the edge of the glossy print.

The door clicked shut. The sudden silence pressed against Marti's eardrums, broken only by the hum of electronics and the scratch of her lighter. She flicked it once, twice, before the flame caught. The first drag of her cigarette burned all the way down, the familiar tightness spreading across her chest. She knew better. Did it anyway.

Smoke spiraled toward the water-stained ceiling as she leaned back in her chair, the springs protesting beneath her weight. Her gaze drifted to the window. Outside, a siren cut through the night. Someone else's emergency, someone else's nightmare. Red and blue lights flickered against distant buildings, then faded around a corner.

The silence returned, heavier now.

Marti turned back to the monitor, eyes burning from too many hours of staring at nothing important. LaLoLa last seen forty-eight hours ago. No trace since.

Marti stubbed out her cigarette, the ember dying against porcelain with a soft hiss. Her fingers returned to the case file Lori had so kindly printed for her.

Tomorrow would bring new leads or new dead ends, but tonight belonged to the fragments that wouldn't fit together, the puzzle with missing edges.

"See you in the morning, LaLoLa," she whispered, closing the file. Her reflection stared back from the darkened screen, hollow-eyed and grim. "Wherever the hell you are."

Chapter 9

Smoke curled around Marti's fingers as she jabbed numbers into her burner with the grace of a pissed-off raccoon. She slung her feet onto the desk, leaned back until the chair creaked, and stared at the stained ceiling as if it held the secret of life. Somewhere outside, a cat yowled: a real banshee wail. Given the rain hammering down, it made sense something out there was miserable.

The cigarette burned down to its bitter nub between her lips. She flicked it into the ashtray, missed by half an inch. Didn't matter.

Rat had OD'd. Time to call. Marti dialed the hospital to check if he was still alive, or at least still breathing.

"I'm looking for an overdose patient, came in last night," she said as soon as someone picked up.

Tone-deaf cheer on the other end: "Sure hun, what's the name?"

Marti paused to click her tongue. Names were for birth certificates and obituaries. This was Falls City; nobody had proper names unless they were carved into brass plaques or granite slabs.

"Rat," she said. "That's what I know him by. Scrawny white guy, looks as if he's been screaming at pigeons since Peterson left office."

Click-clack of keys on the other end. "Rat... Rat... Mmm. Don't see anyone by that name."

"Yeah, no shit," Marti muttered and hung up.

"Where the fuck did he go?" she asked the ceiling tiles.

"How the fuck should I know?" Lori called from the next room.

Marti barked out a laugh. "That's what worries me; he's bound to show up eventually."

She chewed her lip, fingers drumming on denim while her brain connected all the ugly little dots: Hitchcock was in LaLoLa's territory and he overdosed. Rat overdosed. Maybe LaLoLa overdosed, maybe she caused it. She was still gone without a trace. Or came back to give her competition a hot shot.

Marti stood and stretched like a cat with arthritis. "Let's check Hitchcock's haunt."

Lori appeared in the doorway, zipping up her coat, eyes glinting with something between concern and thrill-seeking kink. "That's such a weird way to refer to a death scene."

"Dark humor I picked up on the Force." Marti jammed her cigarettes into her coat pocket and followed Lori out the door because she liked the view.

They stepped out onto Sutton street, walking side-by-side under a war zone of sputtering neon signs blinking as if they were sending desperate morse code signals into the night.

* * *

A drunk stumbled out of a bar ahead of them. He smacked into a wall hard enough to leave DNA behind. The bricks scraped his hand; he didn't flinch, just kept shambling forward as if gravity didn't apply to assholes anymore.

"Jesus. It's, what, 9 AM?" Lori said as she watched him walk-ish away.

The rain wrapped around them like someone else's sweat-soaked bedsheet: intimate, gross, impossible to shake off. They reached Kransten Park where Hitchcock cashed his exit ticket.

Marti had purposefully chosen her office years ago, based on its proximity to Kransten. Close to her dealer. To any dealer.

No sirens left over. No tape fluttering in memorial breeze. Just soggy grass and apathy where some poor bastard's death registered as another Tuesday OD.

Marti crouched low near a weeping tree and started scanning as if something might jump out and explain itself.

"Let's take a look around," she muttered.

Lori shadowed her steps, close enough that their jackets brushed every few feet. Maybe that was intentional.

Lori caught Marti's wrist just long enough to make it weird in a good way. "Please don't do anything fucking stupid," she said, not begging or mothering but asking for Marti to stay alive tonight.

Marti smiled. "When am I not careful?"

Lori raised an eyebrow so hard it practically slapped her forehead.

Marti kept moving, fingers brushing trash bins, benches, bits of plastic junk washed from upstream. A figure hunched on a park bench caught her attention. Skeletal thin, jacket three sizes too big, the telltale tremor of someone riding the edge.

"Hey." She approached slowly, hands visible. "You been here all night?"

The man looked up with eyes like broken glass. Needle tracks dotted his neck like a roadmap to nowhere. He had it bad. "Depends who's asking."

"Someone who's not a cop." Marti pulled out a twenty, held it where he could see. "You know anything about an overdose around here last night? Someone died."

He stared at the bill, then at her face, calculating. "Don't know nothing about no overdose."

"But?"

"But cops were crawling all over the place to the east. Lot of activity for a Thursday night, you know?"

Marti handed him the twenty. He palmed it like a magician.

Somewhere between observation and repetition, watching him pocket the cash with junkie desperation, she gave in.

Shadow was sweating in her palm: a tiny inhaler that looked like medicine if you didn't know better.

She turned away from Lori under cover of nothing but habit and took one quick hit behind cupped hands as if it meant nothing (which it didn't unless you counted everything else before this moment) and let herself drop into that warm numb swell just long enough to forget how cold everything was.

The junkie was already shuffling away, twenty dollars richer and none the wiser that the woman who'd questioned him was just as lost as he was.

Then Lori called out sharply: "Marti."

Back spun tight with reality snapping back into place like rubber bands across skin.

She jogged over, high retreating under adrenaline's boot heel.

Lori pointed toward one tree in particular; it had three bullet wounds as if someone had tried to kill God with bad aim. Lodged inside one scarred hole sat a bullet streaked with blood and tangled hair like some fucked-up souvenir left behind for effect.

Marti squinted at it until focus settled in like fog condensing on glass. She stepped closer and lit another cigarette off instinct alone. She turned back to the junkie's bench to the west.

"Three rounds," she said. "Hair still stuck to one."

Her voice dropped colder than wet marble under bare feet as she exhaled smoke through barely parted lips.

"Is this where Hitchcock died?" Lori died as she scanned the area.

"It's east of the junkie," Marti said like she was a fucking Sphynx.

"But this? Clearly not an overdose," she said, eyes narrowed at nothing in particular except memory maybe.

"Well, you're the one who said he overdosed. Not the police feed," Lori said as she tapped Marti's shoulder.

"Fine. Look it up, what the fuck does it say?"

Lori pulled out her phone and called up the FCPD feed. "Got it. Homicide called to scene overnight...investigation ongoing...no outstanding suspects."

"No arrest announced?" Marti asked as she wiped her hand down her face.

"No. It ends there," Lori said as she looked up at the bullets. "Why would they leave those here?"

"Because they don't give a shit. No one outstanding and no one arrested means they closed it as a suicide. Somebody wants us stupid enough to believe a junkie shot himself three times."

"Who could've done this?" Lori asked, her voice caught somewhere between awe and full-blown nope.

Marti took a long drag. "Take your pick: anyone with half an agenda and worse aim."

Lori didn't reply, just watched rain drip off everything as if nature was rinsing off a crime scene. The leaves above them filtered out light in all the wrong ways, making every-thing feel quieter than it should have been.

"So is this coincidence?" Lori asked.

Marti barked out a laugh and flicked ash onto the wet ground like that was an answer. "Not coincidence," she said. "But it's something. We don't need proof; we need a name." She nudged her chin toward the embedded bullet. "Bag that."

Lori reached into her coat and pulled out a glove, a folding knife, and a plastic baggie. They'd learned early on not to let Marti near sharp objects when she was pissed or high, or worse, trying not to be either.

She snapped on the glove with a slap of latex against skin, flicked open the knife, and sank it into the pock-marked tree trunk. The bullet came loose after some wig-gling, metallic and ugly as sin. It dropped neatly into the bag.

"Do we get it tested?" she asked.

"For what? STDs? I can contact my Forensic fuck, but get it tested for what? DNA? We have no gun to match this to." Marti stepped away from the tree, scanning the underbrush as if she expected it to confess. "But if there's a gun around here, you know, the suicide weapon, maybe it matches."

Lori shoved the bagged bullet into her pocket and began using her boots and hands to brush aside the overgrowth, looking for the gun.

For about ten seconds, nothing happened. Rain hissed through leaves and Marti smoked as if it could hold back entropy. Then Lori stopped dead.

"Hold up," she said, crouching near a clump of rotting leaves. She used her boot to nudge aside the wet mess, and there it was. A wallet, half-buried, looking as if someone had flung it mid-fuck-it moment.

"Hey," she called, holding it up between two fingers as if it might still bite her. "Marti."

Marti wandered over lazily but then perked up when she saw what Lori was holding. "You touching another man's wallet in front of me? I'm wounded."

"Weirdo," Lori said, flipping open the soaked leather. "This belonged to Hitchcock."

The ID inside confirmed it: government photo, government name: Johnathan William Hitchcock.

Lori thumbed further in and found something else stuck in one of those little transparent sleeves people kept dumb shit in. A hologram flickered to life between her fingers: Hitchcock and LaLoLa leaning close in shitty nightclub lighting, their faces too close for plausible deniability.

Marti made a sound low in her throat. Not quite surprise, definitely impressed. Like confirmation of something she'd already suspected but hoped wasn't true.

"Well damn," she muttered around her cigarette as smoke curled across Lori's arm. "So they were fucking."

Lori raised an eyebrow. "Well, they were close, anyway."

Marti scratched her head. "So maybe he was working with LaLoLa, not taking her territory. LaLoLa goes missing three days ago, we see him with Kane, now he's shot dead. This changes things," Marti added.

"Does it him to LaLoLa's disappearance?" Lori asked.

Marti shook her head once, sharp as a blade swipe. "Nope. But now we know they were connected outside of dealing, which makes this even messier."

A gust of wet wind kicked up just as Marti turned back toward the tree. That's when they both spotted it at once: small cylinder tucked into muck at the roots.

Marti kneeled down fast before Lori could stop her, bare hands and zero hesitation, and picked up what looked unmistakably like a Shadow inhaler.

Only this one was wrong.

The casing shimmered faint green under grime and water drops: a warped version of something too familiar to Marti's bones.

She held it up between thumb and index finger without saying anything at first. Just stared at it as if maybe focusing hard enough could will herself not to want it.

"That Shadow?" Lori asked.

"Yeah," Marti said, flipping the green-tinged inhaler between her fingers like a coin deciding their fate. "Never seen one like this before. Definitely off. Might be important."

Lori shifted beside her, eyes combing the shadows as if someone might spring from bushes wearing a trench coat and bad intentions. "Should we take it?"

Marti held it up to her lips. "I'll take it. Obviously. Could be the key to unwinding this whole rat's nest."

"Jesus Mart! That's not what I meant." Lori's voice sharpened like a cracked whip. "You're not actually gonna use that thing, are you? We don't know where it came from or what it's been laced with. For all we know, it's been up someone's ass."

"Mmmmm, ass." Marti flicked her half-smoked cigarette into the mud and stepped on it. "I'm just taking a taste," she said, tone all sugar and knives. "Field research."

"You're unbelievable," Lori muttered, arms folding in that way Marti dreaded and secretly loved.

Marti raised the inhaler to her lips as if offering communion: blasphemous and holy at once. She pressed down, welcoming the half-hit.

Nothing.

Everything.

The rush didn't come. Instead, nausea punched her in the gut like an angry ex with brass knuckles. Her knees buckled, and she bent double as vomit splattered across the wet ground in technicolor arcs.

"Fuck!" she gasped between coughs, wiping at her mouth with a shaky hand that smelled like stale menthols and regret.

Lori was at her side, catching Marti's shoulder before she face-planted into her own bile. "Goddammit! I told you not to do that!"

"I thought it was just Shadow," Marti croaked out, spitting bile into the grass. "But that wasn't Shadow."

"No shit?" Lori snapped, crouching next to her. She looked pissed now, but underneath that was something else: panic trying not to show.

"It's wrong." Marti breathed through her nose, her stomach threatening round two if she twitched wrong. "Off-color, off-taste, off everything." She leaned back against a tree trunk slick with rain and humiliation.

"Bad batch?" Lori asked, kneeling beside her and brushing damp hair from Marti's forehead as if they weren't standing in a crime scene disguised as a public park.

"Maybe." Marti sucked air between clenched teeth. She puked again. "Or maybe it was tampered with."

Lori frowned as if she'd just done math in her head and didn't like the result. "So what? Someone poisoned it on purpose?"

Marti wiped her sleeve across her mouth and tasted blood or adrenaline; perhaps both. "Could be linked to Hitchcock."

"The dead guy?" Lori asked.

"No, the other Hitchcock," Marti snapped. "Yeah, the dead guy! What if he OD'd on this shit first? Someone panicked, made it look like a hit to cover up the real story."

"But a murder would result in an autopsy anyway." Lori said it fast.

Marti stared down at the blackened grass where she'd puked up whatever passed for breakfast that morning. The inhaler felt heavy in her coat pocket, as if it knew things she didn't.

"You're right," she muttered, more to herself than to Lori. She hated admitting when she was spitballing nonsense just to feel in control of something.

Rain picked up again, slicing sideways through tree branches like tiny scalpels trying to carve them out of the night. Marti fished around inside her coat until she found the crumpled pack of cigarettes that had survived countless beatings. Her fingers found one intact stick: miracle of miracles.

She lit up with a single flick needing neither sight nor sobriety; just muscle memory born from repetition.

Lori stepped back with an eye roll so loud Marti could hear it over the crackle of flame and storm-damp leaves rustling above them.

"You're reckless," Lori said. Arms crossed tight across her chest as if they were scaffolding holding up what remained of her patience.

Marti took a drag and let smoke curl from between parted lips slow enough to make a priest blush; she stared straight ahead as if she could see truth if it got close enough without flinching.

"Maybe," she murmured, eyes narrowing beneath rain-slick lashes as gears clicked behind them. "Or maybe I'm just seeing things clearer than anyone else."

Lori gave her The Look: halfway between concern and full-blown murder. She stayed quiet.

"Maybe the wild theory is the right theory." Marti's voice dropped low; conversational but loaded with landmines under every syllable. "LaLoLa clients dropping dead on this bad shit...she gets pissed, goes missing...Hitchcock goes looking, finds Kane...Kane offs him."

"So you think this," Lori gestured toward the discarded inhaler as if it might bite her fingers off, "is part of some bigger plan?"

"I think we just found something purposeful disguised as pleasure," Marti said. "And someone's been feeding it to people who trust too easily. But it's marked."

Lori froze, her hand halfway to her hair. "Poison?"

"No, Lori. I meant unicorn glitter." Marti flicked ash onto the pavement, eyes tracking something only she could see. "Clients tied to LaLoLa dying off like rats in a flooded cellar. You don't find that a little too convenient?"

"That's just rumor."

"And a hundred years ago, so was MK-ULTRA," Marti countered.

"Fuck," Lori muttered, the syllable barely making it past her lips. "If that's true..."

"Then whoever's cooking this garbage isn't just sloppy; they're making a statement." Marti took another drag. It tasted like rust and every mistake she'd ever made. "We owe it to Rat. And to me, and every other junkie in this shit city."

Lori squared her shoulders, worry slipping behind something sharper. "So what, you want to go play detective in government poison labs?"

Marti gave a half-laugh that sounded like a cough. "Wouldn't be my first fucked-up hobby. This isn't government. Too good for those assholes."

"Where do we even start?" Lori asked.

"Not sure." Marti tossed her cigarette into the gutter and turned toward her as if she might physically shake an answer loose from her spine.

"You trust your instincts," Lori added, softer now, touching Marti's arm with fingers that didn't quite settle. "They've dragged us through worse."

"Oh yeah," Marti said, eyeing the spot where Lori touched her as if it was radioactive. "Because instinct worked out great last time. Remind me again who ended up bleeding out in a warehouse while I smoked my way through three bad inhalers? Oh right, me."

Lori flinched but recovered, rolling her eyes so hard they clicked.

Marti ignored it and flipped the inhaler from her pocket up into the air and back down with precision. She caught it one-handed, then held it out toward Lori like an exhibit in court.

"Look at this casing," she said, gesturing as the metal caught faint light from overhead. "That logo? That's Devall's team's handiwork. Except... not quite."

Lori leaned in without touching it. "Color's off."

"Exactly," Marti said, tapping it against her leg. "Someone's either fucking with his supply or faking his brand."

"But why would Devall torch his own market?" Lori frowned.

Marti snorted. "Not him. He'd just do it, not spend the money on dodgy inhalers. This is a different sociopath."

"Too many of those," Lori replied, crossing her arms tight over her chest. "Gardner? Revenge for his son joining Devall? Or Stirling, trying to get back the market after Thornfield died."

Marti's jaw twitched as she pocketed the inhaler as if it hurt to hold.

Lori put her hands on her hips like someone's angry mama. "You need to be really careful."

"I can handle my Shadow," she said flatly.

"You keep saying that."

"Because it's true."

"You also said you could handle whiskey and gunfights," Lori murmured.

"And I'm still here." Marti spread her arms wide for emphasis; ruined leather jacket flaring like wings off a fallen angel no one prayed to anymore.

"That stuff changes you," Lori said.

"No shit." Marti stepped closer without meaning to, until their breath mingled between them in clouds of nicotine and tension.

Lori stared up at her like someone trying to read graffiti on a wall they weren't supposed to look at too long.

"Promise me you're not going to spiral," she said.

Marti raised one hand over her chest like a scout who'd lost faith but remembered the oath anyway. "Cross my heart."

She paused.

"It's made of coal anyway."

That earned the twitch of a smile from Lori, and maybe something softer, but Marti killed it by stepping closer still, city damp clinging to them both now like second skin.

"You pretend."

"You actually think there's something under all this?" Her voice dropped half an octave into something dangerous and real. "All the pills and inhalers and fuck-ups: that underneath it I care about you? About any of this?"

Lori didn't blink.

"Yes," she said.

She stepped in, arms sliding around Lori as if she'd been drowning and forgot she could float. It was automatic. Instinct. A heat-seeking missile aimed at the only warm thing left in Falls City. She buried her face in Lori's neck, breathed her in: cologne, nerves, coffee from three hours ago, and let out a noise that wasn't quite a moan but didn't belong anywhere else either.

"You really can't help your—"

The phone shrieked in Lori's pocket like it had something to say about all that. They jerked apart like guilty teenagers caught by a parent. The air felt colder.

Lori fumbled for the device with hands that were usually too sure for this kind of shaking. She answered. Her expression flattened, then buckled.

"Who?" Marti asked.

"Dan Devall," Lori whispered, tightening her grip around the phone like it might bite her. "He's outside our office."

Of fucking course he was.

Marti's heart didn't race; it revved, growled low behind her ribs like a car left running too long. Devall didn't just call when he wanted something. He showed up with men and silence and left pieces of you missing.

"Fuck it. Is this a goddamn warning?" Marti muttered, half to herself. "Or the end?"

Chapter 10

The rain came sideways now. Slanting sheets against windshield glass and cracked concrete. Falls City dressed itself in grime and didn't care who noticed.

Marti stomped through puddles like they were leeches. Rain soaked through her jacket, clung to her shirt, dripped past her collarbones as if it had a goddamn vendetta.

"Fucking rain," she spat, swiping at her face.

"It's got a vendetta," Lori said behind her, hugging that expensive coat tighter around herself.

Marti didn't mention that Lori looked good in it. Always did.

The hallway outside their office stank of mildew and rotgut whiskey. Not untypical. But what stood there wasn't typical at all: Dan Devall, flanked by two brick walls pretending to be men. He leaned against peeling drywall as if he owned the building just by existing inside it. Bald head polished to a mirror-shine under flickering fluorescent light, tailored suit clinging to his linebacker frame as if it missed him every time he took it off.

"Starova," Devall said with that voice like broken gravel smoothed over by charm school.

"I can see that." Marti slowed but didn't stop moving. "What is this, date night?"

She flicked her eyes toward the goons; both taller than necessary and carrying the same dead-eyed look she saw right before gunfire started.

"We're not doing this in the damn hallway." She shoved open her office door without waiting for an answer. "Inside."

Lori ghosted in behind her.

Devall followed without ceremony, no dramatics, no threats, which made it worse. The bodyguards tried to step in behind him but Marti shoved one hand backward without looking.

"They stay outside," she snapped over her shoulder, "unless this is some kind of group therapy I wasn't warned about."

Devall lifted two fingers in some kind of signal or benediction or maybe just habit. The goons backed off and shut the door behind them.

Her office felt smaller than usual, full of damp cigarette smoke and whatever electricity Devall dragged around with him for atmosphere. Marti stripped off her wet jacket and slung it onto the radiator where it would not dry but might hiss enough to match her mood.

She dropped into her chair hard enough to make it creak and gestured at the visitor seats: cheap plastic things that cracked if you sat wrong.

"Sit or don't," she said. "But stop looming."

Devall sank into one as if he'd trained for it, body loose but watchful, even as water ran from his cuffs onto the floorboards.

Marti lit up one of her last decent cigarettes and dragged smoke into lungs that never thanked her anymore.

"What do you want?" she asked on exhale. "And spare me the velvet-glove routine. I'm fresh outta patience today. If you're gonna kill me, just shoot."

"I need your services." Devall locked eyes with hers across the desk, the way people did when they were either about to lie or beg.

"No bullshit," he added. Voice low now, almost fragile beneath all that mass.

Marti arched an eyebrow as if entertained by the idea that "bullshit" could be bartered away so cleanly.

"You got my attention." She blew smoke between them as if it might draw new lines on old maps. "Now talk fast before I remember I hate your face."

"Marti."

Just her name. Low, intense, as if he was about to propose or pull a gun.

She didn't flinch. Just blinked at him, lit another cigarette, and waited for the punchline.

"I need your help," Devall said. "Someone's been screwing with my product. People are dying. Dropping like flies in alleyways with their tongues purple and their eyes fucking glassy. I can't keep pretending it's not happening."

Marti leaned back until her chair creaked in protest, smoke curling around her face as if it belonged there more than air did. "You were listening."

Devall shook his head: sharp, final. "Not me. One of my men was."

Lori leaned across the desk, too interested for her own good. "What'd he say?"

"Said two women were sniffing around Kransten Park. Found one of my inhalers. Then the dumb one took a hit and puked."

"That's the idiot," Lori confirmed, pointing straight at her.

Marti tapped ash onto a stack of unpaid bills. "Hi," she said.

He nodded as if that sealed some kind of deal. "That's why you're perfect, Marti."

"Perfectly fucked up," she muttered, dragging on the cigarette until it burned close to the filter.

Lori's fingers tracked a nervous rhythm on the edge of the desk, her mouth tight in that familiar he-should-leave-now shape.

"I want whoever's behind this," Devall said. "Find out who's shitting on my name."

"No." Marti didn't look up.

Devall raised an eyebrow. "Why not?"

Marti exhaled and let her head fall back over the chair rest as if she was communing with ceiling ghosts. "Because I'm working a fraud case, a cheater and a missing person. I'm booked solid: emotionally and recreationally."

"Time to pencil me in," Devall said. "It's my turn for attention, and you're gonna give it to me."

Marti flicked ash into yesterday's coffee mug. "So let me get this straight: you want me to trace your faulty Shadow inhalers? Sounds like an inside job your own boys should be handling while you sit in your gold bathtub counting money."

"I have... reasons," he said.

"Don't we all."

"But you're still the only one who can cross lines without getting shot." He paused. "One hundred thousand."

Marti snorted so hard she choked on smoke. "I've been insulted better than that for free."

"Five hundred thousand," Lori cut in before Devall could open his mouth again, already typing into her laptop.

Devall side-eyed her as if she'd grown another head made of fine print and attitude. "What exactly are you typing?"

Lori smirked over her monitor. "The contract. Quality inspection services. No guarantee of resolution." She clicked twice more and looked up. "Where do I send it?"

Marti waved that off with a lazy hand gesture born from too many near-deaths and not enough sleep.

"What's the catch?" she asked after Lori stopped clicking.

"You shut the fuck up about it," Devall said.

Lori snorted without looking up. "That's not a catch, that's basic professionalism."

Even Marti cracked a laugh at that one: short-lived but real.

Devall raised one hand for silence as if they were under courtroom rules now. "You kept quiet with Stirling."

Marti blinked at him, too stunned by actual research to lie fast enough.

"Who told you that?" she asked.

"You didn't," he said, sitting back against the worn leather seat as if he owned every inch of oxygen in the room. "That's what matters."

She stubbed out her cigarette against the fake wood desk. "Fine." Her voice was flat, businesslike and bored, which meant she was taking it seriously or trying to pretend she wasn't curious. "You get me access to your people: dealers, couriers, lab rats. No leash pulling when I start poking around."

"Granted," Devall said. "As long as no one knows you're mine."

"I'm never yours," she muttered under her breath, too quiet for him but loud enough for Lori to glance sidelong and pretend not to smile.

Marti dug into her coat pocket and pulled out the inhaler: the off-brand bastard child they found near Kransten Park. She tossed it onto Devall's side of the desk like trash she didn't want fingerprints on.

He picked it up between two fingers, turning it over once before squinting at its faded label.

"It looks right," he murmured.

"It looks wrong," Marti corrected him, watching his face more than his hands. "Color's off."

Devall gave a noncommittal grunt but kept staring at it too long for someone unimpressed.

"Where'd you find this?" he asked without looking up.

"You think I'm that easy?" Marti drawled and lit another cigarette.

"My guess is, the park." He smiled and set the inhaler down between them like a broken toy neither wanted anymore. The moment hung there before he broke it with a sharper tone.

"One of my cops got photos from an OD scene last week." His voice lost its polish. No pitchman charm remained; just rot crawling under skin.

"It was bad."

Devall held up his phone as if he was offering proof of life, except the life part was absent. The image on the screen showed five kids sprawled out like broken dolls on a piss-stained floor. Some tangled together, some not. All of them dead.

Marti didn't flinch. Her stomach did that thing it always did: a low, twisting flip, like something sour had rolled through her gut. She'd seen her share of corpses (cops, junkies, friends), but this many at once hit different. They still looked soft around the edges, as if they'd only just started fucking up their lives when someone cut them short.

Devall swiped to another photo before she could speak: a close-up of a hand locked around a cheap plastic inhaler, green-tinged and smeared with blood.

"Send those to Lori's computer," Marti said, eyes fixed on the frozen fingers on the screen.

Devall nodded and got busy while she lit a cigarette with one hand and reached for Lori's knee with the other. Just a tap, grounding herself in skin and warmth.

She straightened up, smoke curling from her lips. "Alright, Devall. I'll take your offer." Her voice had turned to gravel. "Five hundred grand and ten clean Shadow inhalers: real ones. I'll need them for leverage and trade."

Behind her, Lori raised an eyebrow but said nothing. Marti threw her a wink: part apology, part threat, part flirtation. Maybe all three made Lori's lashes flutter.

Devall gave her a cold approving look, the kind usually followed by someone saying she's got balls. He didn't bother saying it out loud.

"I want regular updates," he said.

"Yeah, yeah." Marti took another drag and blew smoke toward his polished shoes just for fun.

Satisfied or bored, or both, Devall turned on his heel and walked out without a wave goodbye.

The door clicked shut behind him as if sealing them in something airtight and dangerous.

Lori let out a breath she'd been holding too long. "Marti... what the hell did we just sign up for? A third job from a drug lord? Branded inhalers full of poison?"

Marti tapped ash into the tray choking with cigarette corpses. "Falls City doesn't have drug lords," she muttered. "It has three bored sociopaths with too much product." Her gaze drifted back to the computer screen where those kids lay frozen in death. "And that shit nearly killed me in micrograms."

Lori stepped closer but didn't reach out; not yet.

"Who would do this?"

"Some asshole who thinks he can take over from Devall," Marti said. Bitterness wasn't even flavor anymore. It was the air.

They stood there while Marti ground out her cigarette so hard it snapped at the filter.

"I gotta go," Marti said. "I'll call."

Chapter 11

Marti zipped up her jacket like armor and headed for the door without looking back. Rain hammered against the windows as if god was taking batting practice outside: a racket loud enough to drown out her self-destructive impulses.

Cold slapped her face when she stepped into it, sharp enough to remind her that people used drugs in this town just to feel warm again.

She stalked past strip clubs and soup lines without breaking stride. The usual crowd gathered near alleyways behind an adult bookstore; the neon sign blinked Girls Girls Girls as if trying to convince someone it still mattered.

A cop patrolled nearby with a German Shepherd that looked more alert than its handler. The mutt paused to sniff where things had happened: things no one wanted written down anywhere official.

The users were easy to spot, huddled under awnings or crouched behind dumpsters, glassy-eyed messes holding each other up or nodding into their sleeves.

The city's underbelly wasn't hidden; it strutted around bold as hell, reeking of desperation wrapped in plastic wrap and hope written on pill bottles.

Marti exhaled into the rain and kept walking toward it all, because somewhere in this dark wet hellhole was someone selling death one breath at a time. She planned to find them before they ran out of teenagers.

"Hey," Marti said, stepping under the cracked awning as if it would do her any good. Rain still found her in the spaces between. She squinted at the gaunt man slouched against the bricks, red-rimmed eyes blinking slow. "I heard there's someone around here selling cheap inhalers. You know anything, or just good at looking useless?"

The man's head tilted, skeletal grin stretching wide enough to show three gold teeth and a graveyard of gaps. "Fuck you," he croaked. "What's that worth to you?"

Marti didn't blink. "Information for information." She slid one hand into her jacket and let the edge of a green inhaler peek out like cleavage at a funeral. "Tell me something real, I'll tell you where to score the stuff that doesn't taste like paint thinner."

He sniffed, eyes flicking down to her pocket as if he wanted to wrap his mouth around the plastic right there on the street. "Francois," he said, licking his lips. "Corner of 8th and Grant."

"Bless your cracked little heart." She gave him Doser West and Fifty-eighth. "Tell him Marti said go fuck yourself." She left him in Kransten Park and turned away before he could start asking questions she didn't care to answer.

Marti staked out 8th and Grant until the little fucker showed up: seven fucking hours.

The corner was dark except for a flickering streetlamp trying its best not to die. Francois leaned under it, water streaming off his hood in rivulets.

"You Francois?" she asked, voice flat enough to slide under a door.

He straightened just enough to care. The look he gave her would've been charming if it wasn't so sharp around the edges. "Never heard of him," he said, but didn't move.

Marti held up her green inhaler like a badge. "I'm looking for a deal," she said. "Cheap shit, decent hit. You got anything or am I wasting my rain-soaked charm on the wrong loser?"

Francois sucked his teeth and glanced down the alley as if someone might be watching; someone who mattered more than her. "Why should I trust you?"

Marti took a step closer and smiled. "Because cops don't walk around with Shadow tucked in their bra straps and desperation leaking out their pores," she said. "Also? I've got money, and I'm running out of patience."

"Alright." He reached into his pocket with fingers twitchy from regret or relapse; it was hard to tell anymore. He came back with a handful of inhalers wrapped in plastic like candy for fucked-up children.

"You didn't get it from me," he muttered.

"If I did," Marti said as she handed over cash folded crisp enough to make him bite it later, "you'd be bleeding."

She stuffed the inhalers into her coat, letting them settle against her hip like weapons or promises.

"One more thing," she said before turning away. "Where's this shit coming from?"

Francois looked ready to lie but chickened out halfway through blinking. His jaw twitched.

Marti's patience snapped like a bone. In one motion, she drew her gun and pressed Francois against the wall with her forearm across his throat. His eyes widened, pupils dilating with fear.

"You think I'm playing?" The tremor in her hands wasn't from weakness: it was restraint wearing thin.

"Listen, I don't—"

The gun barked once in the narrow alley. Brick dust rained down as the bullet tore into the wall inches from Francois's ear. He flinched, a wet stain spreading at his crotch.

"Next one goes through something you'll miss," Marti hissed, her face close enough that he could smell the coffee and cigarettes on her breath. The withdrawal was making her dangerous, unpredictable. They both knew it. "I'm not asking twice."

Francois's resistance crumbled like wet cardboard. His voice came out in a terrified whisper.

"There's... there's a shop on Troy Street," he murmured, stumbling over the words as if they weren't safe in his mouth. "They sell out the back door."

Troy Street was north, in the Ironwood District. At least a forty minute drive if you obeyed the law.

She gave him a look that could sand paint off walls. "Story of my fucking life."

* * *

Troy Street welcomed her like a prison shank. Rain spewed sideways now, wind whipping through alleys as if it chased ghosts no one else could see.

Her boots squelched with every step, soaked clean through so each movement felt like hauling concrete soaked in guilt and gutter water.

She pulled her hood tighter, not that it helped, and dropped low into the shadows when she hit visual range of the warehouse: generic brick tombstone of industry past its prime. The kind of place cops avoided unless someone paid overtime.

Old cars rusted into silence along the curb. Graffiti stretched across dumpsters like angry screams frozen mid-fit.

"478 Troy. 478 Troy." Marti repeated the address like a mantra because it fucking was.

Marti slopped around back and joined the jagged line of buyers. Rainwater crawled into every crevice below her waistline; not sexy cold, just cruel.

Her fingers brushed another inhaler from inside her coat pocket (the real shit), and she took a quick half-hit without ceremony. Not because she needed it (she always needed it) but because recon was better blurry than soaked-in real time misery.

Her breath caught somewhere between lungs and longing as Shadow bloomed behind her eyes: sharper focus, muted pain, heartbeat syncing with city noise.

Inside the shop: movement.

The door opened, a hand came out to snatch the coins and withdraw. A few seconds later, the door opened again and out came the same paw to drop an inhaler into a waiting hand. One shuffle forward. Repeat.

Boarded windows left gaps just wide enough to spy silhouettes pacing between machines that hummed wrong; not factory sounds but bio-lab ones, chemical murmurs laced with intent.

Voices snuck through the plywood seams like rats looking for a way out.

"Hey! You got the new batch ready?"

"Almost. Just finishing up the mix. The Devall packaging came in though."

"Perfect match?"

"Close enough. No one checks the fucking color anyway."

Another voice chimed in, flat and tired. "Boss called. Said he's sending a guy to pick up. Drop off more Salts."

Synthetic cathinones. Bath salts. Mixed with Shadow somehow. No wonder people were dying.

The door opened again, and Hand Boy reached out for the next payment.

A sharp laugh split the air. "Yeah, but too many bodies gets attention. Bad for business."

Voices muffled as the door shut again. Marti ran her tongue across her upper lip, caught rain and metal there, stayed still when thunder cracked like judgment over their heads.

Hand out, inhaler delivered, hand withdrawn.

Shuffle forward. Marti grabbed a handful of bills and waited.

Just as Hand Boy opened the door, headlights sliced across concrete. Marti ducked on instinct as a black sedan crept up to the back door. The engine died mid-growl.

She held her breath as the driver stepped out: broad shoulders, leather jacket, haircut that screamed ex-military or current asshole.

"'Bout time," someone inside shouted as the rear door opened wide with a screech. "Got the whole shipment ready."

Jarhead said nothing, just popped his trunk as if he was on grocery duty instead of pushing poison.

Marti watched them load box after box, each one neat as an apology, into the car's trunk and back seat. The size was familiar: about like a cigarette pack or a Shadow inhaler. Maybe both.

That was enough boxed death to wipe out half of the Riverside neighborhood before breakfast.

"Where's mine?" Marti asked Hand Boy who, for reasons best not explained, had stopped mid-sale to watch. He snatched the bills and stepped away, letting Marti see inside until Jarhead blasted past her with his next armful.

No chatter now. Just soaked footfalls and damp cardboard sliding across vinyl upholstery. Five minutes of silence. The trunk slammed shut again and Jarhead melted back into his car.

Engine caught, headlights flared. He vanished into mist like some suburban grim reaper on salary.

The back door shut. Marti slammed at the door empty-handed because, well, empty-handed. Two men stepped out, followed by Hand Boy. He tossed Marti an inhaler as if he was tossing bread to a duck and kept walking.

Marti walked. The crew scattered: cigarettes flicked into puddles, boots sloshing away in separate directions like guilt trying to outrun consequence.

Marti thought about breaking in for exactly four seconds. The useful shit was already gone, nestled in a moving trunk somewhere between here and hell; whatever was left behind tonight wouldn't hold up in Devall's court.

Besides, she was soaked to the spine and exhaustion clawed at her throat.

She slipped into motion along warehouse edges and chain-link fences glistening with old rain and older secrets, cut through alleys that once sold dresses and now sold dreams that stopped your heart if you took too much too fast.

Three miles of rotting city later she hit her neighborhood; you could barely call it that when every street had its own ghost story and no one wore badges after dark.

The rain finally stopped sometime around sunrise o'clock, but the air clung heavy with wet: the kind of cold that gets under your skin and starts making decisions for you.

She unlocked her door with fingers numb from weather and restraint.

Inside: dim lights casting shadows across cracked tile; radiator groaning in protest; everything smelling like cigarettes, rust, and broken plans.

Peeling off her jeans felt like losing a layer of herself: the part that had squatted behind metal for hours while watching death get packaged.

She shivered once as cold air hit bare skin. Maybe she was shaking more than usual tonight, but it wasn't just from being wet.

Huff first. Shower after.

She pulled out what little Shadow she had left: two hits if she rationed it well. She took one now because sometimes survival meant choosing poison over panic attacks.

When she finally stepped into scalding water, it hit her like absolution: hot enough to hurt but not enough to burn away what clung underneath her ribs, the grime that soap couldn't touch even if she scrubbed till sunrise bled through blinds again.

Steam curled around her body in slow spirals as tiles warmed under her palms. Her muscles uncoiled by degrees, not willingly but inevitably, as if even they were tired of bracing for impact all night.

And then—

Then her thoughts started doing things they weren't supposed to do and her hands drifted toward flesh against tile... fingers tracing hipbones... tips finding pressure points...

She tilted her head back under the stream until it drowned everything except heat and heartbeat.

Drugs or orgasms. Addiction didn't care which one killed you.

Marti leaned against the slick shower tiles, one hand braced above her head, the other sliding south as if it had a mission. Which it absolutely fucking did. The water pounded her spine with all the tenderness of a riot cop. Perfect. She needed this. She needed something. Anything.

The city was still coughing up smoke from last night's arson, her inbox full of missing persons reports that read like bad fiction, and her fucking knee still hadn't healed right from the fall through that skylight six months ago. But now? Now she had five minutes and a locked door and no one asking who she'd shot or why.

Her fingers hovered at the edge of heat and need, body coiled like a wire stretched too tight for too long. "Fuck it," she muttered, and dipped in.

She was already wet; of course she was. It never took much when everything outside her skin felt like gunmetal and ghosts. Marti worked in slow circles, each stroke another "fuck you" to sobriety, to restraint, to whatever dog-eared self-help bullshit Lori had left on her desk that morning.

The hiss of water roared over her moan as she sank into herself, chin tucked, forehead pressed to tile gone cold where the steam hadn't reached. Her other hand found her breast, fingers pinching until sensation surged up through her ribs like a live wire.

"Fuck: I'm good." Not loud. Just affirmation.

She kept going, rhythm sharp now, knuckles white as she fucked herself harder than any memory could. Still, the fantasies came creeping in: Lydia from the precinct locker room with the tattoo down her spine; Calista from Narco who smiled like she knew too much; sometimes both at once if Marti let herself get greedy.

Goddamn right she got greedy.

A tongue here, fingers there. Hands that weren't hers exploring places she'd marked off with yellow tape and DO NOT ENTER signs. Her thighs trembled under the barrage of imagined touch, of ghost lovers tangled in steam.

Pleasure hit like backdraft: sudden and violent. She rode it out biting her lip to keep quiet. The tiles blurred; nothing but heat and skin and release until every muscle screamed surrender.

Then the hiss of water again.

She slumped against the wall while water needled across spent nerves and raw skin. The city hadn't vanished but it got quieter for a minute. That counted for something.

She shut off the spray with a groan that felt older than she was and stepped into air so cold it slapped. A towel hung from its hook; she grabbed it, wrapped it around herself like armor made of threadbare cotton.

Her bed waited: unmade sheets still holding yesterday's secrets. She dropped onto them without grace, damp hair soaking into the pillowcase she never remembered to wash.

"Tomorrow will be better," Marti said aloud. Not because she believed it but because lies needed practice too.

Then sleep took her, hard like blackout. Somewhere between dreams and dread, the city whispered new names to chase come morning.

Chapter 12

Marti woke to the stench of diesel and piss wafting through a cracked window that hadn't shut right in years. The glass was streaked from last night's storm, city light bleeding through like a knife through gauze. Somewhere below, a bus screamed against its brakes and someone screamed back. Falls City, baby: still breathing, still rotting.

Her mouth tasted like cigarettes, her head tasted like Shadow. She sat up slow, bones creaking, undershirt clinging to her chest.

Outside, the fire escape beckoned with its rust and familiarity. Marti shoved open the sticky window and stepped out barefoot onto wet steel. Lit up without thinking. First cigarette of the day was halfway gone before she inhaled proper. Smoke curled around her like something alive.

Down below: cars crawling past puddles slick with oil, street vendors unfolding steam-stained carts, a cop yelling at someone who probably deserved it but maybe didn't. Everything damp. Everything loud. The city smelled like it wanted to hurt somebody.

"Sunshine one day," Marti muttered, flicking ash toward the alley. "Just one fuckin' day."

She ground what was left of the cig against the railing and climbed back inside before she froze her tits off. The Shadow inhaler waited on the dresser beside lace panties someone left behind six months and an actual, real book. Marti stared at it as if it might explode.

Her hand hovered over the inhaler.

Don't do it.

She did it anyway.

Hit fast, hard; like chewing glass wrapped in silk. Her nerves lit up just long enough to pretend they weren't frayed to hell.

"Right," she said, voice rough as gravel. "Let's get this shitshow started."

Shirt, pants, boots. Leather jacket on, torn elbow patched with duct tape. Marti shoved out into morning traffic on foot. She didn't bother dodging puddles; they found her anyway.

Halfway down 6th Street she stepped over some strung-out husk of a man leaking into the sidewalk outside an all-night pawn shop. Eyes open but vacant as hell: either dead or wishing he was.

Marti paused, looking down at him.

"You alive?"

No blink. No twitch.

"Live or die," she muttered as a cab sprayed gutter water across her boots, "it's all the same here."

She called for an ambulance and walked away. He was dead, but he didn't have to rot there.

Lori was at her desk when Marti pushed into the office reeking of damp and nicotine frustration.

The place looked too tidy, as if Lori had cleaned something besides blood for once. That made Marti suspicious by default.

Lori glanced up from a stack of files and smiled in that way that made Marti stumble. Her bright green eyes betrayed her; they always did. Concern flickered beneath practiced calm.

"Rough one?" she asked.

Marti stepped through the doorway, lit a cigarette with shaking fingers and exhaled toward the ceiling tiles stained yellow by years of bad decisions.

"Same shit," she said. "Different flavor."

Lori set her pen down. "Find anything?"

Marti didn't answer right away. She stood in the stale glow of flickering fluorescence, watching smoke curl toward the water-stained tiles like it might spell out something useful. Then, flat:

"Add five hundred to Devall's bill." She tossed last night's inhaler onto Lori's desk. "Merchandise," she clarified, as if Lori might've thought she was just throwing things for sport. "Or are you too busy alphabetizing corpses again?"

That got Lori's fingers moving. One of them, anyway.

"What happened?" she asked, already pulling up the file before Marti could start hurling syllables like knives.

Marti stepped farther inside. The door clicked shut behind her with a finality that matched her mood.

"There's a dirty lab on Troy Street," she said. No inflection. No mercy. "They're cutting Shadow with Salts. God knows what else." Her breath burned like acid and bad choices as she exhaled another drag. "They were selling it out the back until someone came by and cleaned house."

Lori frowned, deep enough to fold the space between her brows into that little wrinkle that Marti deliberately didn't look at most days. The one that made her stupid in ways no chemical ever had.

"We've seen bad batches before," Lori said, turning the inhaler over as if it might talk if she stared hard enough. "Was this Devall's?"

Marti shook her head and pointed with the cigarette like it was a gavel. "Nope." She leaned in closer to watch Lori lock it away in that desk drawer Marti didn't have a key to and would never ask for. "This is sabotage or side hustle or both."

"You have proof?"

"No," Marti said, voice laced with smoke and spite and something sharp underneath. "But I saw a few hundred units walk straight out of the lab into somebody's trunk. Means I'll need to go back."

Lori leaned back in her chair, just slightly, but enough for her blouse to pull across one shoulder and down over curve and skin, fabric catching on shape and making Marti's brain short-circuit in exactly the way it shouldn't.

"So what now?" Lori asked, oblivious or pretending to be.

"We shake Devall's team 'til something falls out." Marti flicked ash into Lori's abandoned coffee mug without breaking stride toward the phone.

Lori reached for the receiver first but paused when her fingers brushed plastic.

"That smart?" she asked.

Marti smiled without mirth. Blew smoke that hung like a dare between them.

"Smart? No." She touched ash to lip, kissed it off like regret caught on fire. "But necessary as hell."

Then she took the phone from Lori who took it right back as if they weren't playing tug-of-war with sanity and lit nerves.

"Be subtle as a fucking landmine," Marti muttered around the cigarette still clinging to her mouth. She turned and disappeared into her office. The door swung closed behind like punctuation.

Click.

Then inhale: from the right inhaler this time, and everything went razor-sharp again.

Out at her desk, Lori breathed deep once, then dialed. Devall picked up on ring three, voice soaked in bourbon and disdain.

"Hold." She jabbed transfer as if it shocked her, then sat back to listen.

Marti didn't do pleasantries.

"Devall," she snapped as soon as he was on the line. "Marti Starova. I need access to your boys at Troy Street."

A pause thickened across airwaves before Devall chuckled low: a sound like rust scraping metal.

"Troy? That lab's worth more than your block, Starova. Why the hell would I throw open doors just because you ask nice?"

"Saw someone last night," Marti replied, pacing now, tight circles forming grooves in cheap carpet tiles. "Ex-military type hauling product out of your building. You have a pickup scheduled I don't know about?"

Silence hung heavy again; this time longer. She could almost hear him biting down on whatever reply he wanted to spit first.

Eventually: "Fine." He sighed through his teeth as if he was doing her a favor instead of hedging his own goddamned bets. "Talk to them."

Her shoulders dropped just enough to feel human again. For half a second at least.

"Don't tell them I'm coming," she added. "I want raw reactions."

"You planning on knocking? It's three then two."

"If they pull guns..." She smiled cold against receiver plastic. "Pick up your fuckin' phone."

She ended it there, before he could get smug again, and stepped back into view just as Lori looked up from the screen.

"I'm in," Marti announced as she flopped onto the couch like victory came with springs poking through worn upholstery.

"What's the plan?" Lori asked.

"Tomorrow morning." Marti stretched one leg out, boots half-off so she could complain later that it hurt when putting them back on. "Hopefully Hand Boy forgot what I look like."

"Who?"

"Hand Boy."

Lori blinked twice, processing. She narrowed suspicious eyes over rimless glasses she wasn't wearing but somehow seemed present anyway.

"Why'd you call him that? Did he…" She finger-fucked the air while her mouth tried not to finish any sentence involving hand stuff and strange men from drug labs.

"Fuck no. No fuck." Marti said, scandalized, as she kicked her boots off with enough force they hit opposite walls at different speeds. "Jesus Christ; I need sleep worse than blow right now."

She curled into herself until only knees and a few strands of hair were visible above couch cushions.

Lori watched her before whispering: "Can I come?"

"I've never heard you, but probably," Marti mumbled from inside whatever blanket of exhaustion she'd wrapped herself in.

"Marti."

"Lori."

"Marti."

Lori won the war of words.

"Fine. I'll go now. You found anything on LaLoLa?" Marti asked as she looked around for her boots.

"I stopped by the address on file. LaLoLa hasn't lived there for a couple of months. Office manager said she couldn't pay rent." Lori walked over to the opposite side of the room and bent down. Marti had to clamp her hand over her mouth just to keep from moaning out loud.

"Here," Lori said as she tossed the boots toward the couch. "Were you just staring at my ass?"

"No."

"Yes."

"No."

"Yes."

Lori won that war of words too.

* * *

The cab left Marti two blocks south of Troy Street so no one would associate her face with the upcoming disaster.

Marti tossed a crumpled bill at the driver and slammed the door with pleasure.

Marti inhaled.

Everything stank: piss, wet metal, old grease clinging to brick walls as if it were mold that learned how to lie. Neon signs buzzed overhead in twitching spasms: CHEAP SMOKES; GIRLS INSIDE; FULL SERVICE.

Water pooled near storm drains clogged with condoms and takeout wrappers. Broken glass crunched underfoot as if someone had thrown last year's promises out a third-story window and never bothered sweeping up.

Marti moved first, cutting through the alley. She passed an old pipe yard fenced by rusted chain-link falling off its hinges. Dogs barked somewhere distant, or kids pretending to be dogs pretending to be monsters. Usual neighborhood soundtrack.

A man stood near a dumpster at the far end of the alley: skinny, twitchy, wearing three jackets that didn't match and shoes held together by duct tape and wishful thinking. Marti recognized his face from other nights; harmless user-type with more paranoia than pulse rate.

Marti nodded once as she passed. He didn't nod back but didn't run either.

The alley stank: urine, old curry, rot cooking under a weak afternoon sun. Marti pulled her jacket tight across her chest, not for warmth but to brace herself. The door at the end of the alley looked like it had survived a few too many raids and stopped caring. Gray paint peeled like sunburned skin, a single bulb twitching overhead as if trying not to scream.

She knocked. Three times, then two, like she'd been told. Silly little ritual for men with guns and ego problems.

A slot in the door scraped open. Eyes blinked at her: bloodshot, suspicious, high but not on their own supply.

"The fuck you want?" Male voice. Gravel soaked in whiskey.

"I'm here for business," Marti said, tone steady, hands visible. "My boss is interested in enhancing his premium product."

A beat of silence. Then another, as if the guy had to translate her words into caveman first.

"Who sent you?"

"No one." She let that hang a second before adding, "My boss has Golden Shadow clients who give enough of a shit about quality to look past your bad manners. We heard there might be something worth seeing."

More mumbling behind the door. Metal clunking on metal. A lock disengaged. Then another.

Marti resisted the urge to roll her eyes.

Door swung open.

The man behind it looked like paper someone had crumpled up and smoothed back out: thin, twitchy, skin drawn tight over cheekbones that could slice glass. Behind him stood his larger friend, a wall of fat with suspicion written all over his face and one hand resting over what was very much not casual: the grip of a gun tucked into his waistband.

"Arms up," Paper-Face said.

Marti lifted them without comment. Fat-Hands stepped forward and got grabby fast; hands sliding along her sides and lingering on her tits. She stared ahead and thought about kittens or tax audits or anything else.

"She's clean," he muttered, disappointed.

Paper-Face jerked his head toward inside. "Quick."

She ducked through the doorway.

The lab smelled exactly how hell might if hell ran on fertilizer and broken dreams: chemical sweetness fighting with ammonia and gasoline until everything smelled like you were gonna puke. Her throat caught halfway to a gag.

Ceiling low enough to headbutt if anyone got excited, concrete floor streaked with stains that didn't look dead yet. Two more guys hunched over scarred tables covered in gear that hummed and buzzed with menace. One wore a respirator like he cared about living; the other had gone for fashion-forward bandana chic and looked like he might taste-test the product when no one was watching.

"So," Paper-Face said from behind her, "you're pushing Golden Shadow? Didn't think anyone outside the Heights was moving that shit."

Marti let her gaze drift as she replied, "Clientele's growing faster than purity's dropping. Boss wants something stronger in the mix without sending our customers into seizures mid-orgasm."

Bandana Guy snorted behind whatever passed for a mask. "Golden Shadow." He spit the name out like it tasted bitter. "Fancy branding for trash."

"Marketing," Marti replied, offering him half a smile sharp enough to bleed on.

Movement caught her eye: a salt creeper sitting open on one of the side trays, tubes snaking into little jugs filled with gasoline and salt crystal nightmares. Synthetic cathinones.

She kept her face schooled while cataloging every corner of this toxic mess, but inside, adrenaline was already lining up its shot glass. This place wasn't just dirty: it was suicidal art under flickering lightbulbs. And she was here to buy in. Or at least pretend she would long enough to make it back out alive.

"Your boss got a name?" asked Paper-Face, voice oily-slick as if it passed for charm.

Marti smiled without warmth. "Everyone's got a name. I want chemicals, not fairy tales."

The big one edged closer, boots creaking on the greasy linoleum. "You work for Devall?"

She didn't blink. "I don't work for Devall."

"Bullshit," said the respirator man; first words out of him and they hissed through the filters like steam under pressure. "Devall's been sniffing around here for weeks. Thinks we're slicing into his turf."

"I couldn't give less of a fuck about Devall's turf," Marti said. "My boss wants new blends. Clients are asking questions. That's all."

Paper-Face glanced at Fat Hands. Something passed between them, twitch of an eyebrow, flex of a jaw: silent agreement or silent threat, hard to tell.

"How'd you find us?" Paper-Face again, tone sour.

Marti shrugged. "Stopped by yesterday. Paid my dues, got a taste." She nodded toward the salt creeper as if it wasn't crawling across her nerves just to look at it. "What's in the mix now? I smell gasoline."

The temperature in the room did something inverted: colder and hotter at once. Fat Hands shifted sideways, cutting off her view of the gear as if he'd practiced it in front of a mirror. Paper-Face's hand disappeared into his pocket.

"You ask too many fucking questions," he said, voice cold enough to snap bone.

"Professional curiosity." Marti didn't move, didn't flinch, but her pulse set fire to her neck. This was going sideways fast. She could see the exit sign flickering like a countdown in reverse. "My boss's chemist would want specifications."

Paper-Face let out a low chuckle that didn't reach his eyes. Bandana Guy joined in, mocking: "Your boss this, your boss that... Boss's clients, boss's chemist... Convenient how we never get names."

"Like I said—"

"Get the fuck out," Paper-Face snapped.

Marti didn't move. "Maybe we're misreading each oth—"

Fat Hands produced a gun from somewhere too smooth to be improvised. Barrel down but not for long.

"He said leave," he growled.

Marti held up her hands enough to show she wasn't interested in getting ventilated today. "Fine," she said. "Clearly I've overstayed my welcome."

She backed up slow and steady, eyes locked on Paper-Face's face as if she was memorizing it just as hard as he might be memorizing hers.

Her hand found the handle.

But before she could turn it, Respirator stepped forward and pulled it down himself.

He met her gaze through fogged lenses and said, "If you come back, you don't leave."

Marti gave him one short nod, no attitude left, and stepped out into air thick with rot and regret. The door clicked shut behind her like a final decision made without appeal.

This wasn't the first shithole Marti had been kicked out of. Not even the first drug lab. It was starting to feel like a fucked-up homecoming ritual.

She climbed the chain-link fence and dropped into the muck on the other side, boots sinking into the mud like it couldn't wait to swallow her. A garbage dumpster leaned sideways nearby, leaking something that smelled like chemical soup and dead ambition.

Perfect.

Chapter 13

Marti crouched beside the fence, pulling her jacket tighter around her and flipping up her hoodie. Rain hammered her leather jacket, steady and annoying. She bit down on a curse and stared at the lab's back entrance like it might blink.

The rain picked up. Marti stayed put.

At some point, a sneeze tried to betray her but she strangled it in her throat. No fucking way she was getting shot because of nasal drama.

An hour passed, or six years, give or take, before headlights knifed through the mist. A black sedan eased into the alley like it didn't want to be there either.

Marti shifted just enough to see better, slick mud painting lines down her jeans.

"What the fuck," she whispered, ducking lower, peeking around the dumpster with slow-motion urgency.

Kane.

Her heart slammed into gear: all adrenaline and old wounds. Damian fucking Kane. Still playing detective, or at least wearing the coat. Her ex-partner from another lifetime.

What was he doing here? Undercover? Moonlighting? Selling them all out for a second pension?

He moved toward the building as if he'd been there a thousand times before, exchanging words with Paper-Face at the door. Marti couldn't hear shit over the rain and garbage orchestra around her.

She edged forward on her stomach, crawling through grass and grime like some noir nostalgia reject from basic training. Mud clung to every inch of her, greedy little bastard, but she kept going until she hit a low spot near the fence with just enough cover and line-of-sight.

Right on cue, Kane's voice cracked through the air, low and sharp, like gravel undercarriage on an empty tank of charm.

"...you call me?"

"Some chick came by earlier," Paper-Face said, eyes flicking toward Kane like he couldn't decide if his visitor was boss or executioner. "Said she was looking for something to mix with Golden Shadow."

"I thought she might be a cop," added Fat Hands.

"Describe her," Kane snapped.

"Uh... short black hair? Blue eyes? Butch dyke type." He hesitated, then added: "Pretty though?"

"Small tits," Fat Hands chimed in from somewhere off-camera.

Marti considered throwing a rock at his head. Or a grenade.

"Leather jacket?" Kane asked.

Shit.

Marti pressed herself flatter to the mud as if it could erase how obvious this just became.

"Yeah," Paper-Face nodded. "Boots too."

Kane held up his phone for confirmation. "This her?"

"Yeah! That's her! Who is she?"

"She's an old colleague of mine," Kane said as he tucked his phone away, but his smile twisted sideways: too sharp to be friendly.

Paper-Face blinked at him, trying to play innocent but clearly tasting something bitter in that answer. "Old colleague?"

Kane's voice dropped lower than Marti liked: pure venom wrapped in silk. "Fucking cunt," he said. "What'd she want?"

Fat Hands shrugged again, scratching at his face as if he'd find answers under his skin. Paper-Face mumbled something Marti missed thanks to another gust of wind and misery soaking through every layer of clothing she owned.

Then Kane shouted: "Starova!"

Marti didn't move a muscle.

Like hell she'd respond just because he yelled loud enough to scare seagulls out of puddles.

He called out again, angrier this time, and then gave up with a dismissive scoff only someone truly dangerous could pull off without theatrics: "Fuck her. She's nothing."

Nice try, asshole.

Marti adjusted one elbow deeper into swampy sludge and smiled to herself. Nothing doesn't crawl through sewer water just to watch your dirty hands collect payoff envelopes in back alleys.

"What about the chick?" Fat Hands asked behind him as Kane turned away from where Marti stayed buried under sky and shame and rainwater slicking off bad memories.

"I'll take care of her again," Kane said as he pocketed his bribe like it weighed nothing at all.

Of course he would.

Because Kane wasn't running shit here. He was just another bent cog in someone else's machine.

Marti crawled backward through the filth; elbows sank into wet ground with a sick squelch every time she moved. Mud sucked at her sleeves like it wanted to keep her. Rain hammered her back, sliding cold and steady through her jacket, her shirt, straight down to skin. She paused every few feet, ears straining for footsteps. Kane's voice. Anything that might mean she'd been seen.

Nothing but the rain: fat drops pinging off dented dumpsters and smashed beer cans in the grass.

By the time she reached the rust-caked dumpster at the edge of the lot, her whole body was shaking; from cold, from adrenaline, from rage disguised as disappointment.

Because she'd thought maybe, just maybe, Kane had cleaned up his act.

She slumped against the dumpster, catching her breath and waiting for something: gunfire, headlights, divine intervention. Nothing came.

Kane and his car were gone. The other guys had slipped into the lab without bothering to look back.

So that's how it is.

She counted to three hundred before peeling herself off the metal and slipping across the gravel toward the fence line. One foot after another through sludge and trash until she found the narrow gap near the far corner. The chain-link bit at her jacket, scraped across clothes already soaked and stained halfway to hell.

She slid out into an alley thick with shadows and silence.

Three blocks later, she ducked under an awning outside a boarded-up pharmacy. Lightless windows, iron gate pulled down tight. Her fingers were numb when they found the paper cigarette pack in her pocket: soggy as tissue paper.

"God-fucking-dammit." She ripped it in half and hurled it toward a trash can ten feet away. It bounced off a discarded umbrella and landed in the gutter where it belonged.

She leaned back against brick radiating cold from a storm now long dead and gone. Mud streaked down her face in ropes that tasted of copper and ash.

Kane.

And this shit?

I'll take care of her...

How many people were dying while he played both sides?

I'll take care of her again...

How many cases had he buried with that same dead-eyed promise?

Again.

What did that even mean?

When had he ever.

Marti pushed off the wall, boots striking puddle water hard enough to splash up past her knees. She didn't know where she was going; she moved so she wouldn't freeze solid or scream herself hoarse under some broken streetlight.

Falls City after midnight was all sharp edges: neon signs flickering like ghosts over mirrored streets slick with oil and regret. The only ones still out were drunks too stubborn to go home or monsters who never belonged there.

Again kept echoing with each step, as if a drumline pounded against bone.

Kane had been her partner for years. Years full of snapped cuffs and bloody noses and whispered threats inside locked interrogation rooms where no one hit record. He'd taught her how to play bad cop without flinching. Called her reckless when she deserved worse, laughed when she punched guys twice her size, and backed her every time she didn't wait for backup.

He never said a word about the drinking: not when it started quiet or when it got ugly.

He covered for her.

Fuck me, Marti thought, stopping beneath a flickering streetlamp as someone brushed past close enough to touch sleeves. Some guy shielding his head with an actual newspaper as if this was 1998. She let him go without blinking because.

The Kogoya case.

Oh fuck no.

Her stomach dropped so fast it left echoes bouncing between ribs. Everything went cold except for one tiny sliver of heat behind her eyes that screamed too late too late too late.

Charlie Gomes had been locked in an interview room under surveillance from three angles. Then he wasn't. Gone like smoke on that night when everything went sideways forever.

Video showed Marti in the room with him before she went out for coffee. Left him alone. Maybe.

By the time they caught him, Sabrina Kogoya was dead on a motel bathroom floor with half her chest missing. Nobody ever found that heart he carved out as if he was looking for something bigger than blood. Just a kid.

Marti staggered forward on legs going rubbery beneath soaked jeans clinging in wrong places.

She'd pored over that file more times than sobriety allowed: the night shift roster, visitor logs, camera feeds turned static fuzz five seconds too early. None of it added up unless.

She'd interviewed everyone who'd been there that night, including Kane himself.

Kane who brought her coffee mid-shift like always.

Kane who told her to take five because "you look fried."

Kane who sat alone with Gomes while Marti pissed in a public toilet two floors down, trying not to cry from withdrawal shakes.

Kane who swore up and down he hadn't noticed anything strange.

Kane took care of her?

"Again?" It came out hoarse, barely louder than rain hitting rusting fire escapes above her head, but it echoed through something deeper than ears or alleyways or wind-blown guilt.

She'd trusted Kane. Not some naive, soft-hearted kind of trust: the real shit. The knife-to-the-throat and still turn-your-back kind of trust. He was her partner. Her backup.

Right?

Marti blinked and realized she was in an alley. Narrow, nameless, some forgotten artery between cheap noodles and cheaper nails; one of a hundred places in Falls City that reeked like piss despite the rain.

Didn't remember getting there.

Rain snuck under her collar, cold enough to sting, but her hand was warm. Pocket warm. Gripped around the inhaler as if she hadn't let go of it for three weeks.

Shadow.

One hit. Just to cut through the noise. Clear the blood-fog Kane left behind.

She popped the inhaler open with a thumb flick, jammed it to her lips, tilted her head back just as rain needled her face like cold little knives. The gas hissed into her lungs: a toxic kiss she hated loving.

First came the spark: warmth in her chest, color on the edges of the world again. Then came sound; bright, sharp, wrong.

Gomes.

Motherfucker.

Another drag. Harder this time.

Kane.

Goddamn him.

Another.

And then everything went sideways.

Her heart seized as if someone had yanked it mid-beat; skipped once, twice, then roared back too fast like a machine chewing itself apart. Her vision pinched down to a tunnel lined in neon streaks: blue and red bleeding into each other like bruises caught mid-bloom.

Her knees cracked pavement before she even thought about falling. Mouth opened but no voice came out. Just silence drowned by rain. Her whole body folded inward and sideways until cold concrete kissed her cheek and water pooled up beside her face as if it wanted to drown her.

Sabrina Kogoya slipped into focus at the last second; eyes wide, tiny fingers wrapped around Marti's own. Guilt carved its name through what was left of her brainstem.

Darkness swallowed everything else whole.

Felt like payback.

* * *

Lori stared at the screen as if it might change if she squinted hard enough. Marti wasn't answering texts. Wasn't picking up calls either. Typical Marti move, except not during an undercover gig. Not when she walked into the lion's den without her fucking gun.

It had been Marti's idea after what happened at the courthouse during Lori's first month: six terrifying hours trapped in a parking garage with a man hunting her, simply because no one knew where she was. "Never again," Marti had insisted, installing the tracking app on Lori's phone. One for her, too.

Now, with the blue dot blinking on her screen, Lori was grateful for Marti's foresight.

Marti's pin glowed on-screen like a warning flare, stalled in some ass-end alley off 22nd where deals got made and lives ended behind dumpsters.

"Fuck."

She grabbed her coat off the hook and bolted down the stairs; wind wailed as if it knew something she didn't. Rain hit fast with sharp slaps against skin, but Lori didn't slow down.

"Don't you dare fucking die on me," she muttered into the wind, hair plastered across one eye, feet slapping wet pavement hard enough to bruise bones beneath boots.

The alley showed up too soon or maybe not soon enough. It was all angles and shadows until.

There she was.

Marti crumpled near the wall as if someone had ripped out all her bones. Inhaler still clutched in one hand like some twisted comfort object for addicts who didn't know when to quit.

"Shit!" Lori dropped beside her. Pain sparked up both knees but she didn't care, not with that color draining from Marti's face, lips tinged gray-blue under streetlight glow that showed too much detail.

Pulse check.

There it was: faint thump against trembling fingertips that felt like salvation wrapped in fear-stained cellophane.

"Come on," Lori whispered, brushing soaked hair from Marti's cheek with shaking hands. "Bitch better not bail on me now."

Marti wheezed once with a shallow breath dragged up from somewhere deep. Lori didn't wait another second before dialing three numbers with soaked fingers slipping across glass screen edges.

Eyes locked on Marti's slack face as sirens echoed closer than they should be for this neighborhood; luck or divine pity or maybe both. Lori sat there in grimy puddles next to a woman who'd burned every bridge before letting herself fall off them drunk or drugged or both.

Praying they still had one miracle left between them.

Chapter 14

Rain clawed at the hospital window as if it was trying to get in and finish the job. Shadows twitched across peeling wallpaper, jerking with every flash of light from some ambulance outside that wasn't for them. Again. Lori hunched in a plastic chair that creaked when she shifted, green eyes fixed on Marti's face as if she could will her back just by watching.

Marti didn't move. The oxygen mask strapped over her mouth made her look barely alive, as if someone had paused her mid-collapse. Tubes ran out of one arm; monitors bleeped like bored robots trying to remember what vital signs were supposed to sound like.

"Well," Lori muttered, rubbing a thumb over the cracked vinyl armrest, "Here we fucking go again."

It had been almost a year since last time. Dead of winter then: some ice-slick night when Marti had tried to outrun herself with Wunk, that cocktail of hallucinations and ego death she called a 'good time.' Lia, one of however many of Marti's girlfriends, had called it what it was: suicide warmed up and served in a pretty glass.

Lia's voice still rang in Lori's head sometimes, panicked and broken through the phone when she'd screamed something incoherent about Marti not breathing, blood on the floor, glass everywhere. Marti's apartment always had glass everywhere, but that night it mattered. Lori remembered running red lights in bare feet and pajamas; there hadn't been time for shoes. She remembered the waiting room: fluorescent-lit purgatory. She sat beside Lia while they waited to hear whether Marti would make it out or become another fucking statistic for the overdose map.

Marti survived that night. Obvs.

The surgeon, a tired-eyed woman who couldn't have picked either of them out of a lineup, said it was luck and stubbornness. Rehab followed. Apologies came after that, sort of. Lia bailed somewhere around week three of detox, whispering I can't do this over hospital coffee before disappearing into her bakery.

And now here they were again. Different drug this time: Shadow instead of Wunk. Same story: Marti chasing a thrill like it owed her salvation.

Lori had already called Pauline, which felt more like betrayal than anything else. Pauline deserved to know. Marti wouldn't care. Both things could be true.

She pressed two fingers into her temple where pain pulsed behind her left eye like a migraine with a grudge.

Marti stirred, or maybe just twitched, and Lori leaned forward so fast she nearly slid off the chair.

Still breathing. Barely.

"Doctor said the Medimotes worked," she said, mostly to fill space with something that wasn't machine noise or screaming silence. "So you're technically stable now." Her voice cracked into something brittle. "Big fucking win."

Stable was better than unstable, but stable was still critical.

She stared at the rise and fall of Marti's chest under the scratchy sheet, then reached out and planted a hand on her arm. Cold skin. Small tremors underneath like leftover static from some internal earthquake.

"Y'know," Lori said, voice sharp at the edges, "I really start to wonder if you give a single shit about yourself."

No answer; just the hiss of oxygen and another bleep from the heart monitor.

"Or anyone else," Lori added. "But nah... That's not true, is it? You care too much. It just gets lost somewhere between your last orgasm and your next high."

She tightened her grip until her hand shook.

"I'm still here," Lori said through gritted teeth, jaw clenched so hard it hurt. "Still showing up with duct tape and damage control every goddamn time you decide you're finished playing grown-up."

Her fingers flexed against Marti's arm before letting go entirely.

"I don't even know why," Lori whispered, sitting back so hard her spine jolted against flimsy plastic. Her voice dropped low and savage. "Maybe I'm addicted too; just not to drugs."

The monitor beeped again, faster now, or maybe that was just inside Lori's skull.

"You're better than this," she murmured after a pause that felt like surrender. "Better than licking wounds with strangers and calling that intimacy."

She leaned close because fuck dignity. No one else was listening. She said right into Marti's ear:

"You deserve someone who doesn't have to babysit your death spiral twice a year."

Then silence again except for rain on glass and that goddamn monitor painting lullabies in tones of dread.

Lori stood slowly. Everything hurt, from spine to soul. She stared down at the woman who'd taught her not all love stories get happy endings.

"Pull your shit together," she said, soft but deadly serious now.

Because if Marti didn't?

Lori really didn't know if there'd be another miracle left between them next time.

And next time always came faster than anyone wanted to believe in this city where ghosts pretended they were people worth saving.

The door slammed open and Pauline skidded into the hospital room in heels as if they weren't built for emergencies. Her eyes locked on Marti, still tethered to every goddamn machine in the place. She exhaled sharp.

"Jesus," she barked. "You actually called me."

Lori didn't bother standing. She flicked her gaze up from her chair and offered a deadbeat version of a smile. "Yeah. Figured you'd want to know your girlfriend tried to snort the Grim Reaper under the table."

Pauline crossed to the bed in seconds, ignoring Lori completely now. "Is she...?"

"Stable," Lori said. "For now."

"Fuck." One syllable, packed with fury. She shook her head hard enough to make that perfect hair whip around as if a shampoo commercial was having a breakdown.

Lori shrugged, eyes back on Marti's face. "Magic 8 Ball says 'it'll be okay.'"

Marti stirred then: fluttering eyelashes, twitching fingers, that slow surfacing from whatever chemically-induced hell she'd decided to vacation in this time. Her lip curled upward as if even unconsciousness couldn't rob her of being a smartass.

"Well, shit," she croaked. "This ain't my apartment."

Lori snorted. "Hospital gown's your new couture line now."

Pauline wasted zero seconds lunging forward and planting one on her. Hard kiss, full throttle, all tongue and teeth as if nobody else was in the room except surprise: Lori still very much was.

Marti didn't protest. If anything, she leaned in. The oxygen mask came off and the machine beeped.

Lori stared hard at the IV drip instead of their mouths smashing together like horny teenagers remembering prom night.

When they finally came up for air, Marti blinked as if she was trying to process who was kissing her and why everything smelled like antiseptic and bad choices.

"That's one hell of a wake-up call," she mumbled, voice cracking with something that might've been humor or might've been fear wearing lipstick. The oxygen found its way back up her nose.

Pauline softened: the type of junkie who knew that mistakes happen. She brushed hair off Marti's forehead as if that would fix anything bigger than a cowlick.

"Don't do that baby," she said. A beat passed before she added: "For me?"

Marti hesitated, because who the fuck was she to say that? Her eyes bounced between Pauline's desperate hope and Lori's hundred-yard stare.

"Alright," she whispered.

Lori didn't buy it, but Pauline beamed as if she'd just cured cancer through optimism and started kissing Marti again; deeper this time, eager, as if the promise was foreplay and not a plea against death.

Lori rolled her eyes until it hurt and muttered something about scheduling makeout sessions between cardiac arrests next time.

But Pauline wasn't listening, or maybe she just didn't give a damn, because her hand had vanished under the blanket. Lori caught a glimpse of motion beneath the thin sheet: knuckles shifting low against Marti's ribs, then lower still.

"Oh fuck right off," Lori muttered as she stood up with all the grace of someone forgotten too many times by someone who should've known better.

The door clicked shut behind her as Pauline's mouth claimed Marti's breast through the thin cotton hospital gown, licking circles against blue cloth as if it was skin.

Marti gasped beneath it all: broken but alive. She arched once, twice as fingers found their way into wet heat below.

Whatever pain had landed her here seemed irrelevant now, drowned beneath tongues and hands and this ridiculous need to feel something that wasn't withdrawal or shame.

Outside in the hallway, Lori leaned against cold tile walls painted in colors pretending to be calming: ocean blue or institutional denial or some mix of both.

She heard it, the rustle of desperation masquerading as affection, and crossed her arms tight enough to leave lines in her skin.

This was what moving on looked like: sex in ICU beds while monitors beeped stupid lullabies about staying alive long enough to fuck up one more time.

She closed her eyes for a moment before pushing herself off the wall.

Let them have their moment.

She had ghosts to go argue with anyway.

* * *

Inside the room, Pauline had one hand wrapped around Marti's thigh and the other buried where it counted; fingers working like she had a vendetta against Marti's ability to stay quiet.

Marti bit down on a groan, shoving her oxygen mask off with defiance reserved for bar fights or breaking parole. Whoever said recovery was about restraint hadn't been finger-fucked in a hospital gown.

"Fuck," she breathed, voice low and hoarse. Her hips jerked, chasing that pressure as Pauline curled her fingers as if she'd read the manual on Marti's body and bookmarked the filthiest pages.

Pauline smirked and pressed harder, dragging her thumb up to Marti's clit with surgical precision. The pulse under Marti's skin went from steady twitch to full-blown tremor. Her legs trembled as if they might make a break for it without her. The hospital monitors were still attached. Somewhere in the corner, something beeped too fast and then flatlined into silence.

Marti's eyes slammed shut as if that might stop her from careening off the edge. It didn't. She came against Pauline's hand, with a sound that wasn't quite human.

Pauline leaned in and kissed her neck like she was leaving a signature: something messy and permanent. She didn't say anything; just rode out Marti's spasms with steady hands, cruel fingers easing up once the fight drained out of her.

Then she pulled back.

She licked her fingers clean like someone tasting soup: slow, indulgent, pleased with herself. Then one last kiss, deep enough to taste blood or regret, and she was already reaching for the oxygen mask again.

"Try not to die," she murmured as she fit it back over Marti's face. "I'd hate to fuck a corpse."

She was out the door before Marti could reply, if there'd even been words left in her throat.

Chapter 15

Outside in the hall, Lori stood exactly where she'd been fifteen minutes ago, arms crossed tight enough to crush organs. When Pauline passed by, she offered Lori a wink thick with innuendo and self-satisfaction: a gesture dripping with 'fuck you.'

Lori didn't flinch, just gave a smile sharp enough to cut glass and turned away before her face betrayed anything weaker.

Back inside the room, stale air mingled with sweat and sex and antiseptic in some unholy cocktail none of them could bottle but everyone would recognize on scent.

Lori pushed open the window without asking. Rain blew in sideways, cold enough to cut through whatever afterglow Marti was clinging to.

"Hospital sex? Really?" Lori asked, her voice losing altitude on every syllable. "You're fucking unbelievable."

Marti let out something between a chuckle and a wheeze. "Guess I always did have excellent timing."

Lori glared but stayed put across the room while Marti lay there looking smug and exhausted and pleased with herself. Tubes hung off her like party streamers after a blackout.

Right on cue, Dr. Killjoy strode in wearing his white coat like armor against everything human. "Shit," he said as he scurried over to the window and slammed it shut. "Sorry."

He flipped through Marti's chart as if he didn't already know what it said.

Words weren't his thing. He yanked out her IV without warning and slapped gauze on the bloody spot like he was putting tape over cracks in drywall.

Then he tore off her monitor leads like peeling duct tape. Slipped her a half dozen pain killers.

Marti took the first one dry.

"You're good to go," he said, his delivery straight from med school PowerPoints. "Try not to end up back here."

He didn't wait for gratitude or sarcasm and vanished down the hall.

Marti lay there blinking at the ceiling as if it held answers, or maybe just water stains in vaguely accusatory shapes.

"Thanks, doc," Marti muttered to the wall, swinging her legs over the side of the bed as if she was climbing out of a trench. Her muscles screamed. She winced, scowled, and stood anyway: because fuck showing weakness while Lori was watching. Especially now, when Lori's gaze clung to her like smoke on old velvet.

She dressed in silence, pulling on layers with jerky movements, trying not to look like she wanted to puke or pass out or both. Lori didn't say a word, just kept staring as if she was memorizing Marti's silhouette to identify the chalk version later.

Then they were outside. Marti squinted at the wet neon blur of the city as if it might bite her if she blinked wrong. It was late enough for the streets to look haunted: puddles glowing under half-dead streetlights, alleys stitched together with fog and regret. A car backfired somewhere close (sure, yeah, a backfire), followed by the hiss of steam vents and the occasional slosh of water over ruined sidewalks littered with crushed cans and broken pasts.

Marti lit up, cigarette shaking only a little, and exhaled into the mist hanging in the air like breath on glass. "So I've got a theory," she said around the filter, "about Kane."

"Oh good," Lori said. "Sex was getting too wholesome anyway."

Marti snorted smoke. "Shut up. I'm serious."

Lori tilted her head. "Alright, let's hear it. What's Mr. Tall-Dark-and-Sociopath hiding now?"

"It's more than bribes or backdoor deals this time," Marti said, her eyes tracking shadows as they walked. "I think he's tied to those counterfeit inhalers. Helping someone push into Devall's territory."

Lori paused mid-step. "You mean the green Shadow?"

"What else? People are OD'ing off shit that shouldn't even register on a test strip."

As they turned down a side street that stank of vomit and chemical rain, Marti kept talking, low and sharp as if someone had wired paranoia into her bloodstream along with everything else.

"Could be Kane knows exactly what is going on."

Lori gave her the side-eye. "Or he works for Devall and is in the dark about anything that is being sold out the back of the lab."

Marti snorted at Lori's stupid sensibility.

They passed another collapsed billboard tagged with neon graffiti: missing girls' names and cartoon devils locked in eternal battle.

"So what?" Lori asked. "He gets money for a high body count now?"

"Cops have done worse," Marti muttered.

They walked in silence for a minute or two, boots splashing through oily puddles that didn't deserve names. Somewhere nearby, an old radio crackled out synth-pop from twenty years ago.

"Are we gonna talk about this?" Lori finally asked.

Marti didn't look at her. "Talk about what."

"You nearly died."

"Yeah. That."

"You're not stupid," Lori snapped. "Why'd you take so much?"

Marti blew smoke toward the gutter and shrugged as if it weighed fifty pounds instead of five syllables. "Honestly? I don't fucking remember."

"Bullshit."

But before Lori could press more, they both heard it: a wet coughing sound from nearby that didn't belong to rats or broken plumbing.

They froze.

In the alcove of a boarded-up vape lounge was a guy folded against himself as if trash tossed by the wind. Shaking. Chest quivering more than breathing.

A green inhaler lay next to his twitching hand.

"Fuck," Marti hissed under her breath. Lori was already moving before Marti could say more.

Lori kneeled, phone out with one hand while brushing hair back from the guy's clammy forehead with the other; not gently but not cruel either.

"Medical," she barked at whoever picked up on the other end, rattling off their location while checking his pulse with fingers steadier than anything she felt inside.

Minutes dragged out long and ugly. Then lights came flashing around corners, red and sterile as judgment.

Paramedics swarmed in with big city detachment; Marti stepped back just enough not to get shoved aside.

The guy was still convulsing when they loaded him up, eyes rolled back so far he probably saw heaven's error message blinking in binary.

Lori turned away. Through the jacket, Marti could see tension shaking down her spine.

"It's okay," Marti said quietly, too quietly to believe it herself, but loud enough that maybe Lori would pretend she believed it too.

Lori spun on her instead.

"Fuck you," she said.

Marti blinked. "I'm sorry?"

"You still haven't thanked me," Lori spat. "You remember that part? You'd be dead if I hadn't found your overdosed ass three nights ago."

The words hit harder than any punch Kane had thrown at her; and Kane had thrown plenty.

"Oh," Marti said, guilt creeping up like a tide she'd tried to ignore until it soaked her boots through and started gnawing at bone. "Right... Yeah. Thank you." She stubbed out her cigarette against a rusted dumpster without looking away from Lori's furious face. "I mean that."

"You better," Lori grumbled but didn't walk away this time, which hurt worse than if she had walked forever.

Marti lit another cigarette because pretending not to feel things worked better when nicotine got involved.

She watched as the ambulance disappeared into whatever hell-slick dimension dying people got ferried toward these days.

"He's in on it" she said aloud, but not really to anyone there. Maybe just God if he was still renting space above Fourth Street under an alias.

Then she turned toward Lori again: all business even if her hands wouldn't stop twitching and there were bruises blooming under her skin like bad omens nobody prayed away anymore.

"I'm telling you now," she said tightly, as if every word scraped its way out on gravel and spite. "Kane's behind this shitstorm."

A static-buzz of a memory lit up behind Marti's eyes, jittery and mean. Clarity sharpened it like a knife.

She was back in Homicide. Interrogation Room C. Charlie Gomes sweating through a stained t-shirt on one side of the table. Marti and Kane playing good cop / bad cop slash hungover cop / asshole cop on the other. She'd said something about needing caffeine before she started throwing chairs, then ducked out for coffee that tasted like rust and regret.

When she came back, Kane wasn't in the room; he was out in the hallway bullshitting with a sergeant, laughing at something like there wasn't a murder suspect chilling unsupervised inside.

Only he wasn't inside anymore.

The chair sat empty. The window yawned open like an insult.

"Help!" Her own voice echoed back to her from the corners of memory: panicked, high-pitched, raw enough to bleed from. "Gomes escaped!"

Kane burst in right on cue, face twisted into a perfect mask of righteous fury. Oscar-worthy stuff. "Goddamn it, Marti! I told you not to leave him alone! You went for coffee? Coffee? Jesus Christ, you let him bolt so you could get your fix of burned bean water?" His eyes darted side to side as if cameras might be watching. "I'll try to cover for you, but this one's on you."

The whole thing had tasted wrong then. Now it reeked.

Marti dragged in air as if it might help, but it didn't. Just made her light-headed and pissed off.

"Fuck," she muttered, hand scrubbing over her face as if she could erase time by friction alone. "I'm just not sure anymore." Not sure then. Not sure now.

Lori raised an eyebrow but didn't interrupt whatever Marti was struggling with.

"He's either running poison himself or letting someone else do it because why not? He has logistics down cold: access points, corrupted labs, distribution networks clean enough to avoid sweepers but dirty enough people choke on them." She scoffed without humor. "Only reason this makes sense is if poisoning users is part of the plan."

"Plan?" Lori blinked, as if she'd misheard, as if Marti had casually accused her dad of eating babies or something. "Why the hell would he—"

"Don't know." Marti flicked ash off the end of her cigarette and watched it vanish into the rain-slick street like cotton candy. "But I do know this: he's not stupid. Users can't tell shit apart, not when it comes to inhalers.

Counterfeit, real, laced with whatever death cocktail some jackass cooked up in a bathtub last Tuesday; it all hits the same on first pull."

She took another drag, like maybe nicotine could pin down the chaos.

Nope. Still chaotic.

She texted Devall. She needed to know if he was legit and she was just chasing ghosts. Again.

"Damian Kane one of yours?"

"Could be revenge," she said through smoke. "Could be greed or ego or just Kane being Kane and playing god again because no one ever told him no hard enough. Doesn't matter why. He's bleeding people out. We stop him, or we chalk up more body bags."

Lori nodded, but it was stiff, mechanical. Her arms wrapped tight around herself as if maybe if she squeezed hard enough she'd keep from unraveling.

The fear came in cold and stuck there as if she'd swallowed steel wool. Marti saw it settle behind her eyes before she even opened her mouth.

"No."

Devall's answer was succinct.

"Kane was at Troy. Graft."

Marti's text wasn't as succinct, but it was clear.

"Go home," Marti said, quiet now but no less sharp. "You're shaking like you've already seen the morgue."

"I can help," Lori tried, but her voice wavered at the edges, and she didn't even believe herself halfway through the sentence.

"I've updated Devall on Kane. There's nothing more for you to do." Marti tugged her jacket tighter like armor that hadn't worked in years.

"Not tonight." She forced something close to a smile: more teeth than warmth, and tapped ash again as punctuation. "I've got to get in there and look around. See what the fuck is going on."

Lori hesitated for one breath, then stepped close and wrapped her arms around Marti with a desperation that didn't belong on streets like these.

It took everything Marti had not to melt into it.

"Text me when you're safe," Lori murmured against her shoulder.

Marti didn't say yes or no. She blew smoke over Lori's head and nodded once because promises were expensive and she'd already maxed out on IOUs this month.

Then Lori turned. Walked away, coat clutched tight against rain that hadn't started yet. Her silhouette faded into the endless dark city blur as if watching a final act with no encore.

Marti stood there long after she was gone.

Then rage surged up from somewhere deep and black inside her: less emotion, more weapon-grade pressure building for hours. She slammed a boot into the side of a dented Civic until the alarm wailed like someone else screaming for her.

Fuck Kane.

Fuck counterfeit Shadow.

Fuck this whole city chewing up addicts like winter leftovers no one wanted to admit still smelled like meat.

She stormed toward Troy Street with blood pounding in her ears and murder humming warm beneath her ribs.

The lab waited. It didn't give a shit about humanity. Not one fucking shit.

Marti ducked low beneath a broken fence slat and crept forward until rust bit at her knee and gravel crunched beneath boots she never bothered to clean. One window gaped open just enough to tempt fate or a rock; inside, nothing but shadows stretching long across concrete walls painted with dust and spite.

Empty.

Perfect.

Heart hammering as if trying to burn itself out of her chest, Marti slipped closer until gloved fingers brushed brick coated in grime that remembered better days.

She needed something real. Not lab reports; those were a dime a dozen and twice as fake. She needed the kind of reckless little truths people left behind when they got cocky. A prescription bottle kicked under a table, name half-scratched off but still readable. A napkin with burner numbers scrawled in smudged ink, like a drunk had written them mid-breakup. Crumpled cash slips with hurried tallies in the margins, someone's messy handwriting screaming guilt. Supplier tags only one idiot would think couldn't be traced.

The kind of stupid, beautiful fuckups people made when they thought no one was watching.

Chapter 16

The window bit her on the way in.

Marti hissed through her teeth, glass shredding her palms as she hauled herself over the sill and into the belly of the beast. Blood smeared across the frame behind her like a signature. The stench hit: gasoline-soaked air so thick it could knock a sober girl flat. Not that Marti had been sober in days.

"Goddamn it," she muttered, already regretting every decision that brought her to this moment. Rain pelted through the busted-out ceiling in rhythmic drips, each one slapping against concrete like a countdown.

Gasoline in the air so thick each breath burned her lungs.

Makeshift equipment was cobbled together from stolen medical supplies and repurposed circuit boards. Distorted reflections shimmered in the condensation that coated rows of glass beakers, filled with viscous, discolored liquids.

Click. Click. Click.

Wires snaked across the floor, haphazardly connected to a tangle of electrical equipment. The walls were scarred with electrical and chemical burns, and faded, peeling wallpaper hinted at a forgotten past.

More photos. Click, click. The fumes made her eyes water.

The jerry cans sat in a corner as if they'd been waiting for her: miserable little bastards huddled together like gossipy teenage girls. But Marti barely glanced at them. Gasoline wasn't why she was here, but the vapors strong enough she might get high. Win.

Click.

She moved, boots skidding on slick, oil-stained tile. The lab smelled of sweat, chemicals, and something burned into the walls: an acrid ghost of past mistakes. Her ribs ached with every step, but she forced herself to focus.

Crypto codes. Wire transfer slips. An engraved plaque with someone's name. Anything that could point her toward whoever was running this place. She reached for her cigarettes, but saw some inhalers and, well, they were more important.

The workstations were a mess of crumpled notes, loose tablets, and the discarded inhalers. She flipped through papers, most of them scrawled formulas and shorthand that meant nothing to her. A phone, cracked but still powered on, vibrated with an incoming message. She grabbed it, stuffing it into her jacket.

She needed more. Something solid.

A row of metal drawers lined the back wall. Locked. Figures. She crouched, running her fingers along the edges, searching for anything useful. Her hand brushed a half-empty pill bottle. It rattled, label peeling, the name illegible under layers of grime.

Fentafill. "Score," Marti mumbled as it slipped into her pocket. She paused for a moment; in this joint, it might not be legit Fentafill. Might be lethal. She dropped it back on the floor with a curse.

Marti exhaled and leaned back on her heels. No big revelations yet.

Fuck. She was getting nowhere.

She pulled a cigarette from her pocket and stuck it between her lips. Her nerves were shot, her head pounding so hard she could barely think. She dug out her lighter and flicked.

A spark. The flame caught the lighter. Her brain screamed a warning a split second too late.

The fumes hit her a second later, sharp and thick, wrapping around her like a noose.

Oh, fuck.

The air ignited. A rush of heat, a blinding flash, fire blooming outward like a living thing.

Marti threw herself backward, crashing against the counter as the lab roared to life in an inferno. Her brain struggled to keep up. Move, MOVE. Her boots found the ground and she bolted for the nearest exit.

The door was too far.

The window.

She lunged; what glass remained after entry shattered around her as the explosion chased her heels. The shockwave hit like a sledgehammer.

"Motherfucker!" Her body left the ground before physics dragged her screaming back down.

Pavement met flesh in an explosion of pain. Marti bounced once before skidding into a puddle so deep it could've drowned a lesser bitch right there. Grit embedded itself into every open wound; glass shards still working their way deeper into skin.

Everything hurt: hands, knees, ribs. Even her hair felt concussed.

Her lighter was still clutched in her fingers. The cigarette lost somewhere in the wreckage.

"Yeah," she rasped, spitting blood. "That tracks."

She rolled onto her side with a groan that sounded more animal than human and breathed through clenched teeth until oxygen agreed to cooperate again.

"Jesus fuck." It came out hoarse and reverent: and why not? She was technically alive.

Barely.

Her heart thrashed harder now than any explosion had dared try. She forced herself up on shaking limbs that didn't remember how to balance and staggered away from what used to be a lab and was now an angry pillar of fire chewing its way into the sky.

Behind her, sirens started screaming: the kind that meant flashing lights weren't far behind.

"Well shit," she muttered as adrenaline took a nosedive off a cliff inside her skull. "Guess this counts as burning bridges."

An alley opened up nearby as if offering salvation, or at least temporary fuck-off space, and Marti stumbled into its arms. The brick walls were cold against her back when she collapsed there, breath hitching somewhere between laugh and sob.

Mud squelched under her ass. Rain poured down with zero sympathy for arsonists or drug addicts or women with too many secrets crawling beneath their skin.

With fingers still slick from blood and trembling more than useful, she dug into her jacket pocket and pulled out the inhaler. Shadow stared back at her as if an old lover who hadn't aged well but still knew exactly how to get under your clothes.

She pressed it to her lips and took two hard inhales that knocked everything else quiet for three blessed seconds.

The edge dulled. The pain dipped just low enough for thought to crawl back in around it.

"Fuck it all," she murmured around the aftertaste of chemicals and regret, head tipped back against wet brick while lights flared somewhere too close for comfort. They were closer even than the raging flames right next to her fucking head.

Fire crews swarmed what was left of Troy Street Lab now: bright jackets flashing like warning labels as they doused flames with high-pressure hoses that hissed steam louder than Marti's breathing.

It looked almost beautiful if you ignored what a fuck up it was. She shuffled backward, further into the alley and away from the literal heat.

She watched until visibility blurred at the edges again, not tears exactly but fallout, and drew one more breath laced with ash before pushing off into motion again; she was nowhere near ready but too hunted not to run.

"Did I really do that?" Marti muttered, shoulder pressed against the wall as sirens wailed a few blocks back. "Or is this just some fucked-up Shadow trip and I'm about to wake up in piss-soaked sheets?"

Maybe both. Either way, the lab was gone and she was going to have to explain this shit to Devall.

Or worse, Lori.

She slipped through puddles slick with streetlamp reflection and gasoline shimmer, boots slapping against wet concrete. The stench of industrial fire clung to her clothes as if guilt made wearable: gasoline, burned metal, fried plastic. Her hands wouldn't stop shaking.

She blended right in with the addicts stumbling out of their hives.

By the time she hit her office, her nerves were shredded like city flyers after a riot. She fumbled her keys twice before stabbing the right one home. The lock gave way with a groan, and she shoved inside as if the fire itself might still be chasing her.

She slammed the door shut and leaned back against it, breath ragged. "Fuckin' hell," she whispered to nobody. Not even an echo answered.

The room looked darker than usual, as if the shadows knew what she'd done. The faint hum of the mini-fridge sounded louder than it should.

Marti staggered to her desk. Pulled open the drawer with her whiskey and sucked in a long drink as if it might absolve her. Two swallows later and she could at least pretend she wasn't about to fall apart.

"Goddamn fucking idiot," she hissed between clenched teeth, pacing tight circles around the room like a caged mutt. "What the fuck can I tell Devall without getting killed"

She poured two fingers of whiskey into a chipped mug and knocked it back, making herself cough. Popped a Fentafill.

Still not dead. Shame.

Jacket hit the chair. Shirt next. Pants peeled off sticky from rain and sweat and adrenaline. Her blood. She stood there in an undershirt and black cotton briefs, feeling less disgusting but no less doomed.

Half naked in the office once again, but this time alone.

Marti looked at the clock: Lori would be in soon. So, soon, not alone.

She sank onto the couch, limbs heavy and useless.

"You've really outdone yourself now," she said to the ceiling tiles that had watched too much already. "What the hell are you going to tell Devall? Sorry Danny Boy, just had to have a smoke. Fuck!"

Devall would want answers. Clients always did. The truth: she'd fumbled a cigarette and torched a million-dollar operation. That wasn't an option, not if she wanted to keep breathing.

"Gas explosion?" she muttered, rolling the idea around like a bad taste. "Fuck no. Too convenient. He'd know I'm lying."

She dragged her hands down her face.

"Rival gang hit?" A bitter laugh escaped her. "Right, and then he starts a war looking for people who don't exist."

Her ruined clothes made one final journey into a garbage bag yanked from the collection Lori kept for such an occasion, tied off with jerky hands. She crept down the back stairs barefoot, hoodie thrown over her bare body as a makeshift disguise against dawn patrols or nosy neighbors.

The dumpster swallowed evidence whole. She lingered to make sure nothing suspicious poked out before slinking back upstairs, each step making her skin itch harder.

Back in the office, she paced, mind racing. "What about... kids breaking in? Homeless looking for shelter?" She smacked her palm against the wall. "Great, he'd sweep the streets to kill every person. You're a real piece of crap, Marti."

The shower beckoned. Scrub this shit raw.

Under the water, it came to her. The building was ancient, foundations shifting with every hard rain, walls cracked from decades of settling. She'd seen the water damage, the way the floor tilted slightly toward the back corner. Hadn't she felt the whole structure groan when she'd climbed through that window? The photos she took would support it. Sagging ceiling beams, water stains, crumbling mortar.

"Structural failure," she whispered into the steam. "Old building, heavy equipment, foundation settling after all this rain. Something shifted, knocked over the wrong piece of equipment. Chain reaction waiting to happen."

It was plausible. Maybe even true in a parallel universe where she hadn't been stupid enough to light up in a room full of cooking chemicals.

By the time she collapsed again, cigarette ash smudging into fabric, bruises blooming along her hipbones, her body quit trying to stay conscious. But her mind had found its story: electrical malfunction. Something she could sell Devall without getting herself or anyone else killed.

"Fire."

That's all she had for an update for Devall. It would have to be enough. She was too fucking tired to deal with him.

But even unconsciousness wasn't safe anymore.

The dreams came fast: fire eating walls clean down to bone, screams warped into laughter, someone calling her name in a voice they hadn't used since they were alive.

She twitched once. Twice. Then went still again on that miserable couch under blind-slatted light that crawled across her face as if accusation made visible.

Chapter 17

The door creaked open soft enough that Marti didn't stir.

Lori stepped in oblivious, coat still damp from rain she'd walked through on purpose because fresh air sometimes helped her think after seeing things she couldn't unsee; like Marti lying there looking equal parts angelic and apocalyptic.

A snore from the office: a dead giveaway.

"Christ," Lori breathed, stepping over an overturned ashtray without comment. "Why are you naked, mostly?"

She paused beside the couch long enough for temptation to dig claws in but didn't touch. She wasn't twelve anymore. She could handle desire without acting on it. Probably.

Instead, she crouched low next to Marti's ear and tapped two fingers against her shoulder blade.

"Rise and fucking shine."

Marti jolted upright so fast she nearly punched Lori by reflex. She blinked until memories slotted themselves back into place with all the grace of broken glass being swept across tile.

"Jesus!" Her voice cracked dry from smoke or nightmares or both. "Don't sneak up on me."

"Hard not to. You were passed out cold." Lori leaned back on her heels but didn't move away. "I figured I'd better check if you were breathing before calling in HazMat."

Marti rubbed at one eye with the heel of her hand while trying not to puke from either guilt or hangover; or whatever unholy cocktail panic made when left out overnight.

"What time is it?" she croaked.

Lori checked her phone even though Marti didn't care about specifics. She just needed something tethered to reality before everything spun off again.

"Too early for anyone sane," Lori said. Then added: "I got a ping from Johnny Tangle. Nothing from his end. No uptick in queer bashing. He doesn't know where LaLoLa is."

Good old Johnny.

"Are you..." Lori's voice gentled just enough for Marti to flinch at it. "...okay?"

Marti exhaled sharp through clenched teeth but nodded anyway as if maybe relief was allowed here, even when built on arson and broken rules and sleepless nights stacked high as tombstones.

"Yeah," Marti said. "Yeah."

"Good. So what the fuck? Almost naked. You smell like soap." Lori crossed her arms, eyes narrowing like a lazy cat about to strike. "You wanna tell me what the fuck happened after I left you last night?"

"Nothing much," Marti lied, fingers tapping against the couch cushion like they had somewhere better to be. Her fingers tapped faster. A flash of memory surfaced. Kane, years ago in Interview Room 3, leaning back while a suspect wept across from him. "We've got your prints on the knife," Kane had. that was a lie. The guy confessed in under a minute. Marti had admired it once, how Kane could make lies feel like facts. Now it felt like rot that had been hiding under the floorboards the whole time.

"Nothing much? Why are your clothes playing dead?" Lori asked. "Did you bring someone back? Did she steal your pants and dignity?"

Marti dropped her gaze, then looked up with a grin that could've passed for innocent if it hadn't been taped together with guilt. When Lori didn't blink, she sighed and gave up the fantasy. "I went back to Devall's lab. Burned it down."

"Jesus fucking Christ, Marti."

"It was on accident," she said, hands up as if she was being arrested by common sense. "I just wanted a fucking cigarette. Flame caught on vapor, I think."

Lori stabbed at her phone like she was carving a roast. "At least no one got hurt," she muttered a second later, shoulders relaxing just enough for Marti to breathe again. "News says the place was empty."

"Yeah. Just me and my poor decision-making skills." Marti sank into the couch. "No casualties but plenty of fuckups."

"Spill it." Lori dropped down beside her, still watching her like a scientist waiting for the lab rat to admit it learned nothing.

"You smell really fucking good," Marti said before her brain could wrestle the words back into their cage.

"Spill," Lori snapped.

"I broke in looking for whoever's running that little side hustle," Marti said, leaning in just enough to feel Lori's heat without making it obvious she was chasing it. Goosebumps surged across her arms. She rubbed at them, regretted it when her nipples joined the rebellion.

"I found a phone. It's somewhere over there by your foot." She waited until Lori bent down to grab it before crossing her arms over her chest as if that would stop biology from ruining everything.

"They were cutting with gas or ether or some unstable shit," Marti continued. "I lit a cigarette and boom." She smacked both hands together over her head.

Lori didn't flinch at the dramatics. "And when exactly are you planning to tell Devall?"

"Let him know last night."

"What'd you say? Sorry I can't resist as much as a fucking cigarette?"

Marti groaned, dragging herself upright like a corpse rising for overtime pay. "Something true-adjacent. Electrical fire maybe. I saw wires and motherboards; looked legit messy enough for blame shifting." She grabbed her phone from between the couch cushions and waved it like a magic wand she didn't believe in. "Photos back me up if no one looks too hard."

She crouched near a half-crushed storage bin labeled EMERGENCY PANTS and dug through underwear and mismatched socks like a raccoon sifting for redemption.

"You actually took photos?" Lori raised an eyebrow as Marti yanked on clean underwear.

"Lucky fucking day," Marti muttered, tossing the dirty pair toward Lori's lap with a wink.

"Oh my god, get your biohazards out of my airspace."

Marti laughed and pitched them into the trash. Found jeans next. She pulled them on while balancing on one leg as if sobriety was optional but hygiene wasn't. "Stop looking."

"I wasn't! I was not watching you, Marti. God. Keep your mind out of the gutter for once," Lori grumbled as she stared at the floor.

"The lady doth protest too much, methinks."

Lori's head snapped up. "You got that right. You actually know Shakespeare?"

"Saw it on a Stim Gum wrapper," Marti snorted as she pulled on two mismatched socks.

"Marti, you need to be careful," Lori said as she stood by the door, spine straight as judgment day. "If he suspects you're lying..."

"He won't do shit until insurance kicks in and his official reports come through." Marti zipped up and lit another cigarette. "By my math, I've got four weeks 'til retribution."

Lori retreated toward her desk as if putting physical distance between them might stop Devall from killing them.

Marti watched her go, eyes catching briefly on the curve of Lori's hip before dragging themselves back to reality. She'd set something in motion last night that didn't want to stop rolling downhill.

Not that it mattered now.

The lighter did this, not me.

"Smoking kills," Marti said around smoke and sin.

"Looks like you're right," Lori called back after scrolling through updates on-screen. "No bodies reported. Just ash and headlines."

Marti exhaled through clenched teeth as she pulled on a shirt that still smelled of last week's mistakes. She was going to have to sell this lie hard or drown beneath it if Devall started digging.

Something was going up in flames again soon.

"Fuck this," Marti muttered, grabbing the Shadow inhaler from the disaster zone she called a desk. Her hand shook enough to piss her off. One deep pull, and that chemical comfort slid down her throat like betrayal in a velvet dress.

It didn't clear her head. It never did. But it made the edges fuzzy enough she could pretend they weren't knives.

The door slammed open hard enough to rattle the walls.

Dan Devall stomped in like he owned the office, dragging two beef slabs in cheap suits behind him. Their eyes were the kind that looked for excuses to hurt people.

"Someone blew up my lab!" Devall roared, slamming a fist on Marti's desk hard enough to make her ashtray jump.

Marti didn't flinch, but only because she'd already done that internally and decided it didn't help.

"Told you that last night."

Devall narrowed his eyes. "You didn't tell me shit about this. Was it Kane?"

"I texted you one word." She held up a finger. "'Fire.' You want bonus points for vocabulary?"

He stepped closer. The goons followed, coordinated like synchronized swimmers if swimmers wore imitation leather and smelled of gun oil and cologne knockoffs.

Marti didn't move. "I was there before it happened. Left maybe ten minutes before smoke started pouring out."

Lori tossed over the Holo-Tab without looking away from her screen.

Marti caught it one-handed and tilted it toward Devall. "Here. Your little science nest before the flames."

Footage floated above the cracked screen in grainy projections: tangled wires, machines twitching with purpose or madness, blinking lights on panels no sane person should build outside military contracts or doomed sci-fi pilots.

Devall frowned. "That's Troy Street?"

"Right before shit lit up," Marti said.

Devall squinted at the images. "This isn't our equipment."

"Nope." She popped the P for effect.

He snapped his fingers once and one of his wall-shaped escorts peeled off toward the hallway, phone already out as if they'd expected this answer all along.

Then came the question he'd been dying to lob since minute one: "Did you do this, Starova?"

There it was: the accusation wrapped in bravado and bullshit.

Marti took a drag deep enough to bleach her lungs and blew smoke at the ceiling tiles like they might offer divine intervention.

Do not protest too much, lady.

"Fuck no."

She let silence stretch enough to make it awkward. Then, because he wasn't going to drop it...

"Saw anyone else?"

"Nope."

"Kane?"

That almost made her laugh; almost. Instead she coughed once and gave him side-eye sharp enough to draw blood.

"I told you: I saw Kane earlier that day. Way earlier." She flicked ash into a cup that had once held coffee but now hosted god only knew what lifeforms. "Why would he torch your lab? He's lazy, not suicidal. Maybe it was an accident."

But even as she said it, something twisted in her gut: the part of her that kept secrets from herself when shit got complicated.

"What exactly did you see with Kane?" Devall asked. His voice was quieter now, which made it worse.

"He talked to some of your guys, took an envelope, vanished." She scratched at a burn mark on the desk that hadn't been there yesterday. "I kept my distance so I wouldn't blow my cover."

Which had been blown sky-high anyway. Lucky for her, Devall wasn't smart enough to connect dots unless someone gift-wrapped them with blood and panic.

He stared at her until Marti wondered if today would be one of those days: the kind where bullets ended conversations faster than words ever could.

"Fine," Devall said, his tone pure velvet threat, eyes locked on hers as if he could pry the truth out one twitch at a time. "I'll make you a deal. Find out who torched my lab, I double your fee. But if you fuck this up, there won't be anywhere in Falls City you can hide."

Marti took a drag that burned. Not the time for tremors or guilt. Her brain clicked through half-formed excuses and dead-end lies, trying to reroute the spotlight away from her latest arson hobby.

She blew smoke between them. "You want me to wait until the Fire Marshal calls it suspicious? Fine by me. Happy to take your money. But if I start investigating nothing, and it turns out to be exactly that, well, I'm not the one who'll look stupid."

The silence stretched until she felt it in her spine.

Damn. She was making sense.

Devall's mouth twitched, not quite a smile. "Keep it quiet. If someone's responsible, I don't want him skipping town with a head start."

Someone. Like Marti.

"Half a million," Marti said. "And I keep my eyes open instead of planting evidence."

He moved toward her with the grace of something that kills: no wasted motion, no blinking. His shoes tapped against the floor as if they didn't belong here with the scuffed linoleum and ash stains worked into the grain.

He leaned close enough that she could count every pore on his smooth skin. Underneath whatever overpriced cologne he bathed in, there it was: metal. Blood-tinged paranoia.

"I built that operation from nothing," he murmured against her ear as if it was something tender instead of a threat. "I want names, Marti. Names I can use."

He straightened his jacket as if he hadn't just tried to brand her with fear and turned without another glance at his lackey, who didn't need a signal to leave. Obedience looked good on him.

At the door, Devall paused, one hand on the frame.

"Three days," he said without turning around. "Then I come looking for you."

The door shut with the kind of whisper accountants call final notice and morticians call job security.

Marti didn't breathe again until she heard tires peeling off into the storm.

The room settled into a tense quiet broken only by rain clawing at the windows like it wanted in on their little secret.

Lori stood stiff as wire beside her, one hand twitching near Marti's hip like she didn't know whether to flee or grab on tight.

"Jesusfuck, Marti," she whispered finally, voice paper-thin but sharp around the edges. "What now?"

"Keep your voice down," Marti hissed, pacing hard enough to make old floorboards groan beneath her boots. "We are up to our tits in trouble."

"You think he knows?" Lori asked, but she knew; that wasn't a question so much as wishful denial trying not to choke on itself.

"If Devall finds out it was me?" Marti stopped cold and shot her a look sharp enough to cut bone. "You're dead before me so I can watch you die."

Lori flinched but held ground: a miracle in itself.

"So what do we do?"

Marti snuffed out her cigarette in an ashtray overflowing with crushed dreams and reached for another before her lungs got too comfortable with clean air.

"You leave that part to me." She lit it with hands steadier than she'd earned and blew smoke toward nothing in particular. "Try not to say anything stupid if someone, anyone, starts asking questions."

Lori nodded, worry etched deep enough into her face that Marti had to look away before it started sticking somewhere inconvenient, like her conscience.

"Keep things normal," Marti added.

"Normal?" Lori asked as if sarcasm weren't strangled by panic. "You mean 'don't scream when someone puts a bullet through the mail slot' kind of normal?"

"That's the one."

Outside, thunder rolled across the city as if God had bullets too, and Marti watched rivulets race each other down cracked glass while possibilities unraveled behind her eyes.

She needed distance from this mess. But there was no distance when your fingerprints were soaked into every inch of destruction.

She'd find someone else to pin this on.

Fast.

Because saving Lori wasn't optional anymore.

There was no way in hell Devall would settle for just one body in that fire.

Chapter 18

Marti stared at the wall of notes and photographs, arms crossed and a cigarette dangling from her lips. The room was thick with the stench of over-steeped tea and ghosts of smoke, wrapping around her like a tired old coat.

Marti was an expert at deflection and denial. Can't figure out Devall? Change the subject.

LaLoLa's name was the sole beacon among the chaotic wall collage: circled in red three times like a bullseye, begging for a connection she couldn't quite snag. Somewhere between the fake-drug deaths, the missing dealer, and the burned-out lab (oops), she felt there was a connection, but all she hit was a dead end.

"We're hitting a wall," she muttered, more to herself than to the figure perched on her desk thumbing through her notepad. Lori's eyes flicked up, the green like neon in a power outage.

"Yeah? Well, hit back." Lori was always on the verge of a grin; the corners of her mouth fighting to break free from the seriousness of the case at hand. "LaLoLa was dealing bad product, right? Same kind you were buying to test before you burned the place down."

"Accidentally," Marti said as she nodded, but her focus drifted. "Same kind. So what if she got it from the same lab? And that is connected to her going missing." That idea wasn't a butterfly whispering sweet nothings; it was a hornet nest waiting for a foot to stomp on it.

"What if she saw something she wasn't supposed to, like Kane taking money?" Lori shot it out like a cheap bottle rocket: quick and bright, lighting up a dark corner in Marti's mind.

A tension hung in the air like a fragile spider's web, the mention of Kane curling her lips into a frown. She turned her head, letting the weight of the accusation sink in. "You think Kane killed her?"

Lori shrugged, nonchalant, as if the idea of murder floated around the office like the stale smoke. "I think if someone wanted her quiet, a homicide cop would know what to do."

Marti exhaled, shaking her head. The very thought tasted bitter in her mouth like burned coffee. "No. He's a bastard, but he's not a murderer." The words felt light, buoyed by denial. Yet, somewhere deep inside, that whisper persisted: But what if? If Kane was taking regular protection money from the lab, then maybe he wasn't behind LaLoLa's disappearance; maybe he knew who was. And that made him useful.

"So, what's the next move?" Lori's voice cut through Marti's fog of frustration, the taunt laced with curiosity.

Marti ran a hand through her short black hair, pulling at her roots. "If we keep digging through this garbage, we might just get lucky." But as she looked at the chaos she'd created on the wall, she felt the weight of futility hang over her like an ominous cloud ready to burst. "I just need a hint, anything to tether this floating mess down."

Lori's laughter was sharp, breaking the tension. "A hint? If you wanted hints, you should have brought a Ouija board to the investigation, not a collage of scribbles and frayed edges."

"Yeah, maybe I could ask the universe who the hell is pulling the strings in this shitshow." Marti leaned back against the desk, her gaze dark as she recalled her dealings, her inner turmoil battling between past shadows and present fears.

"Or we could just ask Kane?" Lori suggested, her eyes bright with the spark of reckless mischief.

"Sure, and I could stroll right into the station and hand him my head on a platter while I'm at it," Marti shot back, rolling her eyes.

Lori looked thoughtful for a moment. "You asked."

Sinking back into her chair, Marti rubbed the back of her neck, the memory of Kane's voice creeping in uninvited: I'll take care of her again. She couldn't figure if it was meant to be a threat or if he was just slipping into old habits, acting like she still needed him to fix her messes. The thought got under her skin like a splinter, painful but familiar.

"He knows I was at the lab that day," she thought aloud, and her heart raced at the implications.

Lori's expression sobered at the thought, her quirkiness fading into something serious as thoughts tumbled in her mind. "If Kane knew you were in the area, could he tie you to the fire?"

Marti didn't answer right away. The slow churn of paranoia built behind her ribs, throbbing like an old wound she tried to forget. Kane was smart, smarter than she liked to admit. If he hadn't already figured it out, he was close. If he knew what she'd done, if he even guessed, he'd hold it over her the second it became useful.

But he hadn't called, hadn't taunted. Hadn't black-mailed. Kane had not guessed. Yet.

"No. He doesn't know," she declared. The bravado surged back, an armor against the encroaching dread. "I'll just follow him and let him lead me to who controls the lab." The statement rolled off her tongue like a dare thrown into the face of fate. "I'm going to show him I'm not the same naïve rookie he used to babysit."

Lori tilted her head, curious, prodding for more. "What makes you think he'll slip up in front of you?"

Marti shrugged, suppressing the flicker of doubt that buzzed around her like a pesky fly. "He's arrogant, that much I know. He thinks he's untouchable."

"Untouchable can be vulnerable," Lori pointed out, her eyes earnest. "But don't forget, he's dangerous, too."

"Oh, I'm counting on it," Marti replied, flashing a smirk. The nerves began to slip away as they fell into their familiar rhythm of banter. She needed the reassurance that somewhere in their chaos, they could figure it out. "Now, if I'm following him, I'll need to look the part; don't want him to know I'm onto him."

Lori's brow furrowed. "What does 'the part' even mean? Are you planning to wear a trench coat and sunglasses?"

"Something like that, minus the bad movie vibes." Mar-ti leaned forward, whispering with exaggerated seriousness, "I'm thinking dark jeans, a leather jacket, and enough attitude to make even the shadows jealous."

"Charming," Lori quipped, rolling her eyes. "It's just like you to turn stalking into a goth fashion statement."

"Hey, if I'm going down, I'm going down stylish." Marti shot a wink at her, feeling the pulse of confidence replace her anxiety. "But seriously, I'll bring QuantumSpecs and my lockpicks: never know when you might need to pry open a few doors."

Lori studied her. "You sure you can handle this? If things go sideways, I need you to think on your feet, okay?"

Marti nodded, feeling the weight of Lori's concern settle in her chest like warmth. "If this goes sideways, it lands on me," she affirmed, the edge of fear giving way to determination.

"Good," Lori said, breaking into a smile that reached her green eyes. "Just try not to trip over your own bravado."

"Only if you promise not to trip me with that care package of yours," Marti joked, feeling the adrenaline stir in her veins.

Marti stood, pulling on her jacket, the leather soft against her skin as if molded to her defiance. She flicked ash from her sleeves and took a deep breath, shaking off the nerves that skittered beneath her surface. This was no time for hesitation. This was the moment when she'd either unearth the truth or plunge headfirst into the darkness chasing after it.

"Marti, wait." Lori's voice held apprehension as she gathered her notes, casting glances toward the door as if danger lurked behind it.

"What's the matter?" Marti asked, flipping her collar up like armor. "Did you suddenly remember that we need to call a therapist first?"

"Not even close," Lori replied, humor cutting through her concern. "I just want you to promise me you'll be careful."

"Careful isn't in my vocabulary." Marti's lips twisted into a smirk, brimming with bravado.

But inside, her heart danced a dangerous rhythm as she rummaged through her mind, mapping out Kane's patterns and movements. She visualized the upcoming steps: first, tail him without alerting him. Second, gather whatever leads she could before approaching him. Third, don't screw this up. It wasn't about winning anymore; it was about survival.

"At least promise me you'll check in," Lori pressed, a fierce resolve behind her words.

"I promise," Marti said, though she couldn't shake the unease that this could be her last contact with Lori, a thought that sent chills racing down her spine.

As she crossed to the window and peered out, the neon haze of Falls City crept over her like an embrace, beautiful but filled with shadows. The skyline shimmered as the setting sun reflected off the damp glass like a warning. Kane was in the center of it all, untouchable and confident, circling everything she was working on: LaLoLa, the fake drugs, the lab. It was a bold dance. She was just the puppet struggling to break free of the strings.

Time for thinking was up.

* * *

Buzzing neon shone like an oil spill on the rain slicked streets of Blightwood. Marti stood on the corner of Calder and 9th, reeking of stale smoke and guilt. The garbage stench around her was rank enough to serve as camouflage. She lit a cigarette with shaking hands and told herself it wasn't the drug-induced tremors; it was the cold. Sure. The cold.

Shadow, Fentafill, cigarette, QuantumSpecs. A missing woman.

She'd promised Lori she'd fix it. Not that Lori had asked, but Marti figured setting a drug lab ablaze counted against your karma score, even if you were trying to keep your girlfriend alive.

Girlfriend?

Jesus. Slip of the tongue.

She took a drag and let the word dissolve into smoke. Not the time.

If she could trail Kane and ID who ran the lab, maybe Devall would let her live long enough to hate herself.

The city wore its usual shade of fucked-up. Sirens somewhere uptown, yelling somewhere else. Perfect night for stalking a homicide cop through his latest crime scene.

"Where the fuck are all the cabs?" she muttered, flicking ash at a rat that darted across her boot.

A man shuffled into view from between two dumpsters: skeletal frame, eyes like cracked glass, hair so greasy it repelled the rain. He scratched at his arm as if trying to dig up old sins.

Marti didn't flinch. She watched him size her up like maybe they'd shared a needle once or hid behind a dumpster from the cops.

"Yo," he said, voice gravel-thin, "you holding?"

She exhaled smoke through her teeth without looking at him. "Not tonight."

He licked his lips and rocked on his heels as if she might change her mind if he twitched enough.

"You hear if MethLumina's still moving?" he asked.

"Still moving," she said. Recycling other junkies' bullshit came easy when your brain was made of static.

That was good enough. He nodded with solemn junkie wisdom and melted back into whatever shadow had coughed him out.

Marti scanned the street again, caught headlights slicing through mist, flagged down the cab before it could blow past her like everyone else did these days.

It skidded to a stop with all four tires screaming complaints. Driver leaned halfway across the seat with one eyebrow raised and a mouth full of shitty teeth.

"Fuck dude," Marti said, yanking open the door, "that was a move."

"I got moves." He grinned like someone who hadn't paid taxes in years. "Where you headed?"

"I need you for the night," she said as she climbed in, wet jeans peeling off vinyl seats with an ugly squelch. "Follow someone. You cool with that?"

"You pay up front? I go wherever the fuck you want," Cab Guy said.

Perfect answer. She handed over a folded bill and a Shadow inhaler: currency in both worlds. She settled into her corner like a loaded gun looking for an excuse.

"Twenty-seventh and Gold," she said. Kane's territory. There'd been blood on pavement there an hour ago; she saw it on Falls City PD's socials because cops like to advertise when they find bodies.

And Kane? Kane loved homicide more than God loved judgment.

Cab Guy blew three reds without blinking, swore at every pedestrian who dared exist, and parked on the curb when they reached Gold Street's makeshift morgue perimeter.

"Can I ask questions?" he asked as he idled beside yellow tape flapping in wind that smelled like bleach and fear.

"No." She cracked her window to flick out another finished cigarette before rolling it back up against the slap of rain across her face. "Turn left. I need to see if Kane's flexing."

A rocky bump off the curb. A left turn and they went dark.

They waited twenty minutes, about a cigarette's worth of silence. Marti didn't mind waiting; waiting was half her job these days: waiting for people to fuck up enough to have their boss, lover, enemy or friend hire her to find out just how bad it was.

Eventually Kane showed: clean coat, clean shoes, loud voice barking orders over blue lights and bored uniforms pretending not to hate him on sight.

He lasted ten minutes before slipping back into his black-on-black sedan like some noir cliché.

"Him," Marti murmured as tail lights flared red through steam. "Follow him."

Cab Guy checked his mirrors as if they were hiding secrets from him too. "Sure thing." Pause. Then: "Why we doin' this?"

Marti didn't blink. "I said no questions."

"No," he said, eyes locked on Kane's disappearing bumper, "you said you don't want questions."

He pulled forward, turning onto Kane's trail without waiting for permission: not from her or anyone else breathing tonight.

"But I got questions," he added over his shoulder as if it was gospel truth. "And since I drive? You listen to me."

Rain twisted off rooftops above them like spilled thoughts racing toward gutters no one cleaned anymore. Marti lit another cigarette with fingers that stopped trembling long enough to burn something down again.

This time? Hopefully not herself.

"Why we doin' this?"

Marti huffed, cigarette clenched between her teeth, slapping at her pockets for a lighter as if it was stinging her. "He stole my kid's Christmas gift last year," she said. "I want it the fuck back."

The cab rolled after Kane's car through rain-slick streets, wipers thudding like a lazy metronome for the damned. Cab Guy had one hand on the wheel, the other draped over the gear shift as if he was posing for a calendar called "Grime & Indifference." Marti cracked the window an inch. Smoke curled out to meet the damp air, uninvited but confident.

"Man's in a hurry," Cab Guy muttered as Kane blew through a yellow light that was hanging onto respectability by a thread.

"Keep up."

Cab Guy snorted without looking over. "Of course I will." He let another car slide between them: close enough to keep eyes on Kane, far enough not to spook him. They coasted in silence while Kane sliced through downtown as if he'd lost his GPS and most of his morals.

Eventually, he pulled into the police station lot and killed his lights. He parked as if guilt looked good on him.

Marti watched him step out and disappear through the doors as if he belonged there. And he did. "Now we wait."

Chapter 19

They waited. Together in a stinking cab. For an hour.

Marti ripped through three cigarettes and half her patience. She flicked ash out the cracked window while the city drowned in neon reflections and broken promises. Then Kane reemerged: same swagger, same I-own-this-wet-fucking-world stride. He slid back into his car.

Marti leaned forward. "Go."

Cab Guy peeled out slow enough not to raise flags but fast enough to make Marti's heart remember why it beat at all. His body shifted; looser in parts, tighter in others, like a man slipping into old habits that didn't come with parole papers.

"He's checking his mirrors too much," Cab Guy said.

"And?"

"And we ain't chasing anymore."

He yanked the wheel hard right.

Marti slammed against the door. "What the hell are you doing?"

"Relax," he said, eyes sharp now. "We're just rearrangin'."

The cab skidded into an alley narrow enough to make Marti suck in her breath (not helpful when holding smoke), but somehow Cab Guy missed the dumpster by an eyelash and barreled back onto another street as if he'd done it drunk before.

"What the actual shit was that?" Marti barked.

Cab Guy checked the mirror and smirked. "We ahead. You can't follow someone when you're there first."

Kane's headlights appeared behind them half a second later: sharp, steady, stupid. Then they eased past.

Marti let out a low chuckle. "Okay. That was slick."

"I got layers," Cab Guy said with mock pride.

Every time Kane turned, Cab Guy mirrored it. Sometimes slow. Sometimes quick. Just another cab in a city crawling with them.

"You take some kind of night class in tailing people?" Marti asked as she blew smoke at the windshield.

"Street degree," he said with a grin. "Honors in not getting caught."

Kane took them deeper into smaller roads until he hooked left and disappeared around a corner.

"Dead end," Marti muttered just as Cab Guy kept going straight and pulled over without explanation.

He cut the engine. "He'll come back out if you give him time. You wanna see where he's going? Go ahead. I'll hold your purse."

Marti narrowed her eyes but opened the door. The rain had softened to something less dramatic but still wet enough to ruin plans or mascara. She had neither at this point.

But she had the QuantumSpecs, and they could hold up in the rain.

She slipped along dark building fronts like an idea no one wanted to admit they'd had: a shadowy smear of leather jacket and adrenaline pressed tight against concrete walls that never asked questions.

Wasn't hard finding him again, not when his was the only car still bleeding light down the block. The headlights cut off after a minute, swallowed whole by whatever bad vibe waited ahead.

Kane stepped out and scanned his surroundings, as if instinct had dressed itself as posture, and crossed through a busted fence toward what used to be someone's idea of home but now looked like squatters hadn't even bothered lately.

He knocked once on a splintering door and stood there with all his tension wrapped up in stillness.

She darted toward a side yard down a narrow gap between buildings, boots silent on soaked pavement, praying both gods and strays were taking naps tonight.

For once?

They listened.

The rain was biblical. Gutters choked, street drowning, everything slicked in that particular kind of cold that soaked straight through bitchy weather gear and into your bones. Marti tugged her collar tighter and watched Kane's silhouette vanish through the side door of the Victorian corpse.

Three minutes. She'd give him three minutes to get cozy with whatever devils waited inside.

She'd been on him for hours. Her and fucking Cab Guy, who could tail like a ghost with a vendetta and smelled like pine-scented air freshener masking murder.

The house hunched against the night sky as if it had stopped giving a shit decades ago. Windows boarded up as if they'd seen things best kept out of daylight. A busted downspout pissed water down onto cracked cement, and

Marti slipped along the edge of the siding, keeping low, staying shadow-bound.

One window had a board sagging just enough to leave a sliver; light leaking out, faint voices bleeding into the storm. She pressed her back against the peeling exterior and tilted her head toward the gap.

Rain hammered everything with religious zeal, sweat mixing with it at her temples. She wasn't moving much, but stress had its own plumbing.

Marti tapped record and her QuantumSpecs hummed.

"Couldn't have picked a worse night," Kane said from somewhere inside, his voice slicing through the downpour with all that old homicide anger he used to save for dirty cops and smiling murderers.

"You're the one who insisted on meeting here." That voice? Dunstone. Of-fucking-course. Marti's jaw set tight against memory: cracked ribs, two black eyes, and half a bottle of cheap whiskey puked up from that night he mistook her face for a punching bag.

Oh. So Kane went to them. Not vice versa.

Marti's heartbeat kicked higher.

"Better than someone spotting us at the usual place," said another voice: Fehr, rat bastard number two. The tag team from hell reunited in mildew real estate.

"After that business with Devall's lab going up," Fehr added, "everyone's flinching."

"I'm not here for small talk," Kane snapped. "Word is you're pushing into Westside. That wasn't part of our deal."

Silence held its breath before Dunstone answered, smooth as an oil slick. "Markets evolve. We follow."

"Follow?" Kane sounded as if he wanted to punch drywall or maybe Dunstone's teeth. "You're dragging heat our way. That raid last week almost blew up everything."

"That raid," Fehr said with clinical chill, "was managed. Controlled leak."

"And I wasn't in on it?" Kane wasn't trying to hide his rage now. Good for him.

"Don't take it personal," Dunstone purred as if politeness was a weapon he'd sharpened for this moment. "Shadow's changing shape."

"What does that mean?" Kane asked.

Marti shifted; legs were going pins-and-needles from crouching like a ninja behind rotwood siding. She risked a peek through the crack.

Three shadows stood under a harsh white glow coming off some LED work lamp tossed on peeling hardwood floors: what used to be someone's dining room before squatters or age stripped it bare.

Kane stood with his back to her, tall, tense, hands clenched at his sides, facing barrel-chested Dunstone (still rocking that jarhead haircut as if honor hadn't left his body years ago) and Fehr, gaunt and greasy, twitchy little bastard who probably ran experiments on his own dog growing up.

"The new formula is promising," Fehr said as if he was reading off a test result instead of talking about how to kill people faster this time around. "Addiction's up by sixty percent, withdrawal symptoms more severe across trials. We lost three test subjects last week."

He shrugged as if it was parking tickets they were talking about.

"Fatalities aren't tragic," Kane added. "They're data points."

Dunstone smirked and stepped forward just enough that Marti could see muddy boot prints shaped like exclamation points in front of him.

"We're thinking long-term," he said. "Shadow 2.0 is more than product now; it's leverage."

Leverage meant pain for someone else.

"Control who gets sick," he went on, "and you control who gets better."

"And when you control both..." Kane started.

"You control the streets," Dunstone finished with satisfaction.

Fehr nodded along like some creepy altar boy of capitalism gone cannibalistic.

"This city's falling apart," he whispered through that slime-slick smile of his. "We're tired of pretending to mourn it."

"So your grand plan is drug-induced order." Kane's voice cracked sharp: anger cut with amusement now.

"Not drugs." Dunstone corrected him as if correcting table manners at brunch while loading a gun under the tablecloth. "Territory."

He leaned in closer to Kane until their shadows merged under that white light.

"We pump Shadow 2.0 into neighborhoods we want," he said, savoring each syllable like poison wine. "We flood them until breathing hurts without us."

"And then?"

"We lock supply chains tight as fists." Dunstone smiled again: the kind Marti had seen right before men started shooting in alleyways they swore were safe five minutes prior.

"If they want so much as one clean inhale in those zones?" He grinned wider now.

"They pay us just for existing."

Kane laughed a little, the sick kind of laugh when you are sure nothing is funny but you don't know what other sounds to make.

"The brass doesn't have a clue," Fehr said, voice soaked in contempt like cheap gin. "Half the precincts are off-leash. Narcotics? They're wearing our collars. The west side is Ryker's jungle now, downtown is Wallace's little nepotism nugget."

"Jesus," Kane muttered, the word falling out of his mouth like he tasted something rotten.

"We're not dismantling the system," Dunstone said with a shrug that still felt violent. "Just putting it out of its misery. Department's cracking like ice. Shadow speeds up the avalanche. Five years from now: no cops, no rules, just privately owned muscle, and we will own them."

Marti's stomach twisted hard enough to make her dry heave if she hadn't been too afraid to breathe.

"And Starova?" Kane asked, voice low. "She'd been poking around. Was at the lab the day it went up."

Marti froze. She could hear her own blood screaming.

"You think she lit the fuse?" Dunstone said, with enough interest to piss her off and scare her simultaneously.

"Hell no. Starova's a junkie." Kane snapped it out like it was gospel. "Whatever was left of her brain drowned in whiskey and drugs years ago."

"Don't get cocky," Fehr warned, eyes narrowing as if blades were sharpening themselves. "Addiction doesn't make everyone stupid. Sometimes it makes them dangerous. She's got zero left to lose."

"I can handle Marti again," Kane fired back fast, sure.

"If we find out she did it," Dunstone said smoothly, "she's done."

"That blast burned us both ways." Kane stepped forward, voice tight as he looked down at Dunstone as if he didn't trust himself not to hit him. "Devall's sniffing around now. We're exposed."

"We need to know who did it," Fehr hissed, spitting each word like broken glass. He glared at Kane, accusatory.

"Me? You think I did it? You calling me a traitor?" Kane snarled, jaw clenched tight enough to crack bone. "Because my cut of the profits says I'm still one of you."

Dunstone studied him for one long second that felt like waiting for a gunshot in a silent room. Then he reached inside his jacket.

Marti tensed against the windowsill, heart pounding in her throat.

But instead of steel, he pulled an envelope.

"Your percentage holds," Dunstone said, tossing it over like bones to a dog. "But coordination has to be airtight now. Tell the Fire Marshal the building was empty: electrical short or some bullshit."

"He doesn't wake up for less than two hundred grand," Kane said, palming the envelope without missing a beat.

"Done." Dunstone nodded once. "But what about Starova? If she torched it, we take her out? Kane, I know you can bend an investigation on a dirty cop, but not on a dead one people still remember."

"Remembering and caring are two different things. So what do you want done with Starova?" Kane asked.

Dunstone smiled wide enough to show teeth that probably still had blood behind them from breakfast. "I think your old partner finally needs that relapse everyone's been waiting on." He let that hang there a second before adding, "On Shadow 2.0."

Marti shifted slightly. Her boot scraped metal siding on the windowsill like fingernails dragging over tile in a morgue.

Three heads snapped toward the sound like hounds catching scent.

"What was that?" Fehr whispered.

"Probably just the house settling," Dunstone said even as his hand slid toward his holster.

"I'll check," Kane growled and moved toward the door, gun drawn before Marti could curse his name properly.

She backed away into rain and panic and everything else she'd been trying not to feel tonight. The hedge swallowed her whole as bullets screamed through the branches behind her.

The fucker was shooting randomly into the bushes, hoping to hit something.

It worked.

"Who's out there?" Kane shouted into darkness, stomping across wet grass with murder on his tongue. Dunstone followed close behind, gun raised as if this was just Sunday practice in Hell.

"What'd you see?"

Kane fired again through hedge leaves that shook as if they were laughing at him now. "A fucking dog, I think."

Marti didn't stop moving even when every step hurt more than the last.

When she hit Washington Street, headlights pierced through rain and adrenaline. Cab Guy was already there, engine humming low as if he'd been listening with antennae tuned to trouble.

Of course, the gunfire might have been a fucking clue.

He threw it in reverse before Marti's hand hit the door handle: lights off, tires silent as ghosts over wet asphalt.

Smart bastard.

Within seconds they were ghosts too, fading into traffic nobody cared about because nobody knew better anymore.

Marti didn't fully realize she'd been shot until her side pulsed warm with something thicker than rain. Then came pain: slow and sneaky as an ex-lover with unfinished business.

She pressed shaky fingers into her ribs and winced until vision blurred before whispering, "Sorry for bleeding in your car."

Cab Guy didn't flinch. He glanced at her in the rearview with half a smirk carved into midnight-o'clock stubble.

"Ain't the first time someone leaked all over my upholstery." He shrugged as if he meant it, or maybe just didn't care anymore than she did.

"Fuck." She breathed out between clenched teeth, pressing harder against herself while black spots danced behind her eyes. "1145 Sutton Street."

She slumped back against cracked vinyl seats and closed her eyes just long enough not to die yet.

"Let's call it," Marti said, happy to just be done with it.

Marti slept until Cab Guy woke her up and kicked her out in front of her office.

Marti kicked the office door shut with her boot and made a beeline for the supply cabinet. Her shirt was already glued to her side, soaked through with blood and whatever else came out when you got shot in a fucking shrub at midnight.

She grabbed needle-nose pliers, a tube of BioBuild, two Fentafill tabs, and the last inch of whiskey from her desk drawer. God bless past Marti for leaving that.

Two pills down. Whiskey burn chased them like a friend she didn't want but needed. She collapsed on the cracked leather couch. It groaned beneath her, as if it knew what kind of night she'd had.

"Well," she muttered to no one in particular, "guess we're doing this."

She peeled up her shirt and stared down at the bloated red mess of her abdomen. Blood pooled in the hollows of her ribs. The air stank: coppery and wet. Her fingers trembled briefly before she jabbed the pliers in without warning.

A wet crunch.

The kind of sound that stuck in your ears for days.

Marti bit down on a scream as metal teeth caught bone or maybe bullet; it didn't matter. She yanked. A full-body shudder rocked through her.

The slug popped free with a sick little clink onto the tile, followed by the pliers slipping from her grip.

"Fucking hell," she hissed, gripping the couch with one hand while squeezing BioBuild into herself with the other as if she were some drywall project gone sideways. The compound began to fizz, reacting to heat and open meat. A wisp of steam curled up from her stomach.

"Real cute," Marti muttered as she pressed a cigarette between bloody lips.

Outside, something meowed: a high-pitched complaint just under her skin.

She didn't look. Just grabbed the nearest boot off the floor and chucked it at the window without hesitation.

Glass cracked. Cat fled.

"Fucking cat."

She lit up, took a drag deep enough to burn past pain, and stared out at rain slicing down over neon rooftops beyond the broken glass.

"Cops killing addicts for money." Her voice barely registered over city noise and inner bleeding. "Who'd have thought."

Marti smoked in silence until everything stopped hurting enough to pass for numbness.

Chapter 20

Someone screamed.

Not like horror-movie scream: just Lori-level panic shout that cut through Marti's sleep like barbed wire.

Her brain throbbed against her skull as she fought back into consciousness. Blurry, brutal consciousness.

"Marti! Are you okay?" Lori's voice was too close to her face. Too loud for someone who didn't have any visible bullet wounds.

"Peachy." Marti waved her hand vaguely toward nowhere. "Go away."

Lori didn't go away. Of course she didn't. "There's blood everywhere." She crouched beside the couch and nudged something across the floor with her boot.

A sharp metallic ping confirmed it; bullet meet tile meet Lori's horror.

"What did you do?"

"Failed to duck."

"Marti, what happened?"

"Kane thought I was a dog," Marti mumbled into a cushion soaked in old whiskey and older sex.

There was an offended pause, as if Lori was blinking at nothing while trying not to scream again.

"I'm sorry... what?"

"I'm fine."

"Marti."

"Lori."

"Jesus Christ." Lori exhaled and dragged both hands through her hair before sitting beside Marti as if they were about to watch a romcom instead of recap attempted murder by dirty cops.

Marti stared at the ceiling while trying not to puke or pass out, or both in reverse order. "Cab Guy and I followed Kane last night."

Lori squinted at those words as if they had insulted her masters degree. "Who is Cab Guy?"

"The guy with a cab." Marti tried sitting up, failed, gave up with an annoyed grunt that shook more than it should have. "We tailed Kane near Washington Street."

"You took a goddamn civilian?"

"We're all civilians," Marti snapped without much heat. "But yeah: Kane led me straight to Dunstone and Fehr."

Lori's entire body tensed beside her, a coiled spring dressed like a well paid secretary. "Those assholes from outside The Last Guard?"

Geez, does that woman remember every life threatening bar fight with dirty cops?

"The very same Frick and Frack," Marti said. "Turns out they're not just bruising people up for fun: they're running the labs pushing fake Shadow through half the eastern blocks."

Lori blinked once, slowly, and stopped raking fingers through Marti's hair somewhere mid-bang swipe.

"Wait... Devall's competition is...?"

"Those two fuck-ups," Marti corrected as she shifted against cushions soaked in painkillers and smoke-smell fabric softener from another life ago. "They're carving up turf with Kane running interference anytime real cops poke their noses too close."

"And now you're on their radar."

Marti gave Lori a dry look most people would assume meant 'obviously,' but which meant 'how new are you?'

"So now what?" Lori asked after a long pause, with less panic this time and more grit in her voice than usual.

"You go through my QuantumSpecs footage," Marti said as she looked around for them and gave up halfway through saying it: "Wherever they are."

"They're on your damn head," Lori said before pulling them off as if she was lifting sunglasses off someone too cool to care they were bleeding out on vintage furniture.

Marti smirked despite herself, or maybe just winced enough that it looked intentional.

"See what I caught," she said, "should be good enough if you skip over any shots where I'm actively dying."

Lori stood: not dramatically, but still somehow managed to tap the frame of the QuantumSpecs against Marti's forehead before heading toward her own office like some scolding librarian who moonlit as backup muscle on Wednesday nights.

"You got it, idiot."

"That's Boss Idiot," Marti called after her as Lori disappeared behind their paper-thin office door.

Then silence returned, or well, as much silence as existed when your organs were arguing over which one got dibs on shutting down first.

An hour into rewinding Marti's near-death footage and trying to subtitle her groaning, Lori flinched at the knock on their office door. Sharp. Twice. As if it had somewhere better to be.

She shoved back from her desk. The chair squawked as if it objected to interruptions too. The frosted glass showed nothing but hallway blur; no shape, no silhouette. Just absence in fluorescent lighting.

"Fantastic," she muttered, opening the door with the cautious optimism of someone who'd already dodged a letter bomb this month.

No assassin. Just a box. Shoebox-sized. Light enough Lori thought it might float away if she exhaled too hard.

Her name wasn't on it. Marti's was.

No return address.

Lori stared at it as if it might blink first. A quick scan with a BoomTech3000, a much needed bomb sniffing device thanks to Marti's impeccable choices in clients, and Lori relaxed.

She picked it up with two fingers, like handling a dead rat in an evidence bag, and carried it inside.

She set the box on her desk and took a breath she'd regret. She peeled back the flap.

Then snapped the whole lid off because what the actual fuck?

"Underwear?" she said aloud, more accusation than question.

Not new underwear either; these had seen things. They had probably screamed about them into satin linings.

"Oh my god." She marched across the office suite and launched the box like a volleyball serve straight at Marti's unconscious face.

It landed with a soft thud and the cruel slap of elastic.

Marti woke up swearing in three languages, blinking as two pairs of panties settled in her lap like sleepy cats.

She grinned. "What's this? Christmas again?"

"You got a box of used fucking panties delivered to our office," Lori announced from the doorway, arms crossed, eyebrows higher than God's patience level. "Are you seriously paying women for their dirty laundry now?"

Marti held up something lacey, white, and possibly illegal in six states. "You opened it? It didn't show up pre-defiled?"

"I open all the mail," Lori snapped. "It's called being a professional secretary even when I'm clearly working for an unhinged sex goblin."

Marti pulled out another pair: green this time. She rubbed the fabric between her fingers like some kind of deranged textile sommelier.

"No return address," she muttered. "Did it come with an invoice? Note? Forensics confession?" She dumped all twelve pairs into her lap without flinching.

Lori recoiled as if they were radioactive bees.

"You are a disgusting pervert." She turned to leave but made it exactly one step before Marti raised her voice just enough to halt motion but not enough for sincerity.

"Whoa, hold up! No kink-shaming unless you're wearing a collar and paying me by the hour."

Lori froze mid-stride, cheeks blazing bright enough to power a small city grid.

"This is for work," Marti added, as if that explained anything. "Remember Petrie? Husband thinks wifey's making cash online but doesn't know how?"

Lori spun around as if she'd been accused of writing fanfiction under a pseudonym. "Oh my god, you were serious?"

"I always am when I drop five hundred bucks on crotch couture." Marti sniffed one of the pairs: like testing wine notes. She frowned. "Not strong enough."

Lori gagged and made threatening gestures toward her own eyeballs.

"I ordered them through her PntiPro account," Marti went on, "to prove she's slinging these things for money. But there's no receipt. No confirmation it's hers unless lover-boy can ID his wife's scent by nose alone."

"Can't you just give him these biohazardous napkins and let him run a DNA test?" Lori asked.

Marti looked offended by that suggestion. "Right, because nothing says professional investigator like 'Here's your wife's possible snatchwear; good luck!'"

"Well we could do it. Send them out ourselves. Probably cheaper than building your own panty mountain."

"But what if none match?" Marti said, holding another pair up to the ceiling light as if waiting for divine guidance or secret messages in cotton weave. "What if she has employees? A whole room full of freelancers taking turns rubbing one or two or three out during shifts, like artisanal arousal crafters."

Her voice trailed off: either contemplative or mentally masturbating alongside them in solidarity.

Lori squinted at Marti, who was now quiet.

"You're picturing a room full of women masturbating, aren't you?"

"Oh, hell yes," Marti murmured.

Lori sighed. "Okay, I'm sorry I called you a pervert earlier."

"No need," Marti said, reclining again like Cleopatra draped in her throne of filth. "I am a pervert. Just shut the door when you leave." She grabbed the stolen panties from the floor and piled them over her face like some kind of cotton-scented burial mask. The door clicked shut behind Lori.

Chapter 21

An hour later, Marti came to with the sound of rain trying to beat its way in. Her mouth tasted like dust and evidence. She blinked at the ceiling, then down at the pile on her chest. Empty. Mrs. Petri's panties had slid off somewhere during her nap: traitors.

She swung her legs off the couch and stood up, scooping up what remained of her dignity into the crusty evidence box. She lobbed it onto her desk as if it had personally wronged her, put on a clean shirt, then went hunting for Lori.

"Hey," she said when she found her in her own office, deep in paperwork. "You ever sleep or…?"

"Someone's gotta keep this ship from capsizing. Besides, it's 2:30PM, still working hours," Lori muttered without looking up, before finally catching Marti's gaze and smiling too easily for someone so upright. "Do you know what day it is? How do you feel?"

"No, and I feel like someone chewed me up and spit me into an ashtray," Marti said. Lori was already standing, already motioning Marti over with that look of concern that made Marti's walls wobble.

"Let me check those wounds."

Marti hoisted herself onto Lori's desk with minimal flair and maximum joint clicking. Lori lifted the hem of Marti's shirt with professional fingers that somehow still set off alarms in every nerve ending Marti owned. She poked around the healing bullet hole under the ribline.

Marti winced. "Jesus."

"Healing nicely. BioBuild is amazing, hmm?" Lori said with a note of satisfaction that made Marti want to slap her; except maybe not hard enough to stop whatever was happening between them every time hands got involved. Lori smelled like citrus shampoo and second chances.

"But," Lori continued, "we've got bigger infections than just your body."

"Oh good," Marti deadpanned. "Can't wait."

"I'm serious." Lori stepped back but didn't drop eye contact, which was cheating under whatever rules they were playing with. "Police Chief Franklin needs to know about Kane taking bribes and Dunstone and Fehr's business."

"Ha. Right." Marti snorted, dragging her fingers across the edge of the exam table. "Because that'll fucking fix things."

Lori didn't flinch. "If there's even the smallest chance Franklin's not buried in Kane's back pocket, it puts something, anything, on record."

Marti jammed her finger into the bullet wound on her side.

"Jesus, Marti."

She winced, teeth clenched. Still better than thinking too hard.

"You always said Kane was mixed up with Gomes's escape," Lori tried again, stepping closer.

Marti jabbed herself a second time, straight through BioBuild into whatever lay underneath. Pain bloomed sharp, clean. Reality in its pure form.

"What if Franklin starts digging into Kane for bribery and trips over Gomes on the way? Finds out what really happened?" Lori was full of hope again, as if it hadn't been strangled to death years ago with the rest of this city.

"Franklin doesn't investigate shit," Marti muttered. "That's his brother, William: Head of Internal Affairs."

She yanked her hand out from under the shirt and redirected it to jab Lori's shoulder instead.

Not as satisfying. No flinch. No spark.

"Same difference," Lori said, poking back at Marti's thigh with all the menace of a throw pillow.

"Kane probably owns both Franklins," Marti snapped, poking Lori again; arm this time. "He said he was going to bribe the fucking Fire Marshal to call it an electrical fault. He seemed pretty confident."

Another poke. This one landed squarely below Lori's collarbone.

"He's got everyone in this town by the balls or the pension."

"Well, good." Lori stepped in and poked Marti's ribs, not near the wound but close enough to annoy. "One: it puts space between you and whatever story they write about that fire. And two: you don't know who owns who until somebody makes a move."

"I don't know shit." Marti ramped up: poke to Lori's leg. Another to her hip. "Franklin? Devall? Kane? The fucking Fire Marshal?"

Each name got a jab until Lori grabbed Marti's wrist mid-poke. "This city sold its soul so long ago, it forgot it ever had one."

Marti managed one last jab while she still could, right against Lori's thigh.

"Fuck! That actually hurt," Lori said as she rubbed at it, mouth twitching somewhere between pain and something else entirely.

Marti watched her rub her thigh for too long. She swallowed hard enough to feel it click behind her teeth.

Worth it.

"If you tell Franklin," Lori said, voice low as she leaned past arm's reach, "you're not letting them finger your life anymore." She cocked an eyebrow. "You're fingering theirs."

Poke war back on: shoulder tap from Lori, featherlight but deliberate.

Marti leaned back and fished a crumpled pack of smokes out of her coat pocket. Lighter clicked once, twice. The flame kissed wrapping paper.

She didn't look away from Lori as she dragged smoke into her lungs.

Two years of this woman showing up when no one else would: hospital waiting rooms with vending machine coffee; jail cell drop-ins with fresh bread; crouched in alleyways whispering where not to be when bullets started flying.

More loyal than any lover she'd ever had, which made everything worse somehow.

"If I talk to Franklin," Marti said through smoke and grit, "it creates a trail."

"We want a trail," Lori replied. "We need proof he was told about Kane."

"And Dunstone and Fehr." Another puff. "They handed Kane the bribes personally."

Lori waved away the smoke as if it meant nothing, which pissed Marti off more than it should've.

She rolled her head back and blew another stream toward the ceiling tiles that still had blood spatters from god-knows-when.

"Franklin won't do shit," she muttered, quieter this time but no less certain.

"But you will have." Lori edged closer until their knees brushed and didn't pull back. "You'll have done the right thing."

Marti snorted once but stayed still.

"If Franklin ignores it, and yeah, let's be honest, he probably will. Then Devall can do whatever he wants without you being in his way."

"Kill Dunstone and Fehr," Marti said.

"That would be my guess," Lori said without blinking.

Marti looked down at those red-wrapped hips now inches from her and muttered:

"Fuuuck me."

Then came the look.

Marti sighed and grinned as if she just had the perfect revenge. "Fine. You'll owe me."

Lori lit up as if she'd just beat the devil at cards. "Maybe. What do you want?"

A beat passed between them, sharp and loaded.

"Read me a book," Marti said, the smile curling across her face. "One chapter. My choice."

Lori narrowed her eyes. "Just read? Not act it out with sock puppets? No rooftop nudity?"

Marti leaned back, letting the smile stretch wider. "Nope. Just read. Deal?"

"A real, printed book?"

"Yep."

"Deal," Lori said, but not without side-eyeing her.

Marti grabbed the phone as if it might bite, thumb hovering over the keypad. She didn't need to look up Franklin's number; some things stayed burned in your synapses long after you'd stopped believing knowing them was useful.

"Alright," she muttered, dragging each syllable through a decade of regret, "I'll call him. But don't expect miracles."

"Good," Lori said, already moving toward the desk's mess of tangled wires and half-working tech. "Miracles aren't my thing." She flicked on a recorder with one hand.

With a breath that tasted like old ash and stubbornness, Marti dialed.

Ring. Ring.

Click.

"This is Chief Franklin's line. How may I help you?" A woman's voice: smoothed-out professionalism over brittle exhaustion.

So fucking polite.

"Chief Franklin please."

"I'm sorry, the Chief isn't available right now."

Of course he wasn't. Marti tipped her head back and frowned at the ceiling tiles as if they were conspiring against her too.

"Tell him it's Claire Durren from City Risk Management," she said. "It's time-sensitive."

"One moment, Ms. Durren."

Polite woman had earned herself a gold star and maybe a fruit basket full of Xanax. Or a screaming dress down from Franklin.

Marti glanced toward Lori and murmured, "Get me a drink?"

Lori rolled her eyes hard enough to count as cardio but still made for the drawer, flipping Marti off as she went; one-fingered devotion was still devotion.

"Chief Franklin speaking," came the gravel-and-judgment voice of a man who hadn't liked her before Shadow and sure as hell didn't now.

"Chief," Marti said, "it's Marti Starova. I've got information you need about Dunstone, Fehr, and Kane." Her voice held steady by will and two fingers of dread clawing at her ribcage.

Lori uncorked the bottle with a pop and handed it over like communion.

The silence went on too long. She waited. Then Franklin spoke again.

"Starova?" His voice sharpened like broken glass underfoot. "I don't have time for your lies."

Here it comes.

"Kane already showed me the photos of you outside his house, following his kids." His tone twisted into something disgusted. "You think I'm gonna believe anything from someone stalking an officer's goddamn family?"

Marti blinked. "What? I haven't—"

"I've seen security footage too," he snapped, slicing through her protest.

"Listen," she said, "this is about corruption—"

"And this is about you being a junkie stalker who can't keep her shit together," he barked. "Save it, Starova. Maybe if you weren't so busy sucking on Shadow every time life got difficult, you'd be worth listening to."

The line went dead before she could shove another word into it.

Marti stared at the receiver as if it might apologize if she glared long enough. She slammed it into its cradle hard enough to make Lori flinch behind her recording setup.

"Son of a bitch!" The words tore out raw as she lurched up from the desk and paced across cracked linoleum before spinning back in defeat.

Marti took a long pull of whiskey. "Photos? Video? What the fuck is that all about?"

But she knew.

Kane had won this round. He gave Franklin some doctored images or deepfake videos or both; now Franklin thought she was some glassy-eyed predator with boundary issues and poor fashion choices.

Which she usually was, but not this time.

She took a swig straight from the bottle without asking again or thanking anyone for delivering it.

"Well that went just peachy," Lori muttered behind her gear stack, watching Marti with something between sympathy and fury.

"Did you get that?" Marti asked through clenched teeth.

Lori lifted one shoulder in a casual shrug as she hit stop on the recorder. "'Course I did. Do you—"

But Marti wasn't interested in hearing her verbal evisceration again. She left Lori mid-sentence and stormed into her office, slamming the door so the glass rattled in its frame, held together by spite and old glue. Then she collapsed behind her desk as if gravity had a personal grudge.

Chapter 22

Rain hammered the windows like cops at midnight: relentless and unforgiving. It leaked past the corner of window she'd shattered accidentally (on purpose) during another bout of self-control gone sideways and pooled beneath her chair in slow betrayal.

Across the street, neon from Samir's Discount Liquor bled red against the fire escape and spilled across Marti's face every few seconds as if some idiot heartbeat tried to remind her she was alive despite all evidence to the contrary.

She slouched deeper into her seat until only her eyes cleared desk level, resigned, and let the cigarette burn between two fingers without inhaling because making herself suffer seemed fair tonight.

The metal Shadow inhaler sat where she'd left it, un-capped and unapologetic, on top of case files no one would ever read again. Not unless their author cleaned up or died trying. Both felt equally unlikely.

When Lori had come in, she'd seen it immediately, but Marti hadn't even tried to hide it. What was even worth hiding?

Lori perched on the edge of the desk as if trying not to catch whatever existential rot Marti had been cultivating. She stared at the inhaler without looking at it, a skill you only picked up after two years of watching your boss slow-ly grind herself into dust.

Some things you could let slide. The inhaler? Sure. Dunstone, Fehr, Kane? Not so much.

"Devall's breathing down your neck. Five messages in-cluding one that involved the deaths of your mother, my mother and the Queen of fucking England," Lori said, casual as if she wasn't throwing gasoline on a six-alarm fire. "You can hand him everything he asked for: Dunstone and Fehr, including surveillance footage with time stamps. Tidy little noose. You calling him?"

Marti tilted her head back and blew smoke at the wa-ter-stained ceiling tile that had started sagging as if it knew something she didn't. "Tried saving them. Told Franklin. He shut the door in my face."

"Kane worked his wheels first."

"Kane always gets there before anyone else figures out their pants are down," Marti muttered. She stubbed the cigarette out hard enough to crack ceramic, then lit another because self-control was for people with futures. "That's his specialty."

Lightning flared through the blinds, slit and mean, casting Marti's shadow across the wall as if warning had been scribbled in silhouette. Thunder played three beats behind: polite but inevitable.

"You know where this goes," Lori said, watching Marti's face as if she could catch detachment mid-bloom. "Dunstone and Fehr? Already corpses; they just haven't noticed yet."

Marti flicked her lighter three times before it caught. Tiny sparks lit her numb expression as if she was trying to burn herself awake. "Not my problem anymore," she muttered around smoke and spite. "Steal from the poisoner, you don't get to complain when he won't share the cure."

Lori folded her arms across her chest and leaned heavier against the desk just to feel something solid beneath her. "So what's your next move?"

Marti raised an eyebrow without lifting her head. "Plenty of laundry I've been neglecting."

"Asshole." Lori rolled her eyes, but even that felt tired tonight. "I meant Kane."

Rain slapped against the windows again as if it had beef with everyone inside. Marti swallowed a mouthful of whiskey straight from the bottle: the last decent thing left in the drawer besides an old stapler and a photo of someone she'd never call again.

"I did what I was paid to do," she said, tilting the bottle toward Lori like a toast or threat; it was hard to tell these days. "Find who's making counterfeit Shadow that's killing junkies, gather evidence, and I'll deliver it to Devall with a bow on top. Kane's not part of that."

"The video shows Kane taking bribes," Lori argued, almost pleading now, or maybe just annoyed at having to explain ethics to someone who smoked through every HR meeting.

"And Dunstone and Fehr confessing. Hate to break it to you, but Devall may not care about these differences," Marti shot back with a laugh that didn't make it past her lips. "He'll go for Kane."

The building shuddered as wind shoved against its bones, but neither woman looked away.

"If Franklin's dirty, and I think he is, then he'll give our friends a heads-up tonight," Marti said, her voice low and firm as verdicts were supposed to be. "They'll either kill me or disappear before sunrise."

"And if he's clean?" Lori asked.

"Then he moves tonight too," she shrugged. "Gets the men off the street before the press get wind."

She gestured toward nothing in particular, as if pointing at the office or her whole damn life.

"Take off early," she added as if she hadn't just admitted someone might murder her before breakfast. "I plan to get high, get fucked, maybe enjoy one last exhale before Kane drops a house on me."

"Marti…" There was weight in Lori's voice now; not fear exactly, but something nearby.

"I'm not suicidal," Marti cut in firmly enough to close that door before it opened too wide. "Just statistically aware."

She smiled then: a crooked sort of grin that belonged on a tombstone. She took another swig.

"If tonight's my finale? At least I'll die flipping off Kane with both hands."

Chapter 23

The rain had turned vindictive by the time Marti hit pavement. Icy needles drilled under her collar when wind cornered her between buildings that leaned close together like gossiping drunks.

Streetlights flickered overhead without conviction; neon bled down wet sidewalks where rats hustled harder than half the dealers still left breathing.

She slipped into an alley between Fineman Pawn and a noodle stand that doubled as something illegal before and after midnight. She leaned against cold brick and took a pull from her Shadow inhaler until colors sharpened around her pupils and everything ugly tasted tolerable again.

The burn hit behind her eyes then settled into that familiar ache she tried not to name desire.

She pulled out her phone with fingers that knew exactly where they would end up tonight and dialed fast before logic tackled instinct.

"Hey," she breathed when Pauline answered on the second ring.

"I'm working," came the smoky reply laced with affection or lust or pity depending on the night.

"I don't care if you're juggling chainsaws," Marti replied. "I need you."

Silence stretched long enough for regret to tap at Marti's skull before Pauline finally said: "My place or yours?"

"Mine."

The walk back felt longer than usual even though she cut through alleys where puddles smelled like rust and piss and broken promises. All of which reminded her of home anyway.

Once inside: lights dim enough not to judge her. Locks clicked shut behind habit. Clothes hit floor without ceremony.

In front of the cracked bathroom mirror, the one that made everyone look haunted whether they were or not, Marti stood naked except for bruises and gunshot wounds earned honestly.

She traced along skin still marked by survival: knife scar under ribs from that Cartwright job; bullet graze courtesy of Henry's sloppy aim; burn marks from when Shadow used to come liquid before inhalers made getting high more elegant but less sincere.

Every line told stories no one ever asked about. But they were hers.

And tonight?

They were enough reason to keep breathing just long enough for Pauline's knock to hit the door as if bad habits disguised as salvation, a prayer Marti knew by heart.

When the sound came, Marti was still dripping from the shower, towel slung low around her hips like an after-thought. The knock wasn't loud, polite even, but it carried so much promise. She yanked open the door and stepped back without a word.

Pauline stepped in, wrapped in leather boots and rain-slicked hair, and pulled Marti into one of those hugs she didn't know how to ask for but hadn't stopped craving since the last time. Her skin was cold from the downpour, but her arms felt like fire.

"You good?" Pauline asked over Marti's shoulder as she headed straight for the kitchen table.

Marti gave a shrug and wandered in behind her. "Sure. Aside from wanting to pin you to that wall and fuck you until I forget my name."

Pauline looked up with that trademark smirk, raindrops still clinging to her lashes. "Well then. I guess it's good I showed up when I did." She was already reaching for the towel.

"Damn right," Marti muttered, letting it drop. No use pretending anymore.

The storm outside could collapse the whole city for all Marti cared. The walls of her shitty apartment might be yellowed and cracked, but right now they held something better than hope: skin on skin, breath shared between people who hadn't died yet.

Pauline didn't waste time. Her mouth found Marti's chest like it had a purpose carved in bone. Marti hissed as hot lips closed around a nipple, pulse kicking up like she'd just got shot.

Coat, boots, pants, shirt. Off.

"Fucking hell," she whispered, half prayer, half battle cry, as she dragged Pauline toward the bed with a grin carved out of hunger.

They landed in a tangle of limbs and old sheets that smelled of sweat and cheap detergent. Marti shoved

Pauline flat onto her back, watched her sprawl like some kind of offering.

"You miss this?" Marti asked, already knowing the answer as she ran her palm over Pauline's breasts. The nipples were hard enough to make an impression.

"I missed everything," Pauline mumbled into a moan when Marti bit down on one taut peak.

Marti kept moving. Her mouth trailed over ribs that hadn't seen sunlight in weeks, fingers tracing scars like lines on a treasure map until she reached Pauline's panties and yanked them down. No preamble. No poetry. Just heat and want and muscle memory sharper than anything Shadow could dull.

She dipped her head between Pauline's legs and moaned at the first taste: slick, bitter-sweet, unmistakably hers.

"Oh fuck yes," Pauline gasped above her, hips twitching against Marti's tongue.

And then, because this was them, Pauline held out the small inhaler of Golden Shadow she'd palmed from her coat. One hit later and she was gone, eyes glazed enough to heighten every nerve ending.

Marti grinned against her cunt. "Cheating," she whispered into slick folds before diving back in, tongue pressing against sensitive flesh while two fingers slipped inside with ease.

Pauline swore under her breath, French maybe, or just gibberish made sacred by orgasm, and tugged at Marti's hair as if it was the only thing keeping her tethered to this plane of existence.

"More," she begged through grit teeth that barely sounded human. "Please."

Marti didn't hesitate. "Lube's in the drawer."

Shaky hands fumbled it open while Marti kept her mouth busy with whatever flesh was within reach as Pauline twisted and reached. By the time Pauline handed over the tube, she was vibrating out of herself.

Marti popped the cap open with one hand like a pro and coated two fingers: not because they needed it but because she liked watching Pauline squirm while she worked slow lube circles around that tight ring of muscle no one else got access to.

She pushed inside at first, one finger, and grinned when Pauline clenched around it hard enough to squeeze out a groan from both of them.

"That what you wanted?"

"Yes." The word came out hoarse, wet-eyed and raw.

Marti added another finger without breaking rhythm with her mouth, curling enough to make Pauline arch off the bed as if she'd been lit on fire from within.

"Fuck me harder," Pauline growled, forgetting subtlety.

Marti obliged and watched as sweat pooled along Pauline's collarbone like proof they hadn't wasted their second chance at this fucked-up intimacy they called healing.

The moans turned feral. Loud enough that if anyone was listening through paper-thin walls tonight, they'd get an education; maybe inspiration too if they were lucky or lonely enough.

And somewhere between tongue-flicks and knuckle-deep pumping, right before Pauline shattered like glass under pressure, that storm outside went quiet as if even nature knew when not to interrupt something holy.

"Fuck me harder. Deeper," Pauline gasped, fingers clawing at the sheets. Her thighs trembled under Marti's grip.

Marti didn't answer. She drove her fingers in harder, letting her mouth settle back onto Pauline's clit with the same kind of focus she used every time she prayed. Rhythmic. Precise. Ruthless in the ways that counted.

Pauline let out a strangled cry. "I'm coming. fuck, Marti, don't stop. fuck my ass. please."

Marti shifted without hesitation, two fingers slick and sure as they slid into the tighter entrance with ease. Her tongue didn't slow down, just tormented that swollen nub until Pauline choked on her own scream and came like detonation: spasms rolling through her body, cunt clenching, mouth slack with some combination of bliss and disbelief.

Her cum soaked Marti's chin and lips, and Marti lapped it up like she was starving for it. Which maybe she was.

Then Pauline's hand gripped her jaw: not hard, but firm enough to say stop. She pulled Marti's face away.

She flopped onto her back beside her, chest heaving as if she'd run a marathon instead of just fucked through a thunderstorm. "Your turn," she said between shallow breaths, eyes hazy but hungry.

Marti rolled onto her back and spread her legs wide. The room still smelled like rain and sex and old secrets.

"Go on," she muttered, barely keeping the grin off her face.

Pauline lowered herself between Marti's thighs but paused and reached with trembling fingers to grab the inhaler off the nightstand.

"Seriously?" Marti sat up halfway.

But Pauline didn't answer. Just took another puff of Golden Shadow as if it was candy and not poison wearing a gold label.

That was hit number two tonight. Big mistake.

The shift happened fast: eyes blown wide without focus, breath ragged in a way that wasn't from pleasure anymore. Her limbs twitched as if lightning had licked straight through her bones.

"Hey." Marti's voice dropped into warning territory. "What the fuck is going on?"

Pauline growled.

She lunged downward and sank her teeth into Marti's thigh with animal urgency, breaking skin. Marti screamed, a real one this time, and kicked out on reflex.

"Get off me!" She scrambled backward on the bed as blood welled up around the bite mark: warm and too fucking real for any weird sex game bullshit.

But Pauline was already climbing over her again, clawing, snarling, biting at air as if she'd lost every coherent thought to whatever Golden Shadow had turned her into tonight. A junkie werewolf without a full moon in sight.

Marti shoved back hard enough to send Pauline sprawling onto the floor but not before catching scratches along both arms and one breast where Pauline's nails had landed like talons.

The adrenaline hit next: the kind that came when bullets started flying. Heart pounding too loud in her own ears to think straight as she vaulted off the bed, grabbed Pauline under both armpits, and started dragging toward the door despite the flailing limbs and slurred obscenities still pouring from that beautiful fucking mouth turned rabid.

"You don't get to do this shit," Marti snarled as they reached the threshold. "Fuck off."

She dragged Pauline and kicked her clothes ahead of her.

One final shove knocked Pauline into the hallway, naked except for bruises turning purple across her arms where Marti had grabbed maybe too hard, or not hard enough. Out with the clothes.

Marti slammed the door shut before she could think twice and twisted the deadbolt until it clicked with finality.

Silence followed except for rain hammering against glass again as it always did after guilt settled in.

She leaned against the doorframe, naked, bleeding, still throbbing everywhere Pauline had touched. But all those touches felt like borrowed heat now anyway.

"Fuck you," she whispered, not loud enough for anyone but herself to hear this time. "You crazy goddamn traitor."

And then she slid down until she was sitting on cold hardwood floors with blood drying on her leg and more regret than she knew what to do with.

Pauline's voice came through the door like a dying animal, raw and wet. "Please, Marti. I didn't mean it. It was bad Golden Shadow."

Marti laughed without humor, watching blood seep from where teeth had broken skin.

"Oh, now it's the drug's fault?" she muttered. She wasn't talking to Pauline anymore. Just herself and the blood. "Fuck you."

She got up and hobbled to the bathroom to deal with whatever poison Pauline might have transferred.

The pounding started again, matched to the tremble in Pauline's voice. "Marti, come on. I need you."

"You needed me before you tried to eat me alive," Marti snapped, spitting blood into the sink and watching it swirl pink before disappearing. She pressed a stolen hotel washcloth against her thigh where teeth had broken skin. It did nothing but made her feel less like meat.

The apartment looked wrecked. Lube leaking onto the sheets, a heel jammed under the table as if it were a crime scene clue no one would examine closely enough. Pauline's bra crumpled on the floor like used tissue. She scooped them all up like trash bound for incineration and marched to the front door.

Pauline was still out there, naked and shaking in Falls City's idea of climate control: hallway air cold enough to slap bones awake but never fresh enough to breathe right. Through the peephole: hollow eyes and smeared mascara, lips cracked open as if she still thought words might fix this.

Marti unbolted the door just enough to slide her hand through, then threw the bundle at Pauline's chest hard enough to knock her back a step.

"Take your shit and get lost," she said, dead-eyed and done performing rage for anyone. Not even herself anymore. "You don't get any more chances."

"Marti, please." That last one came out hoarse and pathetic, strings of it clinging between syllables like mucus on rot.

Marti slammed the door so hard dust rained down from somewhere in the ceiling tiles that maintenance hadn't touched in years.

She stood there with one hand pressed against wood and wondered if betrayal always felt this physical, or if today was special.

Then she walked away.

Not far; just to the kitchen chair, but still farther than she'd expected to be from Pauline tonight.

She lit a cigarette with half-dry hands and tried not to look at where red droplets had trickled down flesh and were making their way to the hardwood grain as if it was summer vacation.

Smoke filled her lungs sharp and stale: the kind of high no chemist could synthesize, and exhaled out into nothing useful.

Falls City kept spinning outside as if it hadn't just watched love rot itself out on a Tuesday night.

She watched ash fall onto bloodstains near her foot and thought about edges of knives, of patience, of trust, and how everything eventually dulls or cuts you dead.

"Fuck this city," she muttered.

Then again: "Fuck me for thinking romance here could mean something."

The cigarette burned too fast because nothing good lasted.

She stubbed it out in a shallow pool of blood on the floor, leaving a filthy little crater behind.

Shower water ran. No tears; just muscle memory cleaning up after another failed experiment in intimacy.

Lesson learned: don't let people close enough to bite.

And definitely not twice.

Marti stared down at herself in the glass shower door as blood ran pink-ghostly down skin toward rusted drainpipes familiar with regret.

"This won't happen again."

Not a vow, but a sentence handed down by someone who'd had enough of hope masquerading as connection.

She rinsed what was left of Pauline off her skin and locked whatever remained behind bone and grit where no pulse could reach again.

Chapter 24

The mirror was cracked but not cracked enough to hide the fact that Marti looked like shit. Swollen cheekbone blooming purple, a split lip that still felt like Pauline's teeth were embedded. Blood crusted in spiderwebs over the BioBuild she hadn't scrubbed off yet, and the bite on her thigh hurt like a motherfucker.

That bitch had done her worse than the last time bullet.

She lit a cigarette with hands that wouldn't stop shaking, wincing when the smoke hit the raw spot in her throat. Pauline had gone for the jugular and nearly gotten it. Rain tapped against the window behind her: a slow, mocking rhythm, as if the city never clapped for her unless she was bleeding.

"Fucking perfect," Marti muttered.

She flicked ash into an overflowing tray of yesterday's burnouts, then grabbed her coffee off the radiator where it had transformed into something unholy. Lukewarm sludge washed the toast down like punishment. It scraped past bruises in her esophagus; each swallow was another reminder that opening your bed to junkies with nice smiles led to dental impressions on your windpipe.

She got dressed: hoodie stuck to a shoulder bruise, jeans caught on a bandage along her hip. Every movement was an exercise in fuck-you perseverance. Then she grabbed the garbage bag full of laundry she'd stuffed together post-attack and left before she could change her mind.

Falls City welcomed her as it always did: wet, cold, and mean. Fog wrapped around streetlights like crime scene tape. The whole concrete sprawl smelled like old guilt and cheap cologne. Marti trudged through it all in boots that still had blood on them.

LaLoLa was out there somewhere, dragging danger behind her like a wedding veil made of razors. But first, Marti needed to get Pauline's blood out of her clothes before it set permanently. Couldn't afford to look like a crime scene walking around Falls City asking questions.

She ended up at Aggie's Sudz, where dreams went to spin dry alongside sweat-stained lingerie and bloodied undershirts. She was alone with her suspicious clothes. Perfect.

Into the washer without fanfare, credits fed from her phone to the machine. Hot water and detergent were extra. The hum of machinery and thump of spinning clothes made decent white noise for someone trying not to think too loud.

Marti fed credits into a dryer that looked older than most failed democracies and watched her hoodie swirl around as if it were a drowning victim's final desperate bid for air. She slid onto one of those plastic bench things nobody cleaned and pulled a Fentafill from the secret stash pocket inside her jacket.

It tasted like pharmacy chalk going down dry.

For fifteen seconds after swallowing it, everything stopped hurting just enough for Marti to remember what peace might've felt like once upon a time. Probably back before Falls City pulled down its pants and mooned whatever innocence she'd managed to hold onto during childhood.

But tonight wasn't just bruises and dryer lint.

Tonight was Pauline's teeth on her flesh.

Tonight was betrayal slinking under familiar sheets and curling up nice and warm beside you until it struck hard enough to leave scars and fingerprints in equal measure.

Pauline had used too much Golden Shadow and thought Marti looked more like meat than mercy this time around.

Her fingers drummed against cold metal as fog pressed its face against the laundromat windows like some leering fuckboy who didn't understand rejection. She tuned out everything but the steady heartbeat of dryer rotations until the bell above the door chimed a fairy tale tune.

Marti didn't look right away, not because she wasn't alert, but because falling apart meant not jumping at every creak in this rotting city's bones.

Then came the voice; half-whimper, half-assed swagger: "Bitch, I got something for you."

She pulled her gun and turned so fast the guy flinched and almost fell over his own feet. Maybe he tripped over his dick, which likely hadn't seen action since his veins learned how to purr for chemical affection.

Laundry Man's eyes were red-rimmed and twitchy under layers of grime and regret. The stench told her he hadn't pissed himself before; it had happened just now, poor bastard. His hands shot up toward his face as if that thin skin would stop hollow-point bullets from rearranging his brain matter.

"You better be talking about information or drugs," Marti said. "Because otherwise I will shoot you just for style points."

"Fuck! Don't! Don't shoot!" Laundry Man squealed as he backed toward the vending machine full of expired candy and shattered dreams.

"Then what?" Marti asked, eyes narrowed over the sights of her gun as if they were old friends watching a trainwreck together. "Better start making sense before I get bored."

"Rat told me you're looking for LaLoLa," Laundry Man stammered. His hands shook worse than hers now. But on the upside, it meant Rat was out of the hospital and back in the gutter where he belonged.

"Yeah? So go on," she said as she holstered the pistol but kept one hand near it in case Laundry Man grew balls between now and ten seconds from now.

"Inhaler?" he asked hopefully, as if they were bartering groceries over garden fences instead of information in exchange for synthetic euphoria.

"You pissed yourself," she noted while fishing around in her leather jacket's interior pocket.

"So?" he replied with something close to pride or defiance or both marinated in desperation.

Marti couldn't argue with that logic: it was Falls City standard reasoning after all. She pulled out one of Devall's overpriced gifts: a full Shadow inhaler still sealed in a little box like some sacred relic from an era when consequences mattered less than relief.

She tossed it underhand across the laundromat aisle, casual cruelty on display, and watched Laundry Man snap into motion mid-air; hands transforming into wingspan-hungry talons as the box ripped open like flesh and the inhaler landed between his lips like life blood.

He hit it hard enough you'd think salvation lived inside those fumes instead of just borrowed silence.

Laundry Man coughed once, then whispered through vapor-slick teeth: "Saw LaLoLa five nights ago... Baker Street Sleeps. Bought some Fentafill from her."

Marti blinked once but didn't interrupt and let him keep talking because junkies needed momentum more than permission sometimes. And his gossip was a hell of a lot more recent that Athena's Chemtrail tip, same night Rat saw her.

"Some motherfucker mad at her for selling me pills. I took off," he went on. "But then it went quiet."

"Angry about pills?"

He scratched his neck. "Yah, think that was his gig. She usually sold Shadow, but she said she stopped. Moved to pills. I'm okay with that. I just trade 'em. I walked away. That was it."

Of course it fucking was: Baker Street Sleeps got her closer to LaLoLa than she'd gotten. But now that was almost a week ago. A lifetime.

Outside, fog thickened until headlights looked embarrassed by their own glow. Inside, Marti sat still, hands resting on knees slick with dryer heat, and let Laundry Man's words settle into place like gun oil seeping down brass casing grooves.

It wasn't much, but it was something. And something beat nothing nine days outta ten in Falls City.

"Appreciate it," Marti muttered, handing over one hundred cash. Marti grabbed her half-damp clothes and stomped out the door before the guy could change his story. Dry clothes could wait. A busted trail of pills and shouts couldn't.

The laundromat shrank behind her like an apology no one meant. Neon buzzed to death in the side view while Marti yanked open her car door, tossing laundry into the backseat as if she was kidnapping it. The fog had crawled in thicker now, like something breathing, watching. Shit was always watching in Falls City.

She turned onto Baker Street, past the broken stoplight, past the liquor store with shit stains on its murals, until the

Baker Street Sleeps Motel squatted into view, ugly as ever. A single neon sign sputtered above it like a drunk trying to finish a sentence.

Marti slammed the car door shut and lit a cigarette before she hit the cracked pavement. The motel looked worse than she remembered: two stories of human regret stacked over mildew and murder. The "S" on "Sleeps" blinked enough to look like a dare.

Inside, everything smelled like bleach pretending to be authority. She stepped over someone's vomit-stained hoodie and pushed through the door into reception, if you could call it that. The linoleum floor buckled in places as if it was trying to escape. Behind scratched safety glass sat a man who reeked of sleep deprivation and undercooked bacon.

"I'm looking for someone," Marti said, pausing to drag the crumpled photo from her jacket. "LaLoLa. Might've checked in a couple nights ago."

The manager didn't blink. His eyes were swamp-water red, rimmed with hopelessness and dollar signs.

"We don't do names here," he grunted. "Or IDs. Or cameras. Rooms booked online and paid for through a fucking app. This ain't a damn bed-and-breakfast."

Marti stared at him through the grimy glass.

"You could just say 'no' instead of wasting your oxygen."

He leaned forward, breath fogging his side of the barrier. "You could fuck off instead of wasting yours."

Charming.

She left without another word, flicking her half-smoked cigarette into a puddle shaped like someone's bad night. The fog clung low along the lot.

People loitered around: the kind who'd seen too much or hadn't seen nearly enough. But Marti knew better than to bang on doors here unless she wanted her teeth arranged differently. So she went for eye contact first.

"Seen this woman?" she murmured to one hunched figure by the vending machine. She held up her photo; LaLoLa's photo: all glitter lips and danger eyes.

No answer.

She tried again with two more men (one barely upright on whatever cocktail he'd cooked up in his veins) and an older woman who might've once been beautiful or might've eaten someone who was.

Nothing but shrugs and sidelong glances stitched with bad memories.

Finally, one guy broke silence long enough to slur wisdom between coughs that sounded wet with decay: "You got big eyes."

Marti lit another cigarette. "That's so I can see the little pills better." Asshole.

She turned away from them all. She kicked an empty beer bottle across two parking spaces, then caught sight of something glowing through the haze: a blocky convenience store across the street, lit up as if it didn't know where it lived.

Bright lights meant cameras. Cameras meant truth, or lies caught on tape pretending to be truth. Marti would take either tonight.

Chapter 25

Her boots slapped against asphalt as she made her way across, jaywalking past a taxi idling with no driver inside, as if a ghost had forgotten where they were going halfway through their own murder mystery.

Locked door. She knocked, just like the sign told her to; she was always good at following orders.

The buzzer pinged as she stepped inside. Walls lined with dented cans and expired condoms framed her arrival.

Behind bulletproof glass sat a clerk who looked three minutes away from crying or committing felony arson, or both.

"Lost?" he asked without looking up from some awful magazine with tits on it, AI-warped into oblivion.

Marti didn't answer. She walked straight to the counter, eyes scanning for that black dome camera above the front entrance.

"Does your camera capture the Sleeps across the street?" Marti asked as she dug an inhaler out of her pocket.

The clerk shook his head. "Nope."

Marti pulled out a second inhaler and a couple of hundred dollar bills that smelled like dryer sheets. "How about now?"

The clerk nodded and Marti dropped everything into the cash drawer for him.

"I need footage from five nights ago," she said, nails tapping against acrylic countertop smudged with old fingerprints and candy gunk. "Front camera only."

Clerk raised an eyebrow as he took his booty. "You a cop?"

"Even if I was, the bribe has tainted the evidence. You can't be called to testify. But no, I'm private." She paused. "Investigator."

His tongue flicked across his bottom lip in thought, or maybe just habit. Finally he set down his reading material with a sigh deep enough to collapse lungs elsewhere in sympathy.

"You want chips while you wait?" he asked.

Marti smiled like broken glass catching sunrays for the first time in months. "No thanks," she said. "I've got bigger cravings."

The clerk gave her one last look: half doubt, half curiosity, as if he was trying to figure out if she actually believed her own bullshit. Then he sighed, the kind of sigh people save for lost causes and late-night shifts. "Alright," he muttered, pressing a button that buzzed her past the counter. "Back here."

He led her through a narrow hallway that smelled like old corn chips: an architectural afterthought bolted onto the ass end of capitalism. The "back room" was more of a hell closet, barely lit, stale with fried dust and fluorescent hum.

"Five nights ago," he said, settling in front of an ancient security terminal that looked as if it was three lawsuits past its warranty. "Monday, Monday, Mondayyyy." His fingers skittered over the keyboard like roaches fleeing light as he pulled up the footage.

Marti's pulse spiked before the screen even blinked on. Her eyes locked to the footage like a junkie spotting foil in a stranger's trash. If LaLoLa had walked through this camera's field of view, this dump's outdated tech might've actually been worth something.

With a final, theatrical keystroke (God bless the drama queen in every tech guy), the clerk stood up and left her alone. "Don't steal anything," he muttered over his shoulder.

The room was a cavern of chaos: stacks of off-brand toilet paper rolls, used taser gloves wrapped in duct-tape as if they were war heroes, and wires that looked one spark away from burning down half the block. Nothing worth stealing.

"I wouldn't dream of it," Marti deadpanned, eyes scanning the screen. She took a seat on a stool that creaked its disapproval.

The monitors flickered with grainy black-and-white footage of Baker Street: corner store camera catching both the sidewalk and part of the motel parking lot across the street. There it was, the sacred view. And now she had to do what all great detectives did between breakthroughs: wait and lose her goddamn mind.

An hour passed as she watched. Maybe more. Time lost shape under flickering fluorescence and Marti's complete inability to sit still unless sex or spite were involved.

"I swear to fuck," she muttered, rubbing her temples with nicotine-stained fingertips, "this is worse than my seventh grade health class." She slouched lower, cigarette itch flaring along her spine like a ghost limb.

Then something glimmered.

Not much; a smear of shadow on sidewalk. But enough to get her upright so fast the stool nearly bit it beneath her. A figure with forearm crutches stepped into frame from the fog, moving with purpose. The forearm crutches caught the parking lot lights as LaLoLa navigated the uneven pavement. Even from this grainy footage, Marti could see her clothes. Tight jeans with a pant leg tied off, woven top that hung too light for midnight weather: a silhouette familiar enough to hit Marti square in the chest.

Still trying to look good in a city that didn't give a shit.

"LaLoLa…" She said the name flat, not sure if she was praying or cursing.

Marti paused the footage and sat back, cigarette already between her lips before she realized she'd reached for it. She'd been hoping…what? That LaLoLa would hold up a sign saying 'I'm good, y'all. Leave me alone.' That this would still be a missing person case?"

Marti knew in her gut where this was going.

She leaned close enough for static to kiss her cheeks as LaLoLa crossed Baker Street without looking both ways. Who would? She slipped into the parking lot. No hesitation. No swipe card or registration stop at that sad little motel office shack. Just straight into Room T3 like someone had unlocked it ahead of time and paid through the app for discretion and maybe orgasms.

Or death.

"Bingo," Marti whispered, fingers tapping at greasy keys as she paused the video at 11:42 p.m., Room 3 glowing behind LaLoLa's disappearing outline.

She scribbled both details into her battered field notebook with ink that skipped enough to piss her off. Her chest was tight now; not fear or excitement exactly, but something messier underneath: that dirty cocktail of longing and professional obsession she hadn't learned how to detox from yet.

Marti rewound until she saw Room 3's door open for the first time. She scrubbed back just a few more seconds, and there he was.

Fifteen minutes before LaLoLa showed up, a figure slunk under the motel's dark overhang and opened the door. Nothing but a silhouette against deeper shadows. He slipped in, shut the door, and waited.

Then LaLoLa appeared on screen, each step toward Room 3 sending Marti's stomach plummeting. Marti clawed at her jacket pocket, fingers desperate for the cigarette pack she must have in one of these fucking pockets.

Ten minutes after she goes in, Room 3's door opened again and closed. The same man stepped out, now more visible in the harsh glow of the parking lot lights. His tall frame was no longer concealed by the overhang's shadows, his strides too deliberate not to be guilty about something premeditated. Big and fat, like half of Falls City.

He didn't glance back at the room once, as if whatever went down inside had already been sealed away with Gaffer tape and regret.

He got into a parked ThunderBlade GT that waited for him out front like some overpriced getaway horse. Cherry paint job shone under sodium lights despite one busted headlight blinking toward invisibility. The car shuddered awake and he peeled out from Motel Queasy straight into mystery limbo.

"Well shit," Marti said under her breath, rewinding ten seconds to make sure she hadn't hallucinated it all from lack of caffeine or sex or both.

There he was again: the man who could tell her what happened between 11:42 and 11:52 inside that ugly little motel room where LaLoLa was hiding out.

Now there was blood in the water, and Marti hadn't had a proper hunt in minutes.

Marti leaned closer, as if pressing her face to the screen might squeeze more truth from the pixels. Everything about the video had gone quiet, but her pulse was doing a tap dance behind her ribs. Time crawled forward like a drunk on broken glass.

Then a new actor entered stage left.

Another man. Different build. Skinny. Different rhythm in his stride; twitchy and fast, as if he was late for an alibi. He hustled toward the office, stayed just long enough to leave fingerprints and maybe a few regrets, then bolted straight for Room 3.

Marti narrowed her eyes. "Who the fuck invited you to this party?"

The footage didn't answer. It just played dumb, same as always.

The man reached Room 3. Door opened. He vanished inside.

A beat. Two beats.

Then he flew out of there like a cartoon jackrabbit on meth and made a hard sprint back to the office. Marti didn't need audio to know that scream rattling in his chest. She'd seen it enough times to recognize that flavor of sudden horror.

Another dead girl in Falls City. Another case that ended with a coroner's van instead of a reunion.

A second figure joined him: motel manager, maybe. Balding, nervous energy, holding his glowing cell phone like it could save lives. They ran back to Room 3 and flung the door wide open as if they were expecting bats or ghosts.

Whatever they saw knocked them flat.

Both men recoiled at once. One tripped over the other's foot and smacked into the wall trying to get free from whatever hell had taken root inside that room. The door slammed against hinges not meant for adrenaline-fueled exits and bounced open again.

Marti's thoughts went cold as she watched them panic-dance all the way back into the office like two kids who'd broken into a haunted house and found something actually haunted.

Room 3 remained ajar behind them, bright as a swallowed moonbeam.

Lights showed up next, fast and too late. The video got sketchy as it tried to record bright dark bright dark. Red ambulance lights cut through motel fog with surgical precision. Falls City PD followed, flashing enough blue to light up Marti's insomnia for a week.

Cops spilled onto the scene like rats from a kicked-over nest. They cordoned off entrances with yellow tape that meant business and boredom in equal measure.

Then came the van nobody wanted: white with faded lettering, too calm for comfort. The coroner's meat wagon pulled up slow as if it already knew what waited inside.

Marti lit a cigarette and stared at the frozen image of Room 3's open door. "Rat's not gonna take this well," she muttered.

She rewound, her fingers dancing as if they were made for this kind of necromancy: the digital resurrection of moments best left buried.

Back went time, flickering backward until midnight fog receded from where it had pressed itself against cheap security lenses coated in dust and regret.

She stopped when she saw the red paint job arrive under motel almost-dark, one busted headlight winking at fate again.

Driver's side door cracked open. There he was. Just shadow on shadow at first. No face, dark angles, but Marti knew she had her twist in her puzzle box wearing human skin.

He made a beeline to Room 3 as if he'd done this before, as if he'd planned it all out over instant coffee and murder fantasies.

Timestamp read 11:31 PM.

Which meant LaLoLa had maybe ten minutes left on Earth before someone turned her into another Falls City footnote.

"So you're my little murderer," Marti whispered with something that might've been satisfaction if you squinted hard enough. "Fucking finally."

She copied the footage onto a drive so small it could disappear between two fingers, or down someone's throat if needed. She slipped it into her coat pocket like a relic worth killing over.

Marti skittered out of the room, down the corridor, past the clerk, past the buzzer and into the street.

Outside, morning was trying its best to look hopeful. But Falls City wasn't interested in redemption stories right now; the streets were wet with old fog and new sorrow, slumped under sodium lamps still pretending night hadn't lost yet.

Chapter 26

Lori's fingers hovered over her keyboard, restless as junkie hands. "LaLoLa?" She grabbed her coffee mug like it was the last drink in hell. "You're fucking with me. What does she have to do with Pauline?"

"Laundry. I have her video from a store near a south side motel." Marti's fingers beat a death march against her thigh. A nervous tic Lori had never seen in two years of partnership. "Baker Street Sleeps motel. Five nights back. Room 3. She checked in breathing. Never checked out."

"Christ. OD'd?"

"No." Marti's voice went flat as morgue metal. "Murdered. Pretty sure, anyway. Manager found her. Called it in. Whole circus showed: squad cars, meat wagon, body bag. CSI wannabes picking their asses. They don't bring in Forensics for OD's."

The coffee turned to acid in Lori's mouth. She set the mug down slow, like defusing a bomb. "And you have the whole thing?"

"Red Thunderblade pulled up first. Guy gets out. Goes in, waits." Marti's jaw ground side to side, chewing invisible wire. "She goes in. Couple minutes, the guy walks out casually, no hurry. Drives off like he's going for fucking groceries. Then staff find her."

"Jesus." Lori's throat went tight. "You take this to the cops?"

"With what? Hey, I found surveillance across from your crime scene?" Marti's laugh came out raw and mean. "Besides, what if they already pulled the store's cameras? What if they're building a case right now and Rat just hasn't got a fucking clue and I've been running my ass around for nothing?"

Lori searched Marti's face for the punchline. Found only sleepless bruises under her eyes and something worse underneath.

"Show me."

Marti slid the drive across the desk.

"Yeah." Marti tapped ash into a Day of the Dead skull. A tacky souvenir that felt less cute every year. "Before we spook Rat, I need eyes on the body. Need to know LaLo-La's actually on a slab."

"The video shows—"

"The video isn't enough." Marti cut her off. "You want to tell Rat that his favorite dealer, someone he cares about so much he came to ask for help... That she's dead? Like telling some mother that her baby's dead. Based on grainy surveillance footage? You want that on your conscience?"

Lori's mouth twisted. "No."

"No. So I take a field trip to the meat locker."

"You got time for that?" Lori cocked an eyebrow, fighting down a smirk.

Marti's laugh came thick and oily as alley runoff. "There's always time to count the dead right."

"Your funeral." Lori shoved the cold coffee aside. "I'll run the footage. Enhance what I can. See if there's something your shitty eyes didn't see."

"You're a good partner." Marti headed for the door.

"Marti." Lori's voice stopped her. "Come back vertical."

The door clicked shut. No goodbye needed.

Falls City's rain followed her onto cracked pavement. Ten minutes from the office, after one illegal U-turn and one legal use of profanity, she was parked outside the Coroner's Office with tension riding shotgun.

Inside smelled as if bleach fucked formaldehyde and lost the condom halfway through: a scent nobody forgot once it lodged behind your sinuses. Cold tile hummed underfoot. Fluorescent lights buzzed overhead like pissed-off bees on benzos.

"Why do you always come when death is close?"

It hit her before she saw her: that voice.

Ha-Yoon.

Sweet like honey laced with arsenic.

There she sat behind reinforced bureaucracy and boredom: a mid-sixties Korean woman with silver threading through ink-black hair and glasses perched low on her nose as if she judged every life choice you ever made while waiting for you to make another bad one.

Her eyes found Marti's in half a second; they held there, steady as steel wire pulled taut before slicing skin.

"Looking for the usual?"

Marti's pulse didn't jump. It sprinted straight into memory.

Their arrangement hadn't changed just because Marti stopped wearing a badge; it just got more creative. Sex for information. Ha-Yoon dealt in secrets and submission, and what she wanted from Marti never showed up on paper trails or digital logs.

They'd fucked against autopsy tables that smelled like bleach and bodies, traded intel over orgasms so precise they could've been surgical procedures. Stairwells during lunchtime, broom closets during citywide blackouts, once even pressed against Ha-Yoon's immaculate desk.

Marti crossed the lobby, heels echoing against tile, and stopped short of touching range at the reception desk.

Ha-Yoon didn't ask. She didn't have to.

Because whatever name Marti needed confirmed, whatever whisper might save or sink three more lives tonight, it would come after permission was stripped from Marti's throat in gasps: maybe after Ha-Yoon decided which button-down blouse she'd let get ruined this time.

Information wasn't free in this city, not when it came from women who knew where every body was buried and how far Marti would go to get their hands dirty again.

And right now?

Marti was feeling generous as hell: with everything except forgiveness.

"Marti?" Ha-Yoon's voice cut through the warm, humming quiet of the lobby like a blade dipped in honey. "Who hates you so much to do that to your face?"

She leaned forward on her elbows; cleavage pressed together beneath a tight black neckline that had no business looking that good before noon. Her eyes flicked over Marti's split lip and bruised cheekbone as if she was reading tea leaves.

Marti didn't answer right away, mostly because her pulse had dropped into her cunt and set up a drum line. She hadn't seen Ha-Yoon in months, not since the last time they'd made each other promises they both broke inside an hour. But fuck if Ha-Yoon's smile didn't hit her like a hit after three days sober: sharp, addictive, buzzing with regret.

"It's good to see you," Marti said, voice dragging gravel from somewhere between her ribs.

Ha-Yoon grinned wider, perfume curling around Marti like heat haze. "You look like hell. Still sexy, but hell."

Marti shifted closer. Not touching yet. Just close enough to smell the warm sugar of Ha-Yoon's skin under all that expensive scent.

"What happened?" Ha-Yoon asked again, voice dipping lower without losing its bite. "And don't say nothing. That pretty face got rearranged by more than gravity."

Marti exhaled slow through her teeth. "Girlfriend dumped me."

Ha-Yoon blinked. "She hit you?"

"Hit, bit, scratched." A bitter little laugh escaped from somewhere between Marti's molars. "I think every part of her had teeth."

"And you're here for what? Sympathy? A bandage? A revenge threesome?"

"Death confirmation," Marti said. "Baker Street Sleeps motel. Room 3. Five nights ago."

Ha-Yoon's smile drained out of her face like wine from an empty glass.

"Oh," she said.

"Yeah," Marti confirmed.

They stared at each other.

Ha-Yoon looked away first. "We get one or two a month from there these days." Her fingers twitched on the desk: restless little gestures that didn't match the stillness in her voice. "I might know something."

"Might?"

Ha-Yoon cocked an eyebrow at her. "You think I give away free samples now?"

Marti leaned in, close enough to feel the heat rolling off Ha-Yoon's skin, and let her lips brush just shy of her ear.

"What do you want?" she whispered.

Ha-Yoon shivered but held position like a pro. "Information is power," she murmured back, dry as gin. "And power comes with perks."

Marti smirked against the shell of her ear, not hiding how much she liked the game.

"I hope," Ha-Yoon continued, "you haven't lost your edge just because your face looks like hamburger meat."

"Try me," Marti said.

That was invitation enough.

Ha-Yoon turned toward her, lips parted. She licked them with purpose, upper first, tongue curling up before tracing across the corner and disappearing again with a wet smack. Bottom lip next, slower this time.

Marti watched every second of it with the same reverence people used for eclipses and crime scenes.

Her thighs tightened under her jeans.

She stepped around the desk without asking, without needing to ask, and let Ha-Yoon grab her hand first. The older woman pulled it into both of hers as if it was something precious and fragile instead of connected to someone who'd left bodies behind for less than this kind of tease.

Then she started playing with Marti's fingers: stroking along each tendon, tugging side to side, sketching shapes into her palm like sin came in Braille now.

Every squeeze sent something sharp and electric up Marti's arm and down again between her legs.

She moved closer until their hips brushed, then took control; putting both of Ha-Yoon's hands on her own waist and pressing in between those long legs until there was nothing abstract about any part of this anymore.

Ha-Yoon didn't break eye contact as she slid both palms along Marti's ass, quick detour under her shirt until cool hands landed flat against hot stomach flesh.

Marti hissed through clenched teeth from the pain of all her wounds but didn't pull back an inch.

"Under my desk," Ha-Yoon ordered, not loud enough for anyone else to hear if they tried, but loud enough that refusal wasn't on the table anymore.

Marti grinned sharp and filthy as sin. She dropped fast and crawled between those goddamn high-end office chair wheels until she was centered beneath polished brass edges and perfect posture wrapped in tight fabric.

She pushed Ha-Yoon's skirt up herself; dragged fingertips across smooth thighs and bunched the black hem around those ridiculous hips like packaging she planned on unwrapping later just out of spite.

Little butterflies marched along the waistband of white cotton briefs: pink and pale blue stamped into elastic that probably came from some overpriced boutique where beautiful women found excuses to dress dangerous underneath their work clothes.

Marti dipped forward and kissed right through fabric first. Hard mouth meeting soft cotton soaked dark at center. The gasp echoed off file cabinets and cheap acoustics.

Was she getting so loud she was going to attract attention? Marti decided she didn't care.

And neither did Ha-Yoon. She leaned back on just the edge of the chair, clicked on the foot-brake so nothing would move unless she wanted it to move.

It didn't matter what case Marti had come for anymore. Not when every secret worth having was already blooming open between Ha-Yoon's thighs like confession by invitation only.

Then the sound.

Metal groan. Electric sigh.

The fucking door.

Marti turned statue-still where she kneeled mid-thigh-high sin, but Ha-Yoon? She didn't freeze. Just clutched tighter at Marti's scalp and shoved her face right back in.

So Marti kept going.

Ha-Yoon smoothed her voice out for whoever had entered: possibly the mayor or Satan or some poor intern walking into fire without a hose. Between slow words directed toward the visitor, Ha-Yoon's body told another story: That slight buck of hips against Marti's mouth wasn't an accident; neither was the small cough that covered up a moan.

Then finally: ding. The elevator doors. The visitor gone.

"Go in," Ha-Yoon ordered through grit teeth and a sharp little grin that said everyone upstairs would choke if they knew what she had under her desk right now.

Marti obeyed.

"I'm coming," Ha-Yoon gasped, a litany now. "I'm coming," again, and fuck if Marti wasn't ready to drown in it.

Loud moans spilled out of her mouth unchecked now: fucked-out music echoing against office walls that had heard worse but maybe never this good.

She rode each quake with steady hands and greedy mouth until finally Ha-Yoon sagged back into herself, all spent sunshine and limp limbs, and reached down to tap-tap-tap at Marti's forehead like calling off an attack dog post-massacre.

Marti pulled back from between those thighs as if surfacing from deep-sea treasure hunting: hair wild out of place, lips shining with confirmation bias. She crawled out from under the desk with zero shame and zero apologies left in circulation.

Fucking was currency, and Marti was already bankrupt around this woman.

Ha-Yoon watched her rise with half-lidded admiration and reached toward the drawer without looking, snagged a pack of sanitizing wipes like this was just another meeting gone rogue.

She wiped Marti's hands but, when she tried to wipe her face, Marti pulled away.

"Not yet," Marti said. "You still taste illegal," she muttered with satisfaction as Ha-Yoon snagged her panties from where they'd been crumpled inside her skirt folds.

Panties up, skirt straightened, spine reset. Ha-Yoon sat back proper behind the desk like nothing had happened except everything had, and smiled at Marti.

"Marti, you still have a magic mouth," Ha-Yoon murmured, smoothing her skirt like that would erase the sin of what she had done.

Marti tilted forward for a kiss, eyes heavy-lidded and grinning. Ha-Yoon stopped her with a palm pressed to her chest like a spell. "No kissing," she said. "I know where that mouth's been."

"Well then," Marti said, voice syrupy with mischief, "I'm taking these." She ducked down again; no hesitation this time. She slid those panties off Ha-Yoon's legs with the smooth efficiency of a thief in the night. The scrap of cotton came away damp and defiant.

Ha-Yoon didn't flinch. "You're stealing my underwear?" she asked, shifting in her chair and spreading her legs for the cool air and attention. "God, I like it."

Marti held them up like evidence in court, pressed the crotch to her nose and inhaled, before dragging them across her cheek like they were a holy relic. Then into the pocket they went: trophy claimed.

"But no kiss?" she asked again, half-turning away.

"No," Ha-Yoon said.

Marti paused at the edge of something tender.

"But," Ha-Yoon continued as she swiveled back to her computer. "Here's your part of the bargain." Fingers on keys again like this was any other Tuesday. "Dead from the Baker Street Sleeps Motel for this month." She popped a file onto a drive with speed and held it out, all business again.

Marti reached to take it, but Ha-Yoon pulled back at the last second. Marti blinked.

Then she was grabbed and kissed hard; mouth smashed to mouth in one sinuous snare before being shoved away.

"My mistake," Ha-Yoon laughed against her lips. "Meant yes."

Marti licked her own lip, tasting both of them now.

"Go away," Ha-Yoon said, turning back to the glow of the screen. "But come back often."

Marti tucked the drive into her coat alongside lace and heat-stained memory. "Oh, I will," she said as she slipped out and shut the door behind her like a secret.

The ride back was horns and red lights and something humming low inside her groin she didn't bother naming. She turned the panties over in her pocket like prayer beads every time traffic stopped.

Inhaler in pocket A. Morgue drive in pocket B. Panties in pocket C.

Chapter 27

Lori looked up from her desk mid-keystroke and froze, eyes wide, mouth parted as if she'd just caught Marti making out with a corpse. Well. Close enough.

"Holy fuck," Lori breathed, crossing the room. "What did you do, headbutt a blender?"

"Pauline," Marti grunted as she collapsed into the nearest chair like roadkill. "Golden Shadow binge. Went full banshee on me."

Lori swore under her breath: one of those soft, elegant curses that made space for sympathy without losing heat. She yanked off Marti's coat in one swift motion, careful not to touch anything bleeding.

"You're lucky she didn't kill you," Lori said, voice tight as she guided Marti toward the bathroom they pretended wasn't held together by mold and prayer.

"I'm lucky I didn't kill her." Marti's laugh came out like gravel on glass.

"Let's see."

Marti didn't hesitate.

"Marti!"

Marti stood with her pants around her ankles, innocence in her eyes, and pointed at the bite mark on her thigh. She wondered if she'd wet through her underwear yet.

"Jesus. A bite mark? You'll need a bit of ViaRevive. Gimme a sec," Lori said.

The bathroom light flickered once before settling into its usual half-glow. Lori returned with a vial of help. She wet a cloth under freezing tap water, that old building charm, and turned back to Marti with battlefield tenderness in her eyes.

The sting hit first.

Then came Lori's fingers, cool and deliberate, wiping in the Via Revive as if it could fix everything. Marti was getting excited.

"You said Golden Shadow fucked her up," she muttered, dabbing at Marti's temple as she continued her ministrations. "And now Pauline's trying to get you to use it? Sounds like that stuff doesn't just fry your brain; it turns you into something else."

Marti flinched as Lori found a cut near her jaw. "Yeah," she said through grit teeth. "It turns you into someone who can't feel anything until after they've gutted their lover."

Lori paused mid-cleanse.

There it was: the flicker behind her eyes that meant she wanted to ask more but knew better.

Instead she said, "You're hurting everywhere and still cracking jokes."

"Better than bleeding and crying." Marti tried to smirk but winced. "Hand me the pills."

Lori reached into the cabinet, the one above the sink that only had expired prescription pain killers and imported lube, and passed her two small white tabs of temporary salvation. The expired pills still worked, and served as deniable plausibility should they be raided.

Marti dry-swallowed them like they were breath mints from Hell.

Back in the main room, Marti's pants at her waistline, Lori handed over black coffee (the legal kind) and sat across from her. Rain slapped the sidewalk hard enough to strip skin, sluicing sins and syringes into the gutters as if Falls City wanted to clean up its act but didn't know how.

Fat chance.

Marti leaned back into her chair, smoke curling from the cigarette pinched between two fingers. The leather creaked under her spine like a warning. Across the room, Lori's face flickered blue-green in the glow of her monitor: all sharp cheekbones and sharper eyes.

"You calling Devall about the lab? About Dunstone and Fehr?" she asked, voice casual as poison.

"Not yet." Marti drained what passed for coffee from her chipped mug; lukewarm sludge with a half-life. "We've got time."

Lori gave her that look, part exasperation and part somebody-might-die-and-it'll-be-your-fault. "Not that much. The stakes are high."

"I know the fucking stakes." Marti waved it off like she wasn't neck-deep in problems already. "I've got answers Devall wants bad enough to kill for. So I'm giving his competition a few more hours to keep breathing before their bodies show up bobbing in the canal." She grinned without warmth. "Maybe God'll throw 'em a life raft."

"You believe in God now?"

"Fuck no." A drag off her cigarette. "They're still dead men walking."

A pause. Maybe two.

"Check the report?" she asked, tossing the morgue drive toward Lori's desk like it was a grenade made of answers.

Lori caught it mid-air without flinching: she probably played team sports in highschool. She plugged it while sex still steamed off Marti's skin.

Lori didn't turn around when she spoke, just let her words hang as bait. "I can smell whoever she is."

Marti stepped behind her chair until their shadows tangled on the carpet. She reached into her coat pocket and drew out Ha-Yoon's scrunched underwear as if it were contraband or dessert.

"I got a to-go box too," Marti murmured as she flipped open the fabric and licked across its center seam: long, deliberate, unapologetic.

Lori froze for half a second, not long enough to call attention to, but enough for Marti to catch it. Pupils dilated too far, breath catching between keystrokes.

"You're such a dog," Lori gagged as she turned back to glare at lines of data instead of temptation incarnate beside her.

"Bow wow," Marti replied.

"What's on this drive you gave me?" Lori asked.

"Morgue files."

"I'm not looking at dead bodies!" Lori yanked the morgue drive from her computer and tossed it back at Marti.

"Just check the data. I can check the photos. Hopefully Ha-Yoon gave me a little homemade porn, too," Marti assured her as she tossed the drive right back. "Just check for LaLoLa's name, or anyone meeting her description. I can do the visual check."

Marti dropped into a chair across the desk. Time to give Lori's olfactory senses a break; in all honesty she was the one sniffing like a dog.

"She's not on the list," Lori said happily. Her part of this gruesome search was done. "And the slip drive? Footage shows a red ThunderBlade GT pulling into Baker Street Sleeps Motel the night LaLoLa died."

"Yep. Checked and double-checked the footage. Red, broken headlight. No license plate. There are over two thousand red ThunderBlade GTs registered statewide," Lori said as she watched the ashes from Marti's cigarette fall to the floor.

"Well fuck me with bureaucracy," Marti muttered.

"I narrowed it down. Hundred-mile radius from Falls City. Can we buy one of those robot vacuum things? Clean up after you?"

"No. It might steal my drugs." Marti stood up and rounded the desk again, leaning against Lori's chair; restless energy kept every inch of her body twitchy beneath a calm veneer.

"We're down to thirty-two possibles," Lori said without breaking typing rhythm. She spun the screen toward Marti with triumph in her eyes.

Marti grinned. That number was manageable murder math.

Marti leaned in, breath laced with stale Shadow and vaginal fluids, eyes glittering with mania as she stared down the fresh list as if it fed an addiction: which it did. "Print me a copy." Her voice was flat, but blood lurked behind it. The car was the thing; the final piece of the jigsaw she'd been chasing through every sleepless crack in this city.

Lori hit print. The machine groaned, puking out a sheet as if it hated its own guts. Thirty-two names. Thirty-two assholes who might've driven that red ThunderBlade GT into Baker Street Sleeps motel the night LaLoLa got turned into a corpse.

They hunched over the printout like co-conspirators or survivors: same difference. Marti's finger traced each name down the list, slow and surgical, as if willing one of them to flinch under her touch.

Nothing.

Thirty-two strangers and not a single one made her gut twist in recognition.

"Fuck," she muttered, folding the page with force and shoving it deep into her jeans pocket. The denim was crusted with old coffee and one regrettable parking-lot accident. Paper fit right in.

Time to pivot again. Cars hadn't given up a name. Maybe corpses would.

She hissed out a breath, stuck the morgue drive into her computer, and dropped into her chair with a creak like a porno set for ghosts. Cigarette between her lips, fingers over keys, she clicked through files like some grim Tinder for dead girls.

First one: Female, Black, fifty-six. Washed-out photo. Not her.

Click.

Female, Caucasian. OD, twenty-something. Sad. Not her.

Click.

Female (genetic profile: XY), Black. GSW victim. Leg gone at mid-thigh; old injury flagged.

Marti froze.

The photo confirmed it. LaLoLa's face barely recognizable, but hers. Kind of there, kind of not. Definitely her.

She'd done this before. Dozens of times as a cop. Match the face, make the call. But this one? She could see Rat's yellowed grin talking about his "best connection." Hear him say LaLoLa's name like it meant safety and kindness in a city that didn't offer any. Now she'd have to track him down and watch that grin die.

Marti closed the file carefully and pulled the drive. No point leaving it plugged in. LaLoLa wasn't going any-where.

"LaLoLa is confirmed," she said, testing the words. Clinical. Empty. Like a stripped car.

She stepped into the outer office. Lori saw her face and already knew.

"Rat's going to take this hard," Lori said. "You want me to—"

"No." Marti grabbed her jacket. "This one's mine. Rat ditched his phone. Made him a target for thieves. I'll find him."

She paced toward the window, half to move, half to keep from drowning in other people's disasters. Thunder slammed against the glass like God had opinions about their day.

Chapter 28

Rain hammered every glass surface in Marti's office as if nature was trying to break in for a smoke and some gossip. The place reeked of cigarettes, sweat, and half-vaped Shadow residue baked into every fiber of furniture.

Marti sat behind her desk again and took another drag off an inhaler before lighting a cigarette on top of that hit because fuck moderation; it wasn't paying rent anyway. Shadow softened everything like butter melting on bruises. Made her almost nice if you squinted hard enough and ignored what came after.

"Got an idea!" she called out loud enough for walls to vibrate. About time too. She'd been chewing over Dunstone and Fehr's fate so long she'd nearly convinced herself justice was real again.

Lori appeared without fanfare. She didn't do entrances anymore, not when she'd claimed spiritual squatter's rights inside Marti's headspace months ago.

"What?" she asked sweetly as sin, leaning against Marti's desk with arms crossed tight under tits that could probably be classified as weaponry under federal law. "Careful now: you might sprain something having an actual idea."

Marti twirled her cigarette between two fingers like temptation incarnate before tossing out: "What if we just warn them? Tell Dunstone and Fehr I know what they did and give 'em an hour."

"To run?" Lori asked without blinking. "Might work... might also get you shot in whatever part passes for your brain."

"I'm thinking third party," Marti went on, momentum gathering. "Buy a burner phone, give it to somebody else to make contact. Keeps us clean-ish."

"You think they'll listen?"

"No," Marti said through teeth stained by countless vices. "But it'll help me sleep."

Lori didn't call bullshit, which made it worse. She walked around behind Marti instead, resting one hand on her shoulder before giving it a small squeeze as if they were normal people who touched without consequence.

"You're coming?" Marti asked when Lori reached for her coat but hadn't looked back.

"I'm coming," Lori confirmed as casually as someone ordering coffee. But there was heat under those words that curled low in Marti's stomach like smoke finding dry kindling. She watched Lori walk away from behind and took advantage of the view while pretending not to care; it fooled nobody and made her swallow hard.

That ass deserved its own fucking ballad.

"No, it's safer."

"Yes," Lori snapped, pulling her coat off the back of her chair. "I'm not letting you do this alone. Last time you met them, you came back with two cracked ribs and a concussion."

"Oh, so now you're my designated bodyguard? Gonna throw yourself in front of the next bullet for me?" Marti stood, dragging on her leather jacket like muscle memory. Of course Lori was coming. Marti wasn't about to argue with her better half dressed as moral authority and fucking lingerie model.

"I'm not your protection," Lori said, voice steady as she dug into the drawer and pulled out one of her burner phones as if choosing a weapon. "I'm your conscience."

Which made it worse. Conscience was harder to ignore than bullets.

"Let's go," Marti muttered, shoving cigarettes into her pocket and trying not to think about how nice it felt having someone insist on standing beside her while she did something stupid again.

"Right behind you," Lori said. When their shoulders brushed at the door, Marti didn't move away.

The rain hit like regret: cold, insistent, unrelenting. It didn't just fall; it attacked the windshield in bursts that made the wipers whimper across the glass as if they'd already given up.

The city loomed ahead: gray buildings stacked like busted teeth against a sky smeared charcoal. No sun. No mercy.

Marti steered through it like someone who didn't care if she hydroplaned straight into hell. She parked a block from the precinct, close enough to see who went in and out but far enough that no one would notice them unless they were looking for trouble, which meant they'd probably be noticed in five minutes tops.

Rain softened to a dull spit on concrete: just enough moisture to draw out the desperate ones. Junkies slithered from damp alleyways, twitchy and hopeful and miserable. Like worms after a rainstorm.

"Time to hand off the phone," Marti said without turning her head. Her eyes scanned the sidewalk until they landed on him: a scarecrow of a man with limbs like splinters and a haunted slouch under a soaked bomber jacket that might've once been military-issue.

He'd do nicely.

Marti honked once. He flinched as if kicked but turned toward them anyway. She waved him over with all the warmth of a tax auditor.

He hesitated at their window, eyes darting between Marti's face, Lori's silence, and every shadow within twenty feet.

Marti reached into her jacket and pulled out crumpled bills, unceremonious as fuck, and held it up with one brow cocked in invitation.

His resistance broke fast. Greed didn't take long when your bloodstream screamed louder than your dignity. He shuffled closer, hands trembling like old leaves caught in wind tunnels.

"This is how it's gonna go," Marti said as she shoved the burner phone into his hand along with the cash. "You're delivering this to two cops inside that station over there."

"Carter and Cherry?" His voice croaked around broken teeth, as if he'd done this dance before.

Marti narrowed her eyes. "Dunstone and Fehr."

"Third floor," he said. "Fifth office on the right."

She blinked once. "Well goddamn," she muttered. "You got floor plans memorized or just psychic about dirty cops?"

He grinned wide: too many gaps for it to count as charming. He folded everything into his pocket before heading toward the building without another word.

Marti watched him slink off, knees barely cooperating but driven by need stronger than gravity. Junkies like him couldn't be trusted long-term; but for ten minutes and the prospect of more, later? They were reliable as sunrise.

"You really think he'll make it?" Lori asked beside her, arms folded across her chest but not hiding that little crease between her brows: the one she got when hope started nibbling at her doubt.

"Oh yeah," Marti said as she lit a cigarette from under the dash's shadow. "He'll deliver all right."

And he did. Less than two minutes later he reappeared through the precinct doors like some grimy Lazarus reborn from bureaucracy, glanced toward their car without breaking stride, and disappeared down 9th Street with five bills in his pocket and zero fucks left to give.

Marti took a drag deep enough to hurt.

Falls City justice: outsourced to junkies because you couldn't trust anyone with an actual badge anymore.

Across from her, Lori was quiet. But when Marti looked over?

She wasn't watching Delivery Man anymore. Her eyes were on Marti, and there was something scorching there behind all that morality bullshit. Something that whispered: later, when we're alone, I'm going to remind you why I came along tonight in more ways than one.

Marti exhaled smoke between parted lips and smiled at the fantasy.

Yeah, she'd warn them anyway. But maybe this time she wouldn't dream of drowning ghosts afterward; because some nights ended in violence, but others ended soaked in sweat with fingers tangled in curls that smelled better than victory ever had.

Marti glanced at Lori: jaw tight, pupils huge, her entire vibe one twitch away from feral. She punched in the burner number.

Ring. One. Not even two.

"What the fuck?"

"Listen up, asshole." Marti kept her voice low, coiled with venom. "Devall's onto you. Troy Street? He's got it. You've got one hour to disappear or die. Your call."

The silence after hit like a backhand. Lori didn't speak; she stared out the windshield as if it might bleed answers.

"It's a chick. What kind of fucking joke is this?" Dunstone barked, voice as ugly as his face.

"Who the fuck is this?" That was Fehr, further off but no less pissed, as if he sensed his whole scumbag world teetering on the edge of a toilet bowl.

Marti let them dangle a beat before twisting the knife. "Tick-tock, bitches. One hour." She killed the call, tossing the phone onto the dash as if it offended her.

Lori blinked at her. "Think they bought it?"

Marti dragged smoke deep into her lungs and let it burn all the way out. "If they sprint out in under ten seconds? Yeah. If they stroll out laughing in ten minutes? They're fucked."

Nine minutes later: laughter.

"Oh for fuck's sake," Lori muttered, squinting through the rain-slick window. "They're laughing?"

Marti rolled her window halfway and slouched low, patting Lori's shoulder before dragging her down too. Both stayed hidden while smug masculine voices trailed through water-static and wind.

"Time's up, assholes!" Dunstone crowed, in full parody mode. "Tick-tock!"

Fehr chuckled like someone who hadn't been laid in years and flung the burner toward a sewer grate with all the grace of an ape throwing its shit in protest. The phone bounced once, twice. Then it sat there like a ghost with unfinished business.

Fehr stomped over and kicked it straight into hell.

"Dumb fuck," he growled.

"Let's roll, partner," Dunstone said loud enough to echo off wet concrete.

They got in their cruiser without looking back because cowards never do when they think they've won. It pulled off into traffic like nothing mattered: no warning call, no threat. Just two walking erections fueling their egos on invincibility and maybe meth fumes.

Marti stared after them as if she could set their tires on fire by will alone. "Arrogant dickbags." Her hands gripped the steering wheel so hard it looked like she might snap it clean off.

Lori shrugged. "Their funerals," she said with a chuckle that was more about being serious than being funny.

Marti started the ignition and coasted into the police station lot for a quick U-turn. That's when both women stopped breathing.

There it was.

Red ThunderBlade GT parked cocky among cruisers and SUVs that screamed municipal apathy. Front headlamp cracked like a guilty conscience.

"That's the car from LaLoLa's video," Lori whispered, clutching her phone as if it might explode if she blinked wrong.

Marti's stomach twisted: not metaphorical, just raw recoil. "Yeah," she muttered. "That headlight doesn't lie."

The implication settled over them thick as oil slicks in rainwater: someone inside was dirty. Marti hoped it was Kane because she wanted an excuse to ruin him down to his perfect hair follicles.

Lori snapped pics; still no license plate. Because subtlety was for people who didn't leave trails of blood behind them.

As they peeled out toward home base, Lori said, "When we get back I'll find PD staff names and cross-check vehicle registration records..."

"Nope." Marti cut her off with a snort sharp enough to wound pride. "Ever since those fuckwits realized posting 'Most Hated' blue-line dogshit online wasn't good for their safety, personnel records are under triple lockdown."

"We still have that list of thirty-something possibles..."

"Which we've gone through a dozen goddamn times." Marti hissed through clenched teeth as she cut off a blue coupe doing everything right except existing near her rage vortex. Horns blared behind them. Marti flipped it off without looking back.

She turned onto Sutton Street and slid between two parked sedans outside their office: a miracle given her driving style and mood both rated as extinction-level event.

Inside, wet coats flung over chairs, boots thudding against floorboards worn smooth from stress pacing and case files thrown harder than necessary.

"I've got an idea," Marti said as she stalked toward her desk drawer with familiar desperation; alcohol didn't ask stupid questions, it just burned going down.

Lori groaned behind her. "God help us all. You're forcing your single brain cell to overtime again."

"The car has to have clearance to park there. We need to find out who has the clearance for that car," Marti said as she reached into the desk drawer and pulled out an empty whiskey bottle.

Marti shook the whiskey bottle as if she had Buzzman's Twitch. Nothing but empty disappointment inside. She sighed, muttered something obscene, and chucked it into the trash with a hollow clunk.

There was another bottle. There was always another fucking bottle.

Chapter 29

"Drink?" Marti asked, already elbow-deep in her desk drawer, fishing out a dusty glass that looked as if it had survived nuclear fallout and grown mold out of spite.

"Asshole," Lori called from across the room. "I don't drink fungus-infused brain acid."

Marti poured anyway, tossed back a double that hit like regret and coughed so hard she nearly saw God.

"Before you kill your last neuron," Lori continued, "what's this brilliant idea?"

Marti cleared her throat and grinned around the burn. "Keira Persky: one hell of a bottom."

Lori snapped her gaze over, eyes sharp enough to file steel. A pause. The corner of her mouth twitched; jealousy or disgust, Marti couldn't tell. Maybe both.

"She works in HR at Falls City PD. She might have a list of people with benefits."

"She keeps a list of people she fucks?" Lori asked, slightly aghast and intrigued that she'd need a spreadsheet or something.

Marti smirked. "Not that kind of benefit, genius. Parking is a taxable benefit; she'll have names. Addresses too."

"And you think she'll just hand that over?" Lori leaned against the desk, arms crossed tight under her chest: a position that did distracting things to her cleavage and Marti's focus alike. "Let me guess: you flutter your lashes and she melts like a sad little puddle."

"She likes it when I make demands," Marti said with a wink, already halfway to her burner phone.

She hit call while Lori muttered something about HR violations and trauma bonding.

"Tell me you need something dirty," Keira answered after two rings, voice lush with amusement and silk.

"I need every employee at Falls City PD with parking benefits. Names and addresses," Marti said without prelude.

Keira made a low sound in her throat. "Jesus Christ, Marti: start with hello next time. Maybe flirt a little before spitting in my face."

"I'll do both if you get me that file in the next ten minutes."

A pause on the other end. Static buzzing quiet between them.

"And what do I get for risking my job?"

"My undivided attention," Marti purred. "Some light restraint if you're good... minimal lying if you're lucky."

Now Keira laughed; low, dirty, thrilled.

"You've still got gall," she said.

"And a tight deadline."

Another pause, and then the soft ding of an incoming email lit up the screen.

"You're still an asshole," Keira said fondly.

"I'm your asshole," Marti replied and hung up before sentiment could infect the airspace.

She swiveled to find Lori looming over her shoulder with an expression of vinegar and curiosity.

"Would she really lick your boots?" she asked.

Marti didn't move or blink, just crooked one brow and murmured, "You wanna watch next time?"

"Oh my god, gross," Lori grumbled, but not before pushing closer to peer at the screen, as if invading Marti's personal space was some passive-aggressive kink she hadn't confessed to. "Open the email."

Her breasts pressed against the back of Marti's neck in that deliberate way that made focusing on files feel like punishment for past sins.

"Come on... come on..." Marti muttered as the spreadsheet loaded, and...

Ctrl+F: ThunderBlade.

Nada.

"Jesus fuck." She slammed one hand on the desk hard enough to rattle a stack of case files.

"They're people's names and addresses," Lori said as she pointed at the screen, still flush against her neck as if this wasn't war by arousal. "Not car makes."

Marti grimaced at the obvious truth sinking in like a cinderblock through glass.

"Fuck!" she snarled again, rubbing at her temples as if caffeine or divine intervention might fix stupidity retroactively.

Lori was already smugging it up beside her. "Should've known better. Bet you thought it'd be a piece of cake."

That caught something behind Marti's eyes: a flicker of mischief or madness or both. Realization crept across her face like sunrise over bad decisions.

"A piece of fucking cake," she whispered.

Lori frowned. "You want dessert now?"

"No." Marti stood fast enough to knock over her chair and stalked toward Lori's desk with purpose dripping off her stride. "Wedding cake!"

Lori backed up half a step as if she expected frosting violence. "Marti, I swear to God, if this is about recipes again..."

"Nope." Marti spun toward her with manic joy radiating from every pore. "I need you to be a good little secretary right now and cross-reference our ThunderBlade suspect list against those parking benefit addresses."

Lori opened her mouth to argue maybe, but closed it when Marti reached out and tucked a strand of hair behind Lori's ear without pretending not to enjoy it.

"Piece of cake," Lori echoed before hip-checking Marti out of the way and dropping into place at the computer as if this was foreplay they did every Thursday night between crimes solved and lines uncrossed but begged for.

A few taps here. A muttered curse there as code sprang to life under keystrokes.

```
> matchaddr -a thunderblade_list.csv -b employee_be
nefits.csv --on address --return name,address
[processing...]
[processing...]
[1 match found]
```

>thunderblade_list.csv: Teli Somram, 34 59th Street East

>employee_benefits.csv: Leo Fehr, 34 59th Street East

There. Right fucking there.

Leo Fehr.

"Shit, Marti... Fehr." Lori's voice barely rose above a whisper.

Marti leaned over, not even bothering to look down Lori's top. The screen blinked. "That bastard. He killed LaLoLa."

"You're brilliant!" Lori shouted, grinning like a lunatic and holding up a triumphant hand for a high-five.

Marti ignored it, grabbed Lori by the collar, and kissed her hard enough to bruise. She tasted lemon soda and desperation. It was stupid, reckless. It lasted until Lori smacked her shoulder as if putting out a fire.

"Shit: sorry," Marti lied through her teeth, pulling back with a grin that didn't reach her eyes. "Good find, Lori. Real A+ detective shit. Almost makes me wish we were into indictments."

Lori blinked at her, flustered in that way Marti wanted to see more of. "You gonna tell Chief Franklin?"

"Nope." Marti cut her off. "Fehr got his warning. So did Dunstone. That was the deal. Besides, prison would be a slow, ugly death for cops like them. This'll be cleaner."

Lori hesitated. "Is it enough? I mean, really enough to say he's the killer?"

Marti leaned against the desk, tapped ash onto an evidence folder, and shook her head. "Are you kidding me? It's better than any cop would ever find. We know what happens next. There's no taking it back. So yeah, we have to be sure as hell. We just need enough to slam the goddamn file shut and stop chasing doubt."

"No judge, no jury; just us." Lori nodded. "We say he's the guy, then he's the guy."

"Exactly." Marti lit another cigarette off the stub of the first. Her fingers shook: the only betrayal she allowed herself.

"I can let Rat know," she added. "Not about Fehr, but LaLoLa. Yeah."

That part could be clean.

But telling Devall? That would be dirty.

She drummed the slip drive on the desk like a metronome of vengeance while everything clicked into place: Fehr and Dunstone slinging bootleg Shadow out of Devall's lab; customers dropping dead because they cut quality with poison; LaLoLa gets pissed that her clients are dying, gets too loud about it, and they arrange a sweet little motel rendezvous to 'talk things over.' Then Fehr beats her to death and leaves her cooling in a rented room with blood on the ceiling.

Morgue picks her up like roadkill. Files her as Jane Doe #3.

Now she's not Jane anymore.

Now she's LaLoLa.

Case closed, Rat.

Marti retreated to her office and took a hit of Shadow. An hour crawled by. She came around and lit up a smoke. Another five minutes.

Marti crushed out her cigarette. "All right," she said, standing up so fast the chair spun behind her like some rusted carnival ride. "Game fucking over. I'm calling Devall." Her eyes flicked toward Lori. "QuantumSpecs footage ready?"

Lori nodded once, tone slick and serious: "Yes."

Marti heard what wasn't said: don't drag me into this. She decided not to pretend either of them had clean hands anymore.

Beep.

"Devall? Starova," she clipped out, leaning into each syllable as if it might bite back. "We need to talk. I know who's running bad Shadow under your brand." A pause for effect; not too long or he'd smell theater. "Call me."

She hung up before sentiment could leak in and lit another cigarette instead.

While smoke curled around old ceiling stains and Marti paced like an animal waiting for slaughter or salvation, Lori moved in that quiet way that made Marti's stomach twist: sliding files onto a drive without looking down, snapping photos into folders like bullets into chambers, red-tagging key documents in Devall-red ink.

She included most notes on the fire; because if all else failed, accidental fires were convenient.

Goddamn it. She made being dangerous look domestic.

Two cigarettes later: which was either ten minutes or forever. Marti was halfway through recreating a crime scene in ash on her blotter when footsteps hit hard against tile outside.

The door slammed open as if it were judgment day.

"Starova," Devall greeted (not a question, not even surprise) as he glided in with two massive bodyguards trailing him like tailored statues.

They didn't look at Lori.

Devall didn't sit. Just stood there radiating controlled violence in a coat worth more than Marti's apartment and eyes that had watched people die without blinking.

"You've got five seconds to convince me why I shouldn't gut you," he said.

Marti didn't flinch. Didn't bow or kneel or fucking curtsy like half this city did around him.

"That's a hell of a way to return a phone message," she said as she eyed his bodyguards.

"Two seconds," Devall snapped.

"It's Fehr and Dunstone," she began, her voice bone-dry and slick with sarcasm-cut venom. "Falls City's fucking finest turned chemists from hell. They've been cooking discount Shadow in your lab like meth-heads with badges."

Devall's eye twitched. Maybe.

"They want your business," she smiled without warmth, "and your head on a spike."

Devall blinked once. "And you have proof?"

Marti cocked her head toward Lori without taking eyes off him. "Of course I do."

"QuantumSpecs footage," Lori added from behind them; now they noticed her voice for real. The Holo-Tab displayed the video footage of Dunstone, Fehr and Kane, voices faint, gunshots louder.

Marti kept going: "Includes their chatter with Damian Kane: you might remember him as my ex-partner turned paid-off piece of shit."

Devall arched an eyebrow as if he enjoyed this part more than he should've. "Ex-partner? You protecting him?"

Marti rolled up her shirt just enough to show the half-healed bio implant beneath pale bruises blooming purple across her ribs: a crappy fill of BioBuild that hadn't sat right since Kane nearly ventilated her during the taping session.

"That fucker shot me," she said. "You'll see it on the video footage, the part where I almost die doing your job."

She let the shirt drop back down slow so they could all feel how much that moment weighed between them now.

"I wouldn't protect Kane from rain," Marti finished.

Lori moved like a whisper, but the folder slapped down with enough fury to make Devall jolt in his chair. His hand twitched toward his holster. Marti didn't hide her smirk.

"Jesus, Devall. Your boys deaf or just dumb?" she asked, cigarette dangling between her fingers like punctuation.

He ignored that. "You got the fire bug?"

"Nope," Lori cut in from her desk, eyes glued to her screen. She had to interrupt before Marti shouted out 'It was me!'

"You're hanging onto your half-mil. Sorry about that. But don't get your hopes up; nobody's gonna cough up a real answer. Listen close to the video and you'll hear them denying everything. Kane paid off the Marshall. Ran him a nice fat bribe for some 'faulty wiring' diagnosis," she added. "Copy's in the file."

Devall turned, eyebrows raised as if she'd sprouted fangs. Then he looked sideways at Marti.

"That true?"

Marti lit up like it was the last smoke before execution. Her hands didn't shake yet, but her guts flipped like a kicked dog.

Here came the sell.

"If Kane is covering, and the Fire Marshall's bought off, and Dunstone and Fehr are playing dumb?" She shrugged. "Then you're fucked six ways from Sunday. No leads left to chase. Take the insurance money and enjoy the profits from selling the block."

She held on to the smoke until it hurt, circulating in her lungs until it burned more than truth ever could. Then she exhaled emptiness, clean filtered air that tasted like surrender.

Devall tapped the folder against his thigh. Once, twice.

"You're a damned good PI, Starova," he said, voice low but sharp around the edges. "Still a mess of a human being, but... fuck, you're good."

"I know," Marti said as she smiled without warmth. "Lori'll send over your final invoice: everything catalogued nice and neat, no red flags."

And while Lori handled that, Marti planned to bury herself in a pile of Shadow so deep she'd need excavation drones by sunrise.

"Good doing business with you," Devall said as he turned away. No handshake offered, no bullshit farewells. He wasn't stupid. Lambs weren't dangerous unless you forgot what wolves looked like.

The boys followed him out without a word, silence folding in behind them as if closing a grave.

Marti watched the door stay shut. Then it hit her.

Harder than it should've.

Dunstone and Fehr were going to die; maybe they deserved it, but she'd still fucking tried to save them. Right up until the fuckers shot her.

She let out a slow sigh through clenched teeth and looked at Lori across the dim room.

Marti sighed and looked at Lori. "You can't save someone who thinks they're untouchable. The higher they climb on other people's misery, the harder they hit the ground when karma finally calls to collect."

Chapter 30

The Shadow wasn't working.

Marti stared at the empty inhaler between her fingers, turning it like a key that wouldn't fit the lock. Three hits in the past hour should have numbed her into oblivion by now. Instead, her nerves jangled like loose wires in a storm. Her hands skittered across the desk, rearranging papers, tapping ash, reaching for cigarettes she barely smoked.

Rain hammered against the windows, no longer the cleansing backdrop of earlier but an accusation in Morse code: You crossed the line. You crossed the line.

The newspaper spread before her like a crime scene, its headline mocking her with thick black letters: "HERO COPS DEAD IN DRUG LAB EXPLOSION." Dunstone and Fehr smiled from the grainy photo, all clean uniforms and practiced humility. The same men who'd laughed when she tried to warn them. The same men who kicked that burner phone into the sewer grate like it was nothing more than street trash.

I tried to save them, she thought, lighting another cigarette with hands that wouldn't stay still. I fucking tried.

She exhaled smoke that hung too thick in the air, refusing to disperse. The office felt smaller tonight, like it was shrinking around her, pressing in with questions she couldn't answer.

When had she stopped being a PI and become... whatever the hell she was now? Judge. Jury. Something worse.

The Shadow churned in her system, fighting her instead of helping. Every time she closed her eyes, she saw Dunstone's smirk, Fehr's derision.

"They deserved it," she muttered to the empty room, but the words rang hollow. The line between justice and revenge had blurred beyond recognition, and the Shadow wouldn't let her hide from that tonight.

Marti crushed out her cigarette and immediately lit another, burning through them like she could somehow smoke away the image of Devall's face when she handed him what he needed. The slight nod that meant death warrants were being signed. The knowledge that her investigation was never about finding truth. Just ammunition.

She'd gotten exactly what she wanted. So why did victory taste like ash and chemicals?

The smoke coiled around her like a noose as the night stretched toward morning.

* * *

Lori arrived at 7:38 AM, same as always. The office door's familiar creak announced her before her shadow fell across the threshold.

She stopped short at the sight of Marti at her desk, surrounded by cigarette butts, a Shadow inhaler by her hand. In front of her, the newspaper remained open to the hero cops story, now spotted with ash burns and coffee rings.

"Jesus," Lori whispered, but recovered quickly. She hung her coat on the rack, movement precise as she tried to pretend this was just another morning. "Coffee's probably cold."

"Probably," Marti agreed, voice sandpaper-rough from smoke and silence. She yawned and stretched and sat up as smooth as a Bertha on MethLumina.

Gray morning light filtered through dirty windows, casting everything in the pallid glow of a morgue. Lori moved to her desk, powering up her computer with fingers that trembled slightly against the keyboard. She tried to focus on the screen, but her eyes kept drifting to Marti, to the newspaper, to the evidence of a sleepless night spent wrestling demons.

"Any messages?" Marti asked, though they both knew she didn't give a shit about messages.

"Nothing important." Lori's voice was too careful, too measured. She poured coffee that smelled burned and tasted wrong, but drank it anyway because routine was all they had left to cling to.

The silence stretched between them, heavy with unspoken reckonings.

Lori set her mug down with a sharp click. "My father used to bring cases home."

Marti looked up, surprised by the non-sequitur.

"Homicide," Lori continued, eyes fixed on some middle distance. "He'd talk about them over dinner sometimes. Not the details, he was careful about that, but the weight of them. How they changed him."

Marti waited, sensing this wasn't just idle reminiscence.

"He told me once that the hardest part wasn't catching criminals. It was living with what you had to do to catch them." Lori's laugh was brittle as she finally met Marti's gaze. "He'd be so disappointed in me now."

"You did nothing. I did what needed doing," Marti said, the words automatic but not untrue.

"Didn't I?" Lori's hands had stopped shaking, but something in her eyes had fractured. "I always thought I'd be like him. One of the good ones. But good cops don't set up other cops to die, no matter what they've done."

"They shot me, Lori. Fehr killed LaLoLa. They were cooking poison and selling it as Shadow." Marti's voice hardened. "How many deaths on their hands before it balances out?"

"That's not how my father would have measured it."

"Yeah, well, your father isn't here."

"No." Lori's smile was sad. "And I can never tell him what I've done. That's part of the price, isn't it?"

Marti had no answer for that. The distance between who they were and who they'd become yawned between them like an open grave.

Lori turned back to her computer, shoulders squared with a determination that looked too much like her father's. "I've got the Petrie invoice to finish. You should get some sleep."

But they both knew sleep wouldn't come easy anymore.

* * *

The Ironhook district smelled of wet cardboard and desperation. Post-rain dampness rose from concrete in lazy tendrils, mingling with the stench of unwashed bodies and rotting food. Steam hissed from manholes like the sighs of the forgotten, while overhead traffic created a constant metallic drumbeat. The city's heartbeat, regular and indifferent.

Marti picked her way through puddles that reflected nothing, scanning the makeshift shelters under the overpass. The homeless camp had thinned since her last visit. Some moved on when the weather turned; others just disappeared, consumed by the city's hunger.

She found Rat's shelter near the eastern pylon, a precarious construction of shopping carts and blue tarps that leaked when it rained but kept most of the wind out. He scrambled to his feet when he spotted her, hope flickering across his gaunt face. Maybe she had news about LaLoLa. Maybe she had drugs.

"Marti," he called, wiping dirty hands on dirtier jeans. "You got something?"

The question hung between them, weighted with expectation Marti couldn't fulfill.

"Yeah," she said, reaching into her pocket for the envelope of cash she'd brought. Blood money, conscience money. She wasn't sure what to call it anymore. "Got something."

Rat's eyes fixed on the envelope, but he didn't reach for it. Smart enough to know that cash without strings was rare in their world. "What's the deal?"

Marti took a breath that tasted of exhaust and mildew. "No deal. It's about LaLoLa."

Something shifted in Rat's posture: a tightening, a bracing. "You found her?"

"Yeah. I found her." The words felt like stones in her mouth. "She's gone, Rat. Been gone since you saw her last."

"Gone where?" His voice cracked on the question, though he already knew the answer.

"She's dead. Shot in a motel room." Marti forced herself to hold his gaze. "She was a Jane Doe until yesterday."

Rat didn't move. Didn't blink. Then something collapsed behind his eyes. Not grief, exactly, but recognition of a truth he'd been denying. His shoulders folded inward as if absorbing a physical blow.

"Who did it?" he asked, voice flat.

"Doesn't matter. He's dead."

"You kill him?" he asked, the word bitter on his tongue.

Marti handed him the envelope. "No. Not me. He made enemies. Someone else's justice happened."

Rat took the money without looking at it, stuffing it into his pocket like it was contaminated. He didn't cry. Junkies learned early that tears were wasted water. But the hollow emptiness in his expression was worse than any display of grief.

"She looked out for me," he said finally. "Nobody else did that."

The simple truth of it hit Marti harder than she expected. LaLoLa may have been a dealer, but she was also someone's friend, someone's connection to humanity. Rat's loss was clean and uncomplicated in a way that made Marti's moral gymnastics feel like a luxury.

"I know," she said, inadequate but honest.

"No, you don't." Rat shook his head. "But thanks for telling me. Most wouldn't bother."

He retreated into his shelter without another word, the tarp falling closed like a curtain on a stage. End scene. Exit Rat.

Marti stood there longer than she needed to, rain starting to spit again from a sky the color of bruises. She'd been playing detective, drawing connections on whiteboards, building cases and counter-cases. Meanwhile, real people had been living and dying in the margins of her investigation. People like Rat, people like LaLoLa. People whose names wouldn't make the papers.

She turned away finally, boots splashing through puddles that reflected a city indifferent to individual suffering. There was no clean ending here, only consequences that rippled outward, touching lives she'd never see again.

The rain fell harder as she walked back to her car, washing away footprints but not memories. Not guilt. Not the knowledge that victory and defeat sometimes looked exactly the same.

Marti lit a cigarette with hands that still wouldn't quite stay steady, inhaling smoke that burned all the way down. The Shadow hadn't worked because there was no escaping this particular truth: in a city built on shadows, even justice cast a darkness of its own.

She started the car and drove away from Ironhook, leaving Rat to his grief and LaLoLa to whatever peace the dead might find. The case was closed. The file was shut. Dunstone and Fehr wouldn't kill anyone else.

But the cost. Christ, the cost kept mounting.

Continue the Falls City Series

What happens next? Find out in: ***Rain-Soaked***
November 5, 2025
Book 3 in the Marti Starova Thriller series sees PI Marti Starova racing against the clock, and her past, to find a missing girl. She is in the crosshairs and the only way out is through a pile of bodies.

◆

Almost - Coming January 16, 2026
The Familiar Dark - Coming March 11, 2026
Ready to keep reading? Pre-order now!

www.ingramcontent.com/pod-product-compliance
Lightning Source LLC
Chambersburg PA
CBHW030744310726
48969CB00005B/1310